Claire Fontaine
CRIME FIGHTER

Claire Fontaine
CRIME FIGHTER

A Novel of Life and Death . . . and Shoes

TRACEY ENRIGHT

ST. MARTIN'S MINOTAUR THOMAS DUNNE BOOKS
New York

THOMAS DUNNE BOOKS.
An imprint of St. Martin's Press.

www.thomasdunnebooks.com

www.minotaurbooks.com

Book design by Jonathan Bennett

Library of Congress Cataloging-in-Publication Data

Enright, Tracey.
Claire Fontaine, crime fighter : a novel of life and death . . . and shoes / Tracey Enright.
p. cm.
ISBN-13: 978-0-312-31960-1
ISBN-10: 0-312-31960-6
1. Private investigators—California—Los Angeles—Fiction. 2. Los Angeles (Calif.)—Fiction. I. Title.
PS3605.N753C58 2006
813'.6—dc22

2006042501

First Edition: July 2006

10 9 8 7 6 5 4 3 2 1

To my parents for always
encouraging me to dream

If you prick us, do we not bleed? If you tickle us, do we not laugh?
If you poison us, do we not die? And if you wrong us,
shall we not revenge?

—*William Shakespeare,* The Merchant of Venice

Claire Fontaine
CRIME FIGHTER

1

On a rather balmy October day, I had an interview that changed my life.

My father had the right connections and scored me a brief meeting with a notorious homicide detective named Henry Bennett. When I arrived at his office, situated in the Miracle Mile district along Wilshire Boulevard, I was faced with the worst possible working environment. The lobby of the building smelled like dirty dishes and sweaty bodies, and the floor was stained with dark fluids and a lifetime of heel marks. The air felt thick and moist. My pores were already getting clogged and I hadn't even gotten the job yet.

The second floor offered even less decor and smelled more of neglect and mildew than the foyer. It was a poorly lit, narrow corridor surrounded by walls of gray (not the new Ralph Lauren gray, but lifeless, peeling, and antiquated gray). I walked down the hallway in dismay, absorbing the dull environment. Four of the offices belonged to various medical associations, three were law offices, and two were film-production companies. Henry Bennett's office was the last one on the right, at the end of the corridor. The door facing me was dark wood with simple, gold lettering that read: HENRY BENNETT, PRIVATE DETECTIVE.

I adjusted my silk Armani suit and touched up my lip gloss.

The waiting area was small and dank. Absolutely no decor. Not even a faux Monet. An empty, baby-shit yellow desk was strangely aligned with the east wall, and there was a single foldout metal chair against the opposite wall.

And the obligatory neglected dead plant in the corner.

I heard heavy footsteps approaching, reminded me of a dinosaur clumping across old wood. And then a large shapeless man stepped out of his office. He was in his late forties, about six-foot-two, with brownish-gray hair and weary green eyes, and badly dressed. And I mean *badly* dressed. Beige shirt that fit his girth like a stretched glove. Pants that had seen better days in 1980. Shoes that no longer had a definite shape.

He stopped abruptly in the doorway of his office, looking me up and down rudely. "Who are *you?*"

"I'm Claire Fontaine," I said cheerfully. "I'm here about the job."

"Oh," he said, looking me over again. *"Really?"*

"Yes."

A cruel smirk danced across his face as he snorted the words, "This is a joke, right?"

"No."

"My friend Bud from Vice sent you, right? You're the stripper for my birthday?"

"I know no one called Bud, and the only way you'd ever see me naked is by witnessing my autopsy."

When it finally hit him who I was, his face collapsed into a frown. "Oh, yeah. Your daddy knows the mayor." He exhaled like an asthmatic. "Come on in. I forgot all about this. I'm not exactly a team player. But, you know, when the mayor calls, I like to, uh, pacify him. It's important to stay in good graces with the city officials. Makes my job easier."

Sighing and moaning and cursing beneath his breath, he took me into his office and offered me a chair. "So," he grunted. "Why on earth would you want to work for me? In this business of death?"

He really put me on the spot. It was one of those deep, introspective questions, and I felt paralyzed by him, the office, the fluorescent lighting. I wanted to speak, but nothing came out. He waved an impatient hand in front of my face.

"Hello. Anybody awake in there? You a deaf-mute?"

I shook my head, squeezed my Cartier.

"This is what's called an interview," he said sarcastically. "It's part of the hiring process. I ask you a bunch of silly questions, and then I pretend like I'm listening to you when you answer them."

"I have an interest in police work." I finally breathed. "Ever since I was a kid, I've been a bit of a sleuth. But nobody in your line of work is interested in giving someone like me a chance. They take one look at me and think I'm silly and ridiculous and stupid. And that all I know how to do is shop. But really, Detective, I'd put half these bureaucrats to shame. It's difficult for a girl like me to get one foot in the door."

He snorted. "Hardly, babe. Remember I'm the one doing this 'cause the mayor asked nicely. And that's the *only* reason. I don't like much company, much fuss. I'm not exactly a thrill to be around, got my moods. My bowel issues. My language is pretty tough and I'm hesitant about clouding your pink mind with such filth. All of this makes me nervous."

I had to say something. "I'm clever. Intelligent. Loyal. Punctual. Diligent."

He started laughing. "Those are just adjectives." His hands were in the air. "Do you have any experience? Anything?"

The dreaded question. "Experience?"

"Yes. Experience is the collective knowledge gained from past training that would aid in your ability to bring something to this job."

"I know *what* experience is," I said, flushed with anger.

"I need proof that you have a brain."

Henry Bennett reached his fleshy hand into a McDonald's bag and started devouring greasy hash browns. I could see tiny bits of white potato in his mouth.

"I have a college education," I said.

"I don't." He belched. "This job isn't about being educated, in the scholarly sense. It's about instinct, which is what I got going for me. I can read people, pick out the liars from the loonies. Don't mind getting my hands dirty with someone else's blood. Spend most of my time alone, which is the way I like it. I'm a solitary person and never really enjoyed having a partner when I was on the force."

"How do you feel about having one now?"

"A partner?" His head tilted, confused.

"Yeah."

"You *can't* be talking about yourself."

"Yes, I am."

He tumbled forward with laughter. "Listen, honey, you're here to answer phones, do some filing, and stay out of my way. I'm not even sure you could handle the pictures that come across my desk. We're not exactly talking about the spring layout in *Vogue.*"

"Listen, Detective, I know you're bitter about this, some absolute stranger sitting across from you, wearing the best outfit you've probably ever seen—but could you just lighten up for one week?"

"That's a long time to put up with bullshit and Burberry."

"You might be surprised," I said.

"Shocked would be more like it." He looked at my suit, shook his head. "You might want to consider dressing a bit more casual for the job. This isn't the cleanest place on earth."

"I noticed."

"Feel free to wear jeans or sweatpants, if you want. I applaud comfort. My clients might be put off by all your . . . sparkles."

"If they can handle death," I said, "they can handle a woman who knows how to accessorize."

"Whatever." He tossed the McDonald's bag into an already overflowing trashcan. "You'll be on call, by the way. Hope that won't interfere with manicures and pedicures and the annual Barneys sale."

"I'll manage."

"We'll see. And always keep your phone turned on."

"You mean in case there's an emergency and you need me right away?"

"No, in case I'm hungry and want you to stop by Fromin's and pick up my breakfast. And lunch. And dinner. I love food, it's the American way. So don't be bringing me any hoity-toity crap. If it's raw, I ain't eating it. If it's green, I won't like it. If it's fat-free, I'm allergic."

"Morbidly obese looks good on you," I said. "So be it, I won't try to change that."

"Good." He pulled himself from the chair with a sigh. "How 'bout we start with you running an errand for me."

"Okay." My first official duty.

He removed a small plastic bag from the top drawer of his desk. A smile grew across his face when he said, "Take this *finger* to the Anatomical Pound at the Los Angeles County Morgue."

"What?"

"You heard me." He shook the plastic in my face. "This finger. To the Anatomical Pound. The assistant coroner, Ralph Manning, is expecting it."

I took the bag, glanced down at the bone, slender and charred. "Who did it belong to?"

"Buck Cooper."

"Where's the rest of him?"

"Scattered across the Angeles National Forest. Hikers and outdoorsy types are still finding parts of his body. 'Course, everything was burned up in the fire. It was your basic dismember-and-torch routine. But what people don't understand is that human bone is incredibly fire-resistant. So now we're putting the bastard back together. And it's a real bitch."

"That's so lovely."

"You can start tomorrow, nine o'clock sharp. I hate tardiness, gives me gas. So be on time and be dressed for *work*, in fabric that will actually allow you to move. To file. To clean."

"Yes, sir. I look forward to the challenge."

He started to close the door in my face. "Yeah, bet you do."

The plastic could not prevent the odor from seeping into my nostrils like overcooked pork that had been left in a frying pan for three days. I knew that it was bound to stink up my Mercedes, and no amount of Chanel No. 5 would be able to eradicate the stench.

2

The building seemed too small and angular to house the army of dead bodies that must have passed through on a daily basis. The LAC-USC General Hospital loomed in the distance, multileveled and impressive, casting a shadow over the coroner's office. I was hoping for a drive-thru lane, something quick and easy, where I could just toss the bag out the window and get on with my day. No such luck. And parking was a total nightmare because of too many boxy sedans with government plates. I finally found a spot close to the door, parked, and passed a couple of wide-eyed medical types on my way inside.

The receptionist didn't even budge when I shook the bag in her face. "I've got a delivery for Ralph Manning."

"Is he expecting you?"

"I certainly hope so. Because I'm not leaving here until I find a home for"—eyeing the finger—*"him."*

"Down the hall to the left. I'll buzz Manning."

As I pushed my way into the corridor, a gurney rolled passed me, wheels clattering along the floor. I couldn't help noticing the enormous black body bag bouncing around on top, the blue arm that fell to the side, and the inescapable odor of putrefaction. The morgue attendant nodded and I thought about passing out. Acidic mist hung in the air. It was an icebox, this house of death, air-conditioning working overtime, whispering behind old vents that had grown accustomed to the sights and smells that had rolled passed them.

Ralph Manning was a wiry man, small-boned, fair-haired, early thirties. "Detective Bennett said you had a nice rack!" His voice echoed down the hall. The nightmare played out before me, but I pretended not to hear him.

"I've got Buck Cooper's finger."

"Yeah. I know. We're tryin' to put the son of a bitch back together. Like Humpty Dumpty with all the body parts."

"How lovely."

He snatched the bag carelessly, the bone bouncing within the plastic. "How long you been workin' for Henry?"

"About forty-five minutes."

"You just started today?"

"Correct."

"How's it going so far?"

"Have no complaints."

"You will."

"Excuse me?"

"You'll have complaints," he grunted. "Just give it time. He's a tough one, real set in his ways."

"Yeah, I got that part."

"But be patient because you could learn a lot. I mean, if that's your thing. You don't really seem like the law-enforcement type. Too fancy for street work."

"He talked to me about the outfit."

Manning studied me, his eyes rolled along my hips, down my legs, squaring off at my feet. "You wear the threads well, babe, but in this business it's about keeping a low profile. Hard to imagine the likes of you hanging out with all the bottom feeders."

He shook the bag and turned on his heel. "Thanks again. Mr. Owen was looking for this." Manning disappeared behind a metal door. A meat-locker chill crawled into the corridor, colder than the vents from above. Something sinister lurked behind all the linoleum and polished silver. I hated the smell of it all, death and decay, and knew it would forever haunt me.

From the morgue, I drove straight to Ethan Allen and purchased a Chippendale-style cherry-wood office desk. Very elegant with a nice vintage finish. I also bought a Harvard desk chair in brown leather. Feeling compelled to renovate the entire lobby of my new office, I picked out a forged-iron end table from the Collector's Classics line. And I ordered it all for next-day delivery.

After Ethan Allen, I dropped by the Montblanc store and purchased ten Mozart platinum-trim pens and two Legrand pens for my new office. Then I went to Pottery Barn and selected an old-fashioned swing-arm lamp in satin nickel.

3

For me a corpse has a beauty and dignity which a living body could never hold. There is a peace about death that soothes me.

—John Christie

The next morning, dressed in black Escada slacks, a pearl-white Donna Karan oxford shirt, and Sergio Rossi boots, I arrived for my first official day on the job.

The door to Henry Bennett's office was closed, but I could hear the thick deep growl of the man behind it. Probably talking shop on the phone. I stood alone, twisting the strap of my Chanel pocketbook in the waiting area. Glancing around at the out-of-date, dust-covered furniture, I wasn't sure where to begin.

Thankfully within seconds of my arrival, the Ethan Allen deliverymen knocked on the door. Both men were wearing wrinkled uniforms, liberally saturated with their own personal scent—and it wasn't Lagerfeld Photo, if you get my drift.

The larger one approached me, looked down at the clipboard in his hand, and then glanced back up at me. "Claire Fontaine?"

"That's me. Welcome to my nightmare," I said.

They pushed the metal dolly into the waiting area and began to unload. I retracted a stainless-steel pocketknife from my purse and cut into the first box. My new desk. Flushed with excitement, I politely asked the men to remove the piece of crap currently occupying the east wall of the room. "It would be lovely if you guys could throw it away on your way back to the warehouse," I said, pointing to the old desk.

"Okay." The larger one shrugged. "Where do yuz want it?"

"I'z want it gone," I sighed, greasing their palms with crisp hundred-dollar bills. They eyed each other, quite thrilled with the tips.

"No problem, lady. We'll dump it for ya."

They pushed my new Chippendale cherrywood desk into place, and I neatly lined up my Montblanc pens on top. The Harvard desk chair looked beautiful and regal behind the desk. The forged iron end table was placed up against the wall next to the old, foldout chair that Bennett probably got at a garage sale, along with the desk that would soon be on its way to the closest Dumpster.

There is a God.

With the deliverymen gone, I paced the room, studying every lackluster inch of gray paint that draped the walls. The color reminded me of spoiled milk, aged, dull. Vomit-inducing. I shook my head in disgust, realizing the 1970s paint job would kill any hope of an authentic stylish transformation. Just as I was picking up the phone to call my "connection" in the paint department at Home Depot, Detective Bennett emerged from his office.

Dressed slightly better than yesterday, in pants that *actually* fit, he stepped into the waiting area and looked around the room. His eyes narrowed sharply. Lips tight with anger, he said, "What the fuck is all this?"

"It's new furniture. It's called renovation."

"It's called fucked-up," he groaned.

"It's *braaaaand* new," I said defensively. "Gives the office a more sophisticated look. Elegant. Polished."

"This ain't a law firm, lady! I don't give a fuck about aesthetics. People don't come here for the ambience. They come here because a loved one has been hacked to death with a band saw, or has gone missing. Not one person that stands in this room is thinking about their surroundings; they're too encumbered with their own pain and horror. Last thing I need is to look flashy and expensive."

"I'm sorry. I was just trying to help."

"Don't redecorate," he moaned.

"I can send it all back," I offered.

His eyes locked on the Chippendale desk, and then they circled the room. "Where's my metal desk?"

"I had it removed," I said softly.

"You did *whaaat*?"

"I had it thrown out. It was inoperable and very, very, *very* ugly."

Bennett gripped his head with his hands. "My partner gave me that desk twenty years ago, right before he was shot in the head by a drug dealer."

"Egad," I sighed. My chest felt heavy, and it wasn't because of the huge strand of Cartier pearls resting on it.

"I can't believe this," he cried.

He paced the room, his face burning purple and his hands knotted into fists, the knuckles going white. "This is my worst fucking nightmare. Barbie redecorates."

"Detective Bennett." I reached out to him. "I can send all this back. And I'll search every Dumpster in Los Angeles to find that desk."

"In *that* outfit?" he snapped. "Forget it. I don't have time for this shit. In the future, would you please refrain from renovating my work environment? It really pisses me off."

"Yes, sir."

"Don't so much as hang a fucking picture without my approval."

"Yes, sir."

"Don't so much as buy a coffee maker without running it by me first."

"Yes, sir."

"Don't even think about throwing the phone away in order to replace it with some silly, fancy device."

"Yes, sir."

"And no air fresheners or perfumes."

"What about aromatherapy candles?"

Bennett shot me a look that cut right through my soul.

I nodded and said, "Yes, sir."

Huffing and puffing, he walked into his office and slammed the door. I slumped down in my Harvard desk chair and began to cry. Feeling silly, I wiped my eyes as the tears flowed. This was my first day on the job and already he despised me.

Thirty minutes later he emerged from his office, his face having resumed its normal color. His hands were no longer fists of rage, so I felt safe saying, "Detective, I was going to have the office painted, but I called it off."

"Well," he sighed, looking at the walls, "that's one thing I wouldn't mind, a new paint job."

"That can be arranged," I said gingerly.

"I'm sure it can," he snorted. "What did you have in mind? Shirley Temple pink? Cotton-candy blue?"

"White."

"I guess that would be okay."

I reached into my purse and removed the sample swatches. "Ralph Lauren makes *thirty-two* different kinds of white paint."

"He must have a lot of fucking time on his hands," he groaned.

I handed over the samples. Grumbling and moaning and sulking, he thumbed through the swatches. Finally, rolling his eyes, he said, "Aspen Summit White is nice."

"It might look too pink," I countered.

He looked them over again. "Spring Clover is fine. Or Petticoat White."

"Pick one."

"I can't believe I'm standing here looking at paint swatches while people are being murdered and raped."

"You gotta have paint," I said flatly. "Just because there's crime doesn't mean you can't have a nice finish on your walls."

"Petticoat White," he mumbled.

We hadn't gotten off to a good start, but most of the tension had faded, as work needed to be done. He instructed me to begin the process of cleaning up the file room, a room so dusty, filthy, and unorganized, I immediately had surgical masks delivered.

It was long and narrow, cramped with brown file cabinets. Numerous unorganized stacks of newspapers and aged-yellow documents decorated the floor, not to mention a bag of half-eaten chips sitting in the corner next to a carton of chocolate milk that had expired during Reagan's second term.

The dust mites were everywhere, laughing at me.

Just as I was tossing out a trash bag, Bennett appeared in the doorway. "Looks nice," he said numbly. "I'm going to run out and grab a snack. Be back in thirty minutes. I assume you'll cover the office, answer the phone like a professional."

"Of course."

"Don't throw any furniture away."

"I promise."

I waited just long enough for him to get on the elevator and then moved swiftly to his office. This is where my life would change. The case file on his desk was open, in plain sight, and just begging for my attention. I didn't hesitate to thumb through the photos, but suddenly I felt a lump in my throat the size of a lemon. Thirty minutes had passed, like a blink of black lightning, and I could hardly move, hadn't even gotten to the dead girl's name, address, cause of death. The photos alone had put me in my place.

I heard Bennett outside the front door, fumbling with the lock, so I quickly bolted for the filing room, pretending to be the dutiful administrator, albeit a little stiff from all the gore I had just witnessed. He was stuffing a handful of chips down his throat when he said, "How's it going?"

"Fine," I said robotically.

"Good. Maybe you can do something about the carpet."

"The carpet?"

"Yeah, that gray stuff you're standing on."

I was in a daze as I thought about that girl in the pictures, the one with her throat slit wide open.

"Right," I said. "The . . . carpet."

"You okay?"

"Yeah."

He turned on his heel, went into his office, and closed the door. Another blink of a second and he was in my face, saying something like, "You've been going through my shit."

"I wouldn't touch your shit."

"That file on my desk," he said. "It's out of place."

"I don't know what you're talking about."

"You've got a lot of nerve, lady, sniffing around a detective's joint and then lying about it."

I hadn't replied fast enough, confirming his accusation.

He continued. "And, besides, I can see death in your eyes."

"What?" I said.

He waved a hand. "It's an old saying. You've changed, let's put it that way. You've been looking at death photos. It's written all over your face."

Bennett was right. There wasn't a concealer in the world that could disguise my ashen face. "Who is she?" I said. "The one in the pictures."

"A victim. Something I'm working on." His back was to me now. "Not for the faint of heart."

"Wait," I said. "I want *in*."

"This isn't a card game."

"You know what I mean. I can't have you, a layman, waltzing into crime scenes, exposing yourself to danger."

"Technically, it's lay-*wo*man, and I don't expose myself to anything . . . unless, of course, there's a lot of money involved."

"I think you'd be better suited at the office. Painting and sculpting and decorating."

"Don't make me call . . . the mayor."

We walked into his office and he pushed the file over to me in a huff. "Victim's name is Beth Valentine. Caucasian. Twenty-two. Five-six. One hundred and twenty pounds. Murdered about two months ago in a Venice warehouse. August twenty-seventh, to be exact."

I stared at the crime-scene photos again.

"She had her throat cut," he said. "I just took on the case a couple days ago, so I'm in the preliminary stages of the investigation. It's frustrating as hell. Her mother hired me, and she doesn't exactly have the cash to spend on a P.I. She's a part-time nurse over at Mercy Hospital."

"The police just handed the case over to you?"

"After a certain period of time, they can't justify the resources. It just goes cold. And now I'm walking the same old tracks Homicide walked when they were on the beat. But, you know, big police departments have an influx of new cases and murders and missing girls. Eventually, cases get tossed aside. And, if they're lucky, they get tossed aside to me."

"You some kind of genius?"

"No." His smirk was annoying. "Some of the guys on the force used to call me the Sherlock Holmes of L.A."

"Oh, Gawd."

"Anyway, I got good instincts and that's what it's all about. Beth Valentine liked to party, liked to have a good time, and liked to have sex. With a lot of people. She's what I call a high-risk victim in a high-risk environment. Those are the worst cases, because the potential suspects are endless and most of 'em you'll never even know about. Faceless and nameless men who float in and out of people's lives—drifters, grifters, and players, all subject to telling lies and skipping town."

"Suspects in this case?"

"Nothing solid. Uniforms interviewed more than seventy people. Valentine was likable and beautiful but didn't have any stable relationships. It was hard to find anyone that really knew her, other than her mother. The girl lived fast and hard and died young. Motive could never be established, and a crime without motive is especially difficult to solve."

I stood from the chair, walked into the partially renovated lobby, and pulled my limited-edition spyglasses from my purse. These glasses looked like ordinary reading glasses, but they were actually custom-designed close-range specs that functioned like a high-definition magnifying glass.

Bennett studied me as I held the picture to my face. "What the hell are you doing?" he asked.

"I'm looking at the picture with my special glasses."

"You're going to *read* the picture?" he said bitterly.

"These glasses were designed by the Dutch," I said matter-of-factly. "Their high-def lenses can identify something as small as a fiber. I could find *anything* with these."

"Oh, really," he snorted. "Why don't you find her killer with them?"

"The lenses will pick up only small objects."

Agitated, he flinched, leaned across the desk, and snatched the photo from my moisturized hand.

"Claire," he growled, "this is going to be a long fucking week if you're going to be pulling out all your James Bond trinkets."

"I'll have you know these glasses cost twelve thousand dollars."

"Clearly you didn't wait for your change," he snorted.

"Very funny," I said. "Who found the body?"

"I was just getting to that," he said. "Kids. Two thirteen-year-old boys. Looking to have a smoke inside the warehouse, they removed the plywood from one of the windows. Crawled inside. Awful mess. The stink was pretty bad, being August and all. Hottest day of the year."

"Estimated time of death?"

"Roughly two in the morning," he said, reaching into the top drawer of the desk. "Here's a replica of the type of blade used to cut her throat." The knife was approximately eight inches in length with a sturdy wooden handle and a jagged edge. "Whoever killed her knew exactly what they were doing. He hit the jugular, and it was over. And he split without leaving a single print, fiber, or DNA sample. It was a clean job, very methodical and careful. But the guy likes risk."

"How do you know that?"

"Because he took something from her." He removed more photos, different angles. "He was willing to stick around after he did the job. I figure he needed something extra, a souvenir."

She wasn't missing any body parts and I didn't quite understand until I caught a close-up of the head. Strands of blond hair were scattered, revealing a glimmer of exposed scalp. "He took hair," I said.

"That's right. Hasn't really worked his way up to flesh and bones. It's a starting point, though, and that's what makes me nervous."

"Maybe he likes blondes."

"I don't think he likes women, *period.* Deep down, on an emotional level, he's your basic misogynist. And don't make any jokes about him being a hairdresser. I already heard enough of that crap from the guys over at the department. They got all sorts of cutesy names for the creep. Pisses me off, how trivial we've gotten about murder. If it's not a headline, nobody gives a shit."

"Didn't mean to get you all riled up."

He shrugged. "It's just the culture these days. I bear witness to the demise of society."

Bennett didn't spend much time on the emotional stuff and removed another manila file folder from the top drawer of his desk. "Here's a copy of the case file in its entirety. Case number 137521-37A-2005."

"Thanks."

"Toxicology reports, crime-scene photos, autopsy results. The whole shebang. Give it a read. Let me know if you have any questions."

"Will do," I said. "May I pay her mother a visit?"

"You're an administrator, not an investigator. What is it *you're* going to find that I couldn't?"

"I don't know. Nothing, probably. But I'm a woman . . ."

"Meaning what, exactly?"

"Meaning, well, you know. Woman-to-woman kind of thing. I might be some kind of support system for her. She might talk about different things. She'll see me as a person, not a detective taking notes."

Defensive and agitated, Bennett crossed his arms in front of his chest and studied me as if I were a thief in the night. "You're a real piece of work, Claire."

"What does *that* mean?"

"You're just a piece of work. Con artist. Charmer. Whatever."

"I'll take that as a compliment."

"Take it however you like," he said. "I'll call her. See if she wants a visitor."

"That would be great."

Studying me again, more intensely, he said, "And tone yourself down before you meet her. Nix all the diamonds and fur and shit. I don't want her to think the Republican National Committee has come calling."

4

My housekeeper was standing in the kitchen when I got home. She had, unfortunately, become a permanent fixture in my life, kind of like depression and overpriced shoes. Her name was Rosa Fernandez, and she had been born and raised in some obscure part of Mexico. Now pushing fifty-one, she had lived in the United States for years but still hung on to a fairly thick Spanish accent. Proud to be the worst-dressed maid in Southern California, she was round-faced and olive-skinned, and her acidic, back-talking tone kept me honest.

For a price.

She despised my luxurious lifestyle, complained about my only pet, and tried to put a lock on the house bar. For all the trouble and criticism she brought me, I just couldn't fire her. She was like the eccentric overbearing aunt you loved to hate. And she had become a staple of reality in fantasyland.

"I got the job," I said, tossing my purse onto the counter.

"The one your father *bought* you."

"He didn't buy me anything. He made a few calls to city officials, that's all."

"Whatever the case," she sighed, "I'm glad to see Miss Claire have a job now. Twenty-eight is a good age to join the workforce."

"You could at least congratulate me, Rosa."

"Congratulations."

I walked over to the bar, poured myself a glass of Pellegrino. "I am now working with the finest homicide detective in Los Angeles. He gave me the case file on a girl who's been dead for some time now, but he's just starting to work it. I think it's going to be interesting, going to take me to some very dark places."

"I didn't even know you left Brentwood."

"I do now."

"That's nice, I'll have the house to myself."

"Good. Maybe you'll have time to actually clean it."

She rolled her eyes at me, then jerked a thumb toward the patio. "That animal you got, Claire. What a nuisance. You don't even have a license for it."

"It's a rabbit."

"With pit bull blood. You know, I took that *thing* to the vet last week. Guy said it was twenty pounds overweight, like it was taking hormones or something."

"It's all the . . ."

"What?"

"The sleeping pills." I shrugged, a bit helpless. "Sergeant's very high-strung, anxious. I just give him half of one at night. It helps him rest."

She just stood there, paralyzed with shock, her face frozen, eyes unblinking. I grabbed my purse from the counter and left her standing there, hoping she would thaw out in time to make dinner.

A few hours later, after I had eaten a lonely meal in front of the television, had a cocktail and a hot shower, Bennett rang my cell phone. I was quite surprised to hear from him.

"Claire," he barked. "I talked to Nina Valentine. She wants company tonight."

"Tonight?" I looked at my watch.

"Yes, *to*night. She's a night owl. Has insomnia. I'll give you her address. Be there at nine o'clock."

"As in thirty minutes from now?"

"Yeeees," he said, annoyed.

"Okay. Give me her digits."

Bennett rambled off her address. "No funny stuff," he said.

"What does that mean?"

"It means . . . this is serious business. Don't be an idiot. Don't pull out a bunch of spy equipment in front of this poor woman. And leave all your fucking bangles and pearls at home. Don't want to intimidate her with your bling-bling."

"I'll dress down."

"Dress *normal,*" he said coldly.

Standing in front of my closet, searching for something normal to wear, I realized this on-call crap was going to kill me. I slid into a red Prada tracksuit, then removed my diamond earrings, pulled my hair back into a ponytail, and slid my cold feet into tennis shoes. One simple strand of pearls would suffice.

5

Nina Valentine lived in a forgotten neighborhood.

Her backyard was set against the old train tracks that hadn't been in operation since the seventies. Now it was just a metal graveyard that glistened in the distance like a slimy creature. The streets were narrow and lined with trees, a rustic ambience that had probably once been charming. But the quaintness had been overshadowed by blue-collar apathy. Mud-encrusted trucks were parked at the curb, brown lawns had gone bald from neglect, and beer bottles rolling aimlessly in the wind.

I pulled into the driveway, parked behind an old gray Pontiac, and then found my way onto the front porch. Ceramic blue chimes sang in the breeze as I, almost hesitantly, knocked on the front door. I stood in the darkness for a while, trying to compose myself, thinking of the unspeakable evil that had destroyed this woman's life.

I was a little on edge when the door opened. We formally introduced ourselves and I felt like a used-car saleswoman, greasy palms, too much fragrance, grinning ear to ear.

"Nice to meet you," she said, waving me inside. "Can I get you a drink?"

"No, ma'am. I'm fine."

She wore a paisley housedress that revealed ample cleavage, fleshy arms, a body lost to age and gravity. Her face was specked with freckles, heavily lined, and set in a permanent frown. Once-blond hair had grown gray around the temples, and I imagined beneath the extra weight she had cheekbones and a square jaw. She moved like a heavy woman, exhausted by heartache and hard times.

"Have a seat." She jerked a thumb toward the sofa. "Sorry about the mess. Haven't really been myself since my daughter was murdered."

"Understandably."

A glint of rage poked out at me, and I wondered if she resented me for having been spared such a gruesome fate. I suddenly regretted the strand of pearls around my neck. And the Mercedes sitting in her driveway seemed so pretentious. As I sat on her worn sofa, mindlessly plucking at the loose foam, I envisioned a nightmare unfolding in this very house. The inevitable visit from the police department. Identifying the body. Answering endless questions about her daughter's personal affairs, from parties to pap smears. The stoic air of loss filled every inch of the place with a certain despair that would linger forever.

She walked out of the kitchen carrying a bottle of Jim Beam and a glass of ice. "You're not what I expected."

"I'm sorry."

"No, no." She sat down across from me. "Don't be. I didn't mean it like that. When Detective Bennett called and said his assistant was going to drop by, well, I had this image in my head. Stocky woman with a buzz cut and a chip on her shoulder."

"Well, I'm not stocky and don't have a buzz cut."

"Chip on the shoulder?"

"Of course."

She poured the alcohol over the ice, her face perpetually twisted in anger. "I'm sure you've seen the photos?"

"Yes."

"So awful." Her drink went down like a shot. "Hard to imagine someone could do such a thing, especially to my baby. Bastard cut her neck like he was skinning a deer. No second thought. No hesitation. That's hate, I tell you. No other way around it."

She looked at me pensively, waiting for a response.

"I agree."

"She had a reputation, you know. I'm sure Bennett told you."

"We've discussed her history. She liked to have a good time, made many friends."

"Makes it hard for you, doesn't it?" She shrugged. "All those nameless people out there, mostly men. She had a way with them. And, obviously, they had a way with her. I had a time of it when the police were working this case. A couple of those boys wanted to paint her as a whore and I wouldn't have it. They even asked if she was involved with an out-call service. Or if she took off her clothes for money. My daughter was many things, but a prostitute she was not."

Nina Valentine was white-knuckling the glass of Jim Beam.

"I wish I could . . ." My words trailed off.

She lit a cigarette. "What?"

I shrugged helplessly.

"There is nothing you can offer me. I know, deep down, you'd like to send me to AA and paint my house and maybe even loan me your psychiatrist for a few months. But it won't help."

"Then what?" I said. "What will help?"

"Catch him." She exhaled like a dragon blowing fire. "And maybe I'll be able to sleep again. That's the biggest problem these days. Insomnia. Tossing and turning, watching the clock as the hours tick by. I think maybe I'm afraid to actually *fall* asleep. Because that's when I dream about him, the face in the window."

"The face in the window?"

"That was my recurring nightmare before I gave up sleep." She poured another shot, rattled the ice against the glass. "He would come to me in my dreams. His white face just beyond the glass, looking into my bedroom like some kind of nocturnal lunatic. No distinct features, really. No identifiable shape, no nose. Something terribly inhuman and rotten about him."

She took a long drag on the cigarette. "It's always the same, this dream. And I always walk to the window, drapes pulled back, hoping that I'll catch a glimpse of something real. But I never do. It's like my daughter's killer haunts me, but it's just his spirit, not his body. He likes to watch me while I sleep, full of pride and ego, laughing at how those cops couldn't find a decent lead."

"Don't give up." I felt ridiculous saying it. "Bennett is very smart, the best in the business. He's got great instincts. And me, well . . . Let's just say watch out."

"You don't look so tough." She wanted to smile. "In fact, you don't look like you could kill an insect."

"Oooooh, Ms. Valentine, you have no idea. I've killed ants. Some spiders. Couple of roaches. Even a mouse."

"Wow." Her voice was laced with sarcasm. "You're a real . . . exterminator."

She clicked on the television and muted the sound. Blue light flickered on picture-less walls, and we watched, in silence, as Lucy Ricardo did a comedic dance across the screen, with Ricky frozen in laughter. The wind tickled the old windows and I thought I heard a train in the distance, like an old ghost passing through out of habit. But I knew there was nothing left but crippled steel and tar and deformed tracks.

She let out a haggard sigh. "Well, tell me something about yourself, Claire. From around here? Got a fella?" Her eyes drifted to the floor.

"I didn't come here to talk about me. Or the fella I don't have. I just wanted to introduce myself, get to know you, see where Beth grew up. I know it seems sophomoric."

"Not at all. You got that investigation ritual down. Get inside the victim's head, live their life, try and walk in those shoes. Bennett spent an hour in her room, even though she hasn't lived here for years. When we cleaned out her apartment, I moved all the boxes in there. Keep the door closed. Never go in. Maybe someday I'll unpack her things and be able to smell her clothes again."

I asked to see Beth's old room and Nina obliged. Tilting her head toward the hallway. "Have a look," she said. "On your own. Too hard for me right now. I apologize profusely for the dust."

My footsteps were blanketed by thick beige carpet and I opened the last door on the right, listening as the volume finally came to Lucy's voice. "Riiiiicky!" Automated audience laughter. I shut out all the noise and closed the door behind me.

Beth's youthful years were spent in a lavender room with one window, a small closet, and a twin mattress with a brass headboard. Old movie posters were now peeling from the walls, everything was tinged yellow from age, except for a red lava lamp in the corner, still as bright as a cherry, although sitting in the shadow of cardboard boxes. Gray dust covered the place like fallen snow. The ancient dresser had faded to a diluted pink, knobs were missing, and the drawers had been emptied out. I was left standing there, in the stillness of it all, wondering what this girl dreamed about as a child.

I wasn't really sure what I was looking for. But I knew in my heart I wouldn't find it in this room.

I Love Lucy was over, the sound muted again. Nina had managed to empty half the bottle since my arrival. It felt late, like hours had passed and three A.M. was waiting on the front porch.

"You sure you don't wanna drink?"

"No, thank you," I said. "I better get going. Don't want to wear out my welcome."

"You can stay as long as you like. I'm not going to sleep anytime soon."

The face in the window.

She walked me to the front door, a little wobbly from the booze. "You will come back, won't you?" Her voice was flooded with desperation.

"Of course."

"Did Bennett tell you I'm a nurse?"

"He mentioned something about it."

"Don't work that much anymore. The hospital has been very understanding. I'm on nights, twice a week. They rotate the schedule, but I'm usually there on Wednesdays and Fridays. Graveyard shift. It works perfect for me since I'm up all night anyway."

"Mercy Hospital, right?"

"That's correct. It's a gem of a place, been there for ten years. Used to love it. But I'm old and broken now and there's no sense trying to find happiness in bedpans and broken bones. It's a job, though, and I need the insurance. The rent money."

The streets were quiet, a full moon rising like a white globe in the sky. Trees rustled in the wind, casting ever-changing shadows on drooping sidewalks and archaic vehicles. I passed an elderly man walking his dog and he gave me a friendly wave. Suddenly this forgotten neighborhood didn't seem so dangerous, so foreign.

6

I arrived home just in time to spy on my neighbor, John Armstrong. He had been living next door for almost a year and had proven to be the perfect neighbor, a quiet, unobtrusive world-traveler.

He was tall, six-four, I guessed, with broad shoulders and a lean build, silvery-gray hair that was always tousled and sexy, bedroom eyes. Rugged but elegant. He clearly had money, since he was living next door to me. And, of course, he seemed completely, irrevocably emotionally unavailable and uninterested in me. Which made him so very, very, very desirable and appealing.

Backstory: Six months ago, Sergeant, my impulsive rabbit, dug through the backyard, crossed over into John Armstrong's, and tore his entire yard to shreds. We were introduced when he handed me a landscaping bill for five thousand dollars. I distinctly remember attempting to flirt with him, but it had proved useless. He was flushed with anger and didn't even notice the La Perla peeking through the sheer Gucci blouse.

But I remember being immediately smitten with him, regardless of the fact that he was much older and seemingly hated me. Armstrong was unapproachable, mysterious, and gone a lot. *What's not to love?*

On this very balmy California night, I retired the idea of having my apple martini and watching *Law & Order*. I had more exciting plans that involved a Pier One wicker chair and night-vision goggles.

Standing in the darkness of my backyard, peering through my

night specs, I watched Armstrong pace his backyard while talking on the phone. He appeared green through the lens, but still desirable. As he paced back and forth, mumbling and growling on his cellular, I silently perched on the wicker chair, steadily adjusting my goggles.

Darkness allowed me to be invisible. Darkness allows all of us to be invisible. I suppose that's the danger of night.

Armstrong clicked off his cell in a huff, walked back inside his house, and pulled the sliding glass door shut with a thump. My night spying had come to an abrupt end.

No less than three minutes later, I was responding to a heavy-handed knock on my front door. He stood before me wearing khaki pants and a Ralph Lauren oxford shirt. Sexy windblown hair. Mysterious, twinkling eyes. His voice was thick with suspicion. "Claire, is it?"

"Yes, Claire Fontaine," I said, extending my hand.

"John Armstrong," he said as he shook my hand.

"Yes, we met about six months ago."

"We did?" he asked curiously. "Oh, yeah, when your gerbil ate my backyard."

"Rabbit. My rabbit," I said.

I invited him inside my house and he entered with trepidation, as if this wasn't a social call and he didn't want to be cornered.

"What can I do for you?" I said awkwardly.

"Why do you have night-vision goggles?"

"Huh?" I said, feeling the sudden heat climb my neck to my face.

"Why do you have night-vision goggles?"

"I'm not sure," I said. "They come in handy sometimes."

"Like when you want to spy on your neighbor?"

"Well. You know. I'm just. It wasn't like—"

"May I see them?" he interrupted coldly.

I walked quickly to the kitchen, removed them from the counter, and scurried back to the living room. I was certain my face had turned a strange shade of purple and my hands were moist with perspiration. Flushed and anxious, I handed the goggles to him. "It's the Dipol 2MV. It can be used as a night-vision goggle or, detached, as a night-vision binocular," I said. "It has a built-in infrared illuminator for operation in low-light conditions or total darkness."

"Like your backyard?" he grunted. Methodically, he detached the binocular from the mask and said, "What's the viewing distance?"

"Up to two hundred meters in normal conditions, and about a hundred in hazy conditions," I said matter-of-factly.

Eyeing me suspiciously, he declared, "You'd make a terrible spy."

"Well, thankfully, I'm not one," I retorted.

He continued to study the specs. His silence was alarming.

I blinked at him. "Are you going to use them against me in a court of law?"

"Not yet," he said dryly.

Seemingly uninterested in the entire experience, he reattached the binocular to the mask and handed it back to me. Shrugging his broad shoulders, he said, "You might want to consider the B21 Military Night-Vision Binoculars. Very high resolution, viewing distance of two hundred and fifty meters."

"Oh, okay," I said.

"I mean," he added, smirking, "if you're going to be spying on me, you should have the proper equipment."

An awkward moment. Alone with him, I found myself uninteresting, nervous, and, worse, a terrible hostess. He had not left my house as I had expected him to, and I seemed incapable of entertaining a man. It had been so long since I was alone with one, and now it appeared as if he was possibly, maybe, sort of flirting with me. I felt flustered, light-headed, and the Xanax was upstairs. But the Grey Goose was only ten steps away. "Would you like a drink?"

"No, thanks," he said. "I wasn't planning on staying long."

"That's too bad," I mumbled, "because I really wanted a drink."

"How long do you plan on spying on me?"

"I hadn't really given it any thought," I said with a shrug.

"Well, just so you know my schedule, I'll be in London next week and then I'll be back. Two weeks from Sunday I'll be in Tokyo."

"I appreciate that," I said, laughing. "Should I call you Mr. Armstrong?"

"John is fine," he said coolly.

He turned around and let himself out.

The man disappeared so quickly it was as if he had never been there, a flirtatious ghost filling my romantic void. But I could still smell his musky human scent, and I knew he was real.

7

The painters arrived at the office at nine A.M. with five gallons of Ralph Lauren Petticoat White for the lobby and three gallons of Granite Falls for Detective Bennett's office.

We decided to take a drive while the men worked on the renovation. Henry Bennett drove a brown 1985 Buick. It was a real piece of crap, dirty and grimy, falling apart at the seams.

"What a piece of junk you drive," I said, pushing old fast-food cartons from the seat.

"Hey, it works and it's paid for. And it blends. I don't need some flashy red car in my business."

"Where are we going?"

He pulled onto Wilshire Boulevard and hit the gas just hard enough to throw back my head. With an air of pride in his voice, he said, "I'm gonna show you the crime scene. You'll get a sense of how the girl died. It'll be a learning experience. I want you to absorb."

"Absorb *what?*"

"The environment."

"The warehouse?"

"That's right." He tapped the steering wheel. "What's important to remember is that *he* chose this place. Might not look like much, condemned. You wouldn't think twice about tearing it down and building a Versace store in its place."

We parked across the street from the dilapidated warehouse where Beth Valentine's dead body was found. The neighborhood was industrial and artistic, sparse street decor. Mostly concrete. Reminded me of New York. Hard to imagine there was an ocean only four blocks from the building, but I could smell the salt air.

We stood in the middle of the parking lot—cracked, uprooted concrete littered with trash, used condoms, and old clothing someone had discarded. It was unusually hot for October, and Detective Bennett was sweating like a pig. Thankfully, I was wearing a red dress with thin flimsy fabric, which allowed my body to breathe. My hair was pulled off my neck, tied back with a silk scarf. Silver open-toe Jimmy Choo sandals. Clearly, I was overdressed for the occasion.

I followed Bennett's slow and sturdy pace to the metal door. While his fleshy fingers fumbled with the lock, I glanced around at the neglected environment that had invited death inside. The building itself was brown brick with windows that had been shot out and renovated with plywood. Wiry, beige shrubs had grown through the cracks of the cement, and the thick hum of flies swarming created unpleasant music to my ears.

He unlatched the lock and pulled open the door. "It's gonna be ril, ril hot inside," he said. "And it'll probably smell like piss and rot and death."

"I can take it," I said, removing my sunglasses.

The door slammed shut behind us and I covered my mouth.

It was stifling inside, and the heat only brought out the various odors that had been held captive for however many years the warehouse had remained empty. The floor was battleship-gray concrete, skuffed and stained. Blue-black mold grew on the west wall. Hot and muggy, no electricity, foul smelling, eyesore, waste of trendy space, and coffin to Beth Valentine. "You're right," I said. "I would tear this thing down, but I wouldn't replace it with anything. Too many ghosts in this place; the land is probably cursed."

He wasn't even listening to me. "Over here," he said. Standing there, head down, hands shoved into his pockets, he stared at the barren concrete. "This is where they found her."

The snapshots of her death blinked in front of me like a bad flashback. I could see her body, twisted, painted in blood, the blond hair scattered. It was all so awful, but the warehouse gave life to a dead scene. I felt transcended, immersed in the experience.

"Yep," he said. Bennett walked the space, tracing the edges of the warehouse with his finger, and wiping the grime on his unfashionable trousers. He then began to mumble to himself, almost as if summoning up her ghost. "Why did you come here? Did you cross the devil? Where is he? A man like that. Talk to me."

I looked away, felt awkward watching Bennett work. I also felt helpless standing there in my Choos as a trained law-enforcement official called upon the spirits of death to help him catch the living.

I leaned down and flicked a black-winged insect from my leg, then walked to the other side of the warehouse. Noticing a small, ramshackle gray door, I said, "What's in there?"

"Nothing," he said with a shrug. "Used to be the bathroom."

"Oh," I said, curiously pushing open the door. The sink had been ripped out of the wall and discarded in the corner. The toilet had been completely removed, leaving an open hole in the earth and producing a malodorous stench that could rival that of a decomposing body. I covered my mouth, leaned back, and shut the door. Walking toward Bennett, I said, "Christ, what a place to die. This shithole. Someone staked this place out, no?"

"Of course they did. Knew it was empty, condemned, dark as the grave. It's a perfect place to commit a crime. Windows boarded. I mean this is Ted Bundy's wet dream—isolated concrete walls." He kicked a piece of cardboard across the floor. "The perp knew the body wouldn't be found immediately, which gave him time to run while the corpse was subjected to it's own gases. I'm not sayin' he's a genius or anything, but he's smart enough. And he's one angry son of a bitch."

"You got a profile?"

"Of course," he said. "But I don't always rely on those things. FBI lives for that shit, behavioral science, psychological analysis. Some of it's hocus-pocus to an old-timer like myself. Can't always go by a diagram to get inside someone's head. All these shrinks sitting around, with their Harvard degrees and fancy textbooks, telling seasoned cops that *all* serial killers are bed wetters and fire starters as children. Or killed the neighbor's cat. I mean, granted, some of that shit is straight on, but it's not the rule."

"What is the rule?"

"There isn't one," he said. "That's the thing. When you're dealing with evil, there are no rules. No givens. No charts. It's about instinct and perspiration, asking questions, walking in their footsteps. And sometimes, it's all about timing."

"What's your thought on this guy?"

He didn't hesitate for a moment. "White male. Late twenties to early thirties. High school education. Raised by a single parent, probably a dominant female. Below-average student in school, felt ostracized. Turned to violence at a young age. Feels inadequate on the inside, needs to obtain power. Likes to have control over women. Fascinated by knives, probably has a collection. Takes the hair because, for now, it satisfies him. He's not ready for body parts and blood." He looked me in the eye. "But, in time, he will be."

"How do you know that?"

"These guys escalate. Our unsub is no different. He'll get more confident, need to take more risks, spend more time with the body. A chunk of blond hair won't do the trick anymore. He'll want flesh. Something more personal. Trust me. I've seen this shit for twenty years. It don't change. It don't get better."

"Doesn't," I corrected.

"What?"

"It *doesn't* get better. That's proper English. You said, 'It don't get better.' "

His blood pressure must have shot through the roof, and his face turned red with rage. "I don't need some bullshit grammar lesson from the likes of you. Keep in mind, I'm doing you a favor. Letting you along for the ride. People in law enforcement, I mean, *real* people in the business, would kill for a gig like this. They wouldn't dare offer up an English lesson while standing in the middle of a crime scene."

"Just thought maybe I'd help you with—"

"I don't need help." He turned from me, a whiff of his sweat tickling my nose.

The tension between us seemed to raise the temperature in the warehouse, if that was even possible. I reached into my clutch, removed a cream-colored, satin Perry Ellis handkerchief, and blotted my forehead. "See what you did to me? Made me sweat," I groaned.

"About time."

We left the warehouse in silence, the tension still palpable and oppressive. Sitting in the car, I started to think about Bennett and all his machismo and wondered if maybe he was threatened by women in general. Smart women, independent women. He'd spent his life surrounded by men in uniform, men with guns, strong men with hearts that had been hardened by the job.

Shifting uncomfortably in my seat, I turned to him and said, "Are you threatened by me because I have a vagina?"

He fell forward against the steering wheel. *"Whaaat?"*

"You heard me," I said. "It's my feminine power that overwhelms you. You're threatened because I am a woman with a vagina."

"I'd be threatened if you were a woman *without* a vagina."

"I'm serious."

"I am too. This is getting weird," he whined. "I don't want to hear any more about your vagina. And you can ditch all this women's lib shit. I'm not threatened by you, period."

He started the engine, turned the radio up as loud as it could possibly go, and drove recklessly toward the office. I reached into my satchel and removed a postmortem photo of our victim. It didn't get any easier, looking at death, no matter how many times I saw the snapshot. Something surreal about the position of the body, not quite posed but twisted in an unnatural manner. Pooled blood that appeared black, jaw set in permanent agony, eyes cloudy and vacant. Bennett turned the radio station when something classy came on, and we were forced to listen to George Thoroughgood the rest of the way. I buried myself in the girl's loss, studying her piece by piece. Head to toe. I noticed the dark patches of hair at the root of her scalp. She was a bottle blonde, peroxide or home bleach. Not a professional job.

"She did her own hair," I said.

"So?"

I took pride in ignoring him and reached into my clutch for the magnifying lenses I had purchased at the Spy Shop on Sunset Boulevard. Pressing my eyes against the razor-thin glass, I studied her hands again, this time closely. Obsessively.

Bennett looked over at me, curious about the fancy lenses. "Where'd you get those?"

"James Bond gave them to me."

"Right," he snorted.

I removed three more of the crime-scene photos. Studying different angles, trying to see as much of her fingers as possible. I could readily identify her fingernails, at least the ones still on her hands, as white-tipped acrylics. French manicure.

Definitely a professional job.

"She had her nails done," I said. "Professionally."

"So?"

"Did you talk to her manicurist?"

"No," he grunted. "Didn't even know she had one."

"Looks to me she did. I'm willing to bet you she told her manicurist a lot of things. Haven't you ever heard the saying 'A manicurist is someone who holds your hand while you talk about your problems'?"

"Cute."

8

The smell of fresh paint filled my nostrils as I sat at my Chippendale desk dialing Nina Valentine's number. She answered on the second ring, we exchanged the usual pleasantries, and then I asked, "Who was Beth's manicurist?"

"Gosh," she said. "Some little Asian girl."

"The Vietnamese have monopolized the nail industry. They're *all* little Asian girls."

"Gimme a sec. I'll remember. Beth went to her for years—a little shop down on Abbott-Kinney."

"Name?"

"Place is on the corner next to an art gallery. You can't miss it."

"What was her manicurist's name?"

"Gimme another sec." She took a deep breath. "Ling. I'm pretty sure that's it. Hope she's still there. My heart is racing. My goodness, I can't believe I remembered." There was so much emotion in the woman's voice I almost felt guilty for getting her hopes up.

"Thank you, Nina. I'll be in touch."

"Wait. Is there, you know, a lead? Something to feel good about? I'm dyin' to know. You have no idea what it's like to be me."

"We're just exploring other avenues, trying to find a new direction."

"That's real smart of you." She sounded on the verge of tears. "All them cops that come over here never asked about her manicurist. Guess they don't think like that, huh? All they wanted to know was who she was screwing. That was the angle they were working, and it never got nobody anywhere."

"That's why Bennett hired me," I said. "I have a different perspective. A rather unique talent for discovering the obscure. The ridiculous. The fine line between innocuous and insidious."

I hung up feeling like a fool, an impostor, a phony.

But it didn't stop me from pursuing the truth.

Nail Works looked out of place. The little yellow house, with its old windows and lopsided porch, was uncomfortably squeezed between a pretentious art gallery and an overpriced bar. The old broad at the front told me Ling was booked solid for the day. At a feverish pitch, I complained about an ingrown toenail and how I needed an "emergency" pedicure and how I'd pay three times the regular price. Five minutes later I was sitting at Ling's station, looking at her heart-shaped face and tiny spandex dress. She lowered herself to the ground and removed my shoes. "You have hurt foot?" Her Vietnamese accent was thick and I suspected she was barely twenty.

"I need your help."

"I fix you." She put my feet into a basin of water. "Soak for five minutes."

She was about to leave me sitting there. "Wait," I said.

"You need sumting?"

"Yes. I do. Wanted to know if you remember a girl named Beth Valentine?"

She was lost in memory for a moment. "Oh, yes. She was a good client, nice girl. I liked her a lot. She was murdered."

"How did you hear about it?"

"Some other girls that come in here talk about it. They tell me. Said it was awful mess. Baaaad man got to her."

She lowered herself to my feet, clipped a piece of skin from my cuticle, and then said, "You knew her?"

"No."

"Why you ask 'bout her?"

"I'm trying to figure out why she was killed."

"You a cop?"

"No, no," I said, waving a hand.

"But you're working on finding the bad man?"

"That's correct. Did Beth talk about her boyfriends?"

"Sumtime." She nodded. "There were many. Every two week, she had a different boy. Very popular."

Ling avoided eye contact, head down, working robotically on my feet. "Beth liked having many partners. Kind of wild that way," she whispered.

"Did she talk about any of them in particular?"

"Don't 'member. I hear so many stories from so many women. Can't keep track."

"Do you recall if she ever said anything about someone getting violent, making threats?"

She finally looked up. "No. Don't think so. Beth liked everybody, you know. She was touchy-feely that way. Liked to be pretty. Very American girl. She had friend that come in here, too. They potty together."

"Potty?"

"Yeah, you know: potty." She wiggled her body.

"Party?"

"Yeah, potty. They do all sorts of tings like that."

"Remember the girl's name?"

"Isabelle," she said. "Isabelle Minx. Sumtime she still come in and get nails done. I hear she makes dirty movies, sumting like that."

"Know where I can find her?"

"We have phone number in book at front desk. That's all we have. Don't keep no good records at Nail Works."

"That's fine. I appreciate the information. When was the last time you saw this Minx girl?"

Ling looked over my shoulder, eyes clouded in thought. "Maybe a month ago. Not fo' sure."

I had my toes painted cherry red, tipped the girl fifty bucks, and got the number from the schedule book. Walking out of the place, I felt a little rush of adrenaline as I dialed the number on my cell phone.

"Gardenia Productions." A woman answered.

"I'm looking for Isabelle Minx."

"She's out of town."

"Do you know when she'll be back?"

"In the morning," she snapped. "Who is this?"

"Just a friend."

"Right."

The next thing I heard was a dial tone.

9

By the time I got to the office, Detective Bennett had already ruined the new paint job and was growling. "Seeee, this is a fucking mess. The walls are wet. The back of my pants are fucking stained with this Petticoat-white shit. You come in here and mess everything up."

"Looks like you messed everything up," I said, pointing to the ass-print on the wall.

"How'd it go with the salon lady?"

"Quite well," I said proudly.

"Really?"

"Ooooh, yes. I got a name. And a number. And I bet you've never even heard of this chick."

"Give it to me."

"Isabelle Minx."

"You're right. That her real name?"

"Who knows? I got a real number, though. Works at some place called Gardenia Productions. Out of town till tomorrow morning. Manicurist said she was a regular 'potty' girl who spent some time with the victim. I think it's a lead."

"Could be." He was so blasé it irked every nerve in my body.

"I was hoping for a little more enthusiasm, Detective."

"Listen, kid, I've learned not to get too excited with every witness. Gotta be realistic. Most of them turn out to be worthless. But we'll pay her a vist in the morning. You did good. I would've never caught the nail thing. Ever. That manicure shit don't even cross my mind."

"That's what I'm here for."

"Yeah . . ." He let out an exhausted sigh. "I'm going to grab a bite to eat. Be back in thirty." He reached for the door.

And then I put a stain on his plans. "I want to see where she lived."

"Who?"

"The Valentine girl."

"It's not that relevant anymore. And besides, I just went there a few days ago. Waste of time."

"I think it's important that I see where the vic ate and slept and washed her hair. It'll give me insight."

"It'll give me gas." He picked at his dry elbow skin, privately debating whether or not to take me on a tour. "It's not exactly the Plaza," he snorted.

"Neither is this joint."

"Christ. You're a pain in my fucking ass. You just want to stroll around the apartment complex?"

"I think it's a valid request."

Sighing, he shoved his hands into his pockets and jiggled his keys. "Fine," he said, sulking. "Twenty minutes and we're outta there."

"Great."

"And I mean twenty minutes, Claire. Don't even think about redecorating the place."

I slid into the Buick and plucked at the worn, brown leather seats.

More fast-food containers had collected on the floorboard of the passenger's side. I kicked a Del Taco bag out of my way and coldly said, "Maybe we can trash some of this trash."

"Don't push it, Claire."

"Should we make an appointment with management, inform them of our arrival?"

"We're not ambassadors or diplomats arriving at the White House for dinner," he huffed.

"I know. But shouldn't we—"

"This isn't the kind of joint where I need a fucking permit to get on the grounds. And 'management,'" he snorted, making invisible quote marks in the air with his fingers, "consists of one punk actor that thinks he's James Dean."

"Ooooh," I said. "I sense tension."

"How perceptive of you," Bennett said dryly. "You know, the kid's a punk. Typical. Comes to Hollywood thinking he's a big shit. I think his bullshit attitude comes from the fact that he's trying to be James Dean."

"Did you tell him that James Dean is dead and no one should aspire to be dead?"

Bennett found my humor to be annoying and turned up the radio.

I began tossing empty Coke bottles into the backseat until I had enough legroom on the passenger's side. He rolled down his window and hung his arm over the side. Pushing his greasy, nondescript hair from his face, he said, "I just didn't like the kid. I mean he wasn't helpful. He wasn't accessible. I'm running a homicide investigation, and he's annoyed that I gotta have access to the property. I think he missed some audition, got real smug with me. His name is John Dean, or something like that. How ridiculous. John Dean. Of course that's not his *real* name. His birth name is something like Bob Pollock. I can't remember. He's about as relevant as the dirt beneath my fingernails."

"I'm really glad I brought it up."

"If we're lucky," Bennett moaned, "we won't have to deal with the son of a bitch."

We weren't lucky.

The building was three stories of neglected rot: Lime-green paint peeling off the walls in large sections. Broken windows. Sharp, angular pieces of glass glistening in the sun. Grimy metal gates positioned drearily at the front of the building, as uninviting as the surrounding landscape. I rolled down my window and observed the premises. Ghostly. Abandoned.

I turned to Bennett. "Does anyone even live here?"

He killed the engine. "They did a few days ago. Looks like a tornado came through here."

Dirty mattresses were piled outside the front gate, along with an overturned couch and broken furniture. Grass along the side of the complex was brown, overgrown, and littered with discarded shower curtains and rusted kitchen appliances.

Bennett and I stepped out of the car, made our way to the front, and took in the emptiness of the space. He pushed open the gate, which creaked painfully with every inch, and then waved for me to follow. In the courtyard, center of the complex, was a small swimming pool filled with dirt. The place was oddly quiet, desperate for human attention.

And then, suddenly, there was music coming from above.

The elevator remained permanently open and dark, so we climbed the stairs to the third floor. Following the beat of the music, we found ourselves standing in front of apartment 17. Bennett rolled his eyes. "The punk is here," he said.

"How do you know?"

"Recognize the tunes."

Bennett rapped his fist on the door like he was serving a warrant.

The footsteps inside were fast approaching, and then a young man appeared with a Marlboro dangling from his lower lip. Mid-twenties with high cheekbones, perfect skin, and certainly a strong resemblance to the late James Dean. He raised his sculpted nose at Bennett, then ran a hand through his sandy locks. "What do *you* want?"

"Nice to see you, too."

"I'm serious," the kid hissed. "Can't you see there ain't nothing left? Nobody left here but me. And I'm outta here in four days."

"Good for you," Bennett snapped.

"Who's the babe?" the kid asked, tilting his head toward me.

Bennett cleared his throat. "Claire Fontaine. She's working with me."

"You a cop?" He studied me. "Certainly don't look like one, if ya are."

"No," I said. "But I would like to see Valentine's old apartment."

"What for?" he asked, dropping the cigarette to the ground and smashing it out with the heel of his tennis shoe. "This entire place is about to be torn down. Every single inch of it. The assholes that owned this property sold it. They're bringin' in bulldozers on Monday."

"Why the tear-down?" Bennett said.

" 'Cause they're gonna build a fucking Starbucks. And then put another Starbucks next to it."

"Would it be okay if I looked around?" I said.

He opened the door wide enough for me to get a glimpse inside his apartment. Moving boxes lined the walls. "I'm John Dean," he said, looking directly at me. "People call me Johnny."

We shook hands.

Bennett yawned. "Look, kid, I ain't got all day. Show her apartment fourteen."

Johnny stepped back inside, turned down his stereo, and watched the muted television screen in front of him. *"Blade Runner,"* he said, looking at me. "Remember that one? Harrison Ford. Sean Young. One of Ridley Scott's best, I think."

"Yeah, I remember. Sean Young had that awful haircut. Bangs up to the middle of her forehead."

He shoved his hands into his pockets, smiling at the television screen, inadvertently inviting us inside. He picked up a pack of Marlboros and removed a cigarette.

I could hear Bennett sigh—a deep, sulking, stop-wasting-my-fucking-time sigh. "Uh, Johnny, I'd like for you to show Claire the apartment before the building gets torn down."

"Why should I? You don't got nothing on me, don't got a legal document in your hand. You just waltz in here uninvited and start ordering me around."

"I've got connections at the Screen Actors Guild. I could make a few calls, have your SAG card revoked."

"For what?"

"Anything. Could say you harassed other actors on the set, sold drugs, showed up drunk. Depends how creative I feel when I make the call."

"Fine," he groaned. "Lemme grab my lighter."

He sauntered over to the table and purposely knocked a stack of headshots onto the floor, making a loud commotion over them and drawing attention to his raw beauty. Neither Bennett nor I commented on the photos. I watched as frustration danced across his face. He picked one of the black-and-whites up and began to fan himself with it. Bennett rolled his eyes again and then looked at the Timex around his wrist.

As we were heading out the door I could hear footsteps above us. Bennett looked up at the ceiling, taking note of the mysterious thumping. He turned to Johnny, got into his pretty face, and said, "Who's on the roof, kid?"

"My girlfriend," Johnny mumbled. "It's no big deal. She's workin' on her tan. Likes to lay out nude up there. Ain't nobody around to see her."

We could hear the hollow sound of someone trouncing down the stairwell. Within moments, a tan, sultry blonde with huge silicon breasts stood before us. Bennett gulped when he saw her, the enormous plush rack, long tan legs, firm stomach. She was wearing a skimpy leopard-print bikini and flip-flops. I could smell the Hawaiian Tropic on her from ten feet away. The grease on her body caught the brilliant shimmer of sunlight, casting a glare across her taut belly. She eyed Bennett and me suspiciously. "Johnny, who are these people?" she asked, smacking her gum.

"The *po*-lice," he said.

"Really?" she purred, a hint of excitement in her gravelly voice.

"Yeah," he groaned. "Remember that chick that used to rent the studio in the corner? The blonde?"

"Yeah," she smacked. "The sexaholic."

"Right." He smiled wide, flashing his poorly capped teeth, white as fresh snow. "They're here to see the apartment she used to live in."

"Can't imagine why," she said, blowing a pink bubble. "Won't find anything of hers. We rented that apartment out to some Japanese man a week after she got murdered."

"I know," Bennett said. "And I've already seen the place. My associate"—he glanced at me—"would like to have a look. You can blame her for all the inconvenience."

I rolled my eyes and handed Johnny a twenty. "Here," I said. "Here's some cash for your efforts. It'll buy you some smokes."

"Yeah. Cool." He pocketed the cash. His girlfriend was now batting her eyelashes at Bennett, looking for some male attention. "I'm Tess," the girl said, reaching out an oily hand. "I watch the show *Cops* all the time. You guys are, like, totally amazing."

Bennett looked at her with amusement. "Thanks."

"I work at Fantasy Girls," she purred. "The topless joint on Vine."

"Yeah, I know of it," Bennett said, smiling.

"It's a good gig, I guess. The cash is nice. I'm waiting for Johnny over there to hit it big. You know his agent says he's a wonderful actor, very Method, marketable."

"Great." Bennett yawned. "Now. Can. We. See. The. Apartment?"

Johnny kept a cool distance from the rest of us as we walked along the corridor. I followed behind Tess and Bennett, who were numbly engaged in worthless chatter. Tess, sticking out her profitable melons, purred about being an exotic dancer. Bennett nodded robotically.

"Johnny, do you have the key?" Tess said.

"Yeah," he muttered, eyeing her bare skin. "Don't you want to put some clothes on?"

"Not really," she said, circling her tan belly button with a glossy pink fingernail. "Unless the *po*-lice here are gonna arrest me?"

"I'm not the *po*-lice," I said. "Just an innocent bystander."

She ignored me and batted her thick eyelashes at Bennett.

He smiled again. "I ain't gonna arrest ya."

"Then I'm going to stay in the bikini," she giggled.

Johnny inserted the key into apartment 14. Pushing open the door, he said, "Have a look around. It's a studio with a kitchenette." He passed Bennett in the doorway without looking at him, and gave Tess a smack on the buttocks. "Let's leave them to their business."

"I wanna stay," she said, pouting. "How often do we get to be around law-enforcement types?"

"You got a wet one for cops?" Johnny hissed.

"No, baby."

"They ain't nuthin' but trouble," he said, placing another Marlboro between his pretty lips.

"I'll be up in a minute," she purred. Stretching her slim arms around his neck and standing on her tiptoes, she licked his cheek. Bennett tried his best to ignore her oily, plush, gum-chewing presence, but it was difficult, given the number of times she used her hands to stroke some part of her synthetic body. "This is our smallest apartment," she said. "I think the square footage is like four hundred feet or something."

I walked into the small dreary space, taking in the darkness of the room. The air was rife with decay and mildew and I could sense the despair of the apartment's former inhabitants. Turning toward Tess, I said, "Did you ever come in here while Beth was living in this apartment?"

"Fuck no," she smacked. "We weren't exactly friends."

"Were you enemies?"

"No," she said, running a nail under the flimsy strap of the bikini top. "I didn't really know her. And I didn't really want her near Johnny."

"Why's that?" Bennett asked.

"Valentine was one of those girls with an appetite." She licked her glossy lips. "Dripping with sex. She could've made some dough as a dancer, I guess. She had a nice bod and certainly men noticed her. But I wouldn't trust her as far as I could throw her. She's the type to stick her nails in, bite down hard, and take a man away from his woman." Tess brushed the blond hair from her shoulder. "She was cold around the heart."

"You don't seem all that warm," I said.

Her eyes narrowed sharply. "Who are you, *laaaaady?*"

"I'm a lot less greasy than you, that's who I am."

"Listen, bitch—" she said through her gum.

Bennett snapped his fingers, stepping between us just in time. "Ladies, ladies. Let's just get this over with. Put the claws away."

I sulked quietly over to the bathroom. A glimmer of light shone through a small window. The blue-tiled shower was big enough for one adult, and the toilet bowl was brown with rust. Dead moths had accumulated in the light fixture. I pulled open the rickety drawer beneath the sink. Tess stepped into the narrow doorway.

"You won't find anything," she said icily. "The cops tore this place apart looking for evidence, and then we cleaned up the rest so we could rent it out. It would be best if you keep your hands to yourself, lady."

"Go change the oil in your pubic hair," I said dryly.

Bennett appeared at the doorway, squeezing his shapeless body next to us. I felt a *Dynasty* moment coming on—two grown women about to claw at each other with acrylic nails, maybe even end up on the floor, pulling out each other's hair.

We were packed in like sardines now, and I was pressed firmly up against Tess's gigantic melons. Bennett found pleasure in silencing us with his enormous girth. I was fighting for air, trying to maneuver past him without familiarizing myself with Tess's plastic anatomy.

"Okay," I said, wheezing. "We'll be good. Just move. I'm dying here. It's hot. I can't breathe."

Bennett and I left the complex in a rush. He was practically dragging me out of the place. Tess's foul-mouthed commentary soon faded into the distance. When we slid into the Buick, I studied the disheveled property. Located on the busy corner of Washington and LaSalle, it was constantly suffused with traffic. I smiled and said, "This really is a perfect location for a Starbucks. If you think about it, this corner is—"

"Uh-huh," Bennett interrupted. "You almost broke a nail back there. Got pretty catty in that room. Better watch yourself in the future. Girls like Tess are tough and weathered and know how to win a fight. She could've put your eye out with one of her tits."

"Ouch."

When we got back to the office Bennett disappeared into the grimy building without even saying good-bye.

I drove home like a zombie. Tired. Apathetic. Poorly accessorized.

10

My house had an eerie silence that reminded me how lonely life could be in the big, bright city. I ran a hot bath, lit my favorite aromatherapy candle, and crawled into the water. I started to think about the victim. With my eyes closed, I wondered if there was a death reflex after such violence; if she shook, sat up, or convulsed. Or, was a death reflex a myth conceived in various morgues around the nation? *Why did I care? Why am I thinking about this in the late hour while taking a bath to relax? Why isn't the aromatherapy candle working?*

Twenty minutes later, still tense and thinking about blood, I wrapped myself in a terry-cloth robe and started to make myself a drink.

The doorbell rang. *A little late for visitors,* I thought.

I pulled the robe tightly around my body, grabbed the closest nail file, and walked to the front door.

A young, innocuous-looking man in a uniform was standing on my porch.

I unlocked the door, opened it an inch, and said, "Yes?"

"Ma'am," he said sweetly. "Sorry to bother you at this late hour, but there's been a power outage on the block and we just want to make sure you're okay."

"Can't you see my lights are on? There's no power outage."

"Seven houses down the street are without electricity," he said flatly.

"Really?"

I opened the door just enough to get a good look at the fellow. He was appropriately attired for a Los Angeles fireman and clearly flushed with embarrassment. "Terribly sorry to bother you, ma'am."

"No worries," I said, studying his rather toned physique.

"The electricians are working overtime to fix the problem."

"Do they have any idea what might have caused such an outage?"

"Some kind of animal chewed through the electrical circuit. It dug through six feet of soil and then ate through nine high-voltage wires."

"Jesus!" I gasped. "Sir? Can you excuse me for a moment? I've gotta go check on something."

"Certainly." He nodded. "We'll be out front if you need anything."

"Thanks," I said.

Slamming the door, I ran through the living room, tossed the nail file onto the couch, and bolted through the French doors. Just as I suspected, Sergeant was nowhere in sight. His cage was empty and there was a sizable hole between the fence and yard. He was on the loose, destroying valuable Brentwood property and high-voltage electrical wires. Standing in the backyard, I could hear the distant hum of men working on the power line. Sadness washed over me as I realized Sergeant probably couldn't have survived the chewing frenzy, and I would stumble upon his lifeless, charred rabbit carcass in the coming hours.

After wiping my tears and putting on Chanel lipgloss, I found myself mingling with my neighbors down the street. I roamed around in my robe, drinking coffee with the fire department and pretending to be innocent. My superb peripheral vision detected a very tall gray-haired man hastily making his way toward me. I hoped it was Clint Eastwood, because if it was John Armstrong, I knew exactly what he was going to say.

"Where's the gerbil?" he hollered.

"What're you talking about?"

"The Los Angeles Fire Department just told me a small *burrowing* animal chewed through the electrical wires that accompany our block."

"I don't own a gerbil," I hissed.

"Where is he?"

"If you mean Sergeant, he's in his cage," I said nervously.

"Prove it."

"Okay, I will."

He followed close behind as we approached my house. Bracing myself for a very embarrassing, humbling situation, I kept fidgeting with my robe, chewing on my thumbnail, licking my lips.

I pushed through the French doors and flipped on the porch light that would illuminate Sergeant's cage and prove to Armstrong that I was not only a coward but also a liar. Luckily for me, Sergeant was sitting in his hutch chewing on a piece of hay. *Unfortunately*, he bore the physical evidence of his misadventure with electricity. Most of his whiskers had been singed off and his facial fur was soot-covered and black. His right ear was significantly shorter than the left, and he was hot to the touch. There was even a wisp of smoke billowing from the cage.

I folded my hands and lowered my head shamefully. "Okay," I admitted. "So he got out for a few minutes."

"There is smoke coming from the animal, Claire."

"Yes, I can see that," I said flatly. "Please don't tell. I'll be ostracized from the neighborhood."

"I won't. But this isn't a good way to start a friendship."

"Understood," I said. "I'll never let him out again. Ever."

"I'm not talking about the animal, Claire. I mean the lying."

"Oooooh, that."

Fear and angst had been replaced by sexual tension.

I removed Sergeant from his cage and wrapped him in a Ralph Lauren towel. As I was making my way into the house, Armstrong stared down at me and said, "Do you want to have dinner tomorrow night?"

Trying not to appear desperate, I responded, "Sure. Yes. Absolutely. Of course. Definitely."

"Okay. I'll come over at around eight o'clock."

"Lovely."

11

The next morning, at around ten o'clock, Bennett and I headed to Gardenia Productions. The Valley was hot and sticky and smelled like paint thinner and undeveloped film. It was a section of town dedicated to the art of filmmaking, and that included the kind of films with oily naked people doing squishy things in front of the camera. Bennett pulled the Buick along a narrow winding street, parked directly in front of a seamy gray warehouse, and killed the engine.

"There's more porn produced in this square mile than the rest of Los Angeles combined," he said.

"I'm so proud to be here."

"It's true," he said. "This just might be the porn capital of the world."

"Again. I'm bursting with personal pride."

"Hey," he grunted. "Knowledge is power. And it happens to extend far beyond Saks Fifth Avenue."

We stepped out of the car only to be hit by a dirt storm blowing off the road. I picked gravel out of my mouth as we approached the warehouse. "You'd think with all their skin-flick money they could pave this road."

The warehouse was a movie studio, encrusted by brick and mortar, the exterior built to last. The windows were tinted black, and I had a feeling the structure could survive an earthquake or a riot or a nuclear holocaust. Two Porsches and a Mercedes were parked in the (paved) parking lot, and a fancy sign was placed above the entrance: WELCOME TO GARDENIA PRODUCTIONS.

Stepping into the lobby, I immediately felt out of my element despite the serene and tasteful decor. Classical music drifted from invisible speakers, and sleek modern furniture gave the place a hip minimalist appearance. Fresh-cut gardenias were an added touch, emanating their lovely scent from Swarovski vases. Black-and-white photographs graced the walls and gave warmth to a rather cool, steely environment; the pictures portrayed the foamy rage of crashing waves on a mysterious shoreline, the solitary oak in Northern California, the migratory flight of seagulls across a stark white sky.

I leaned toward Bennett. "I feel like I'm in an Ian Schrager hotel."

"Well, you're not. So let me do all the talking."

"These people have a lot of nerve," I said. "They think a fancy lobby and a production company named after a flower will give them class. It's the pretty shiny wrapping on their ugly sour business."

"You're still talking."

When we approached the reception desk, Bennett asked to see Isabelle Minx and we were told to have a seat. While we waited, I touched up my makeup and Bennett helped himself to a croissant and green tea. "I can already tell this stuff is going to give me the runs," he said, looking into the glass. "But the croissant sure is good."

"Can you please keep your intestinal idiosyncrasies to yourself."

As Bennett reached for another croissant, a strikingly beautiful woman emerged from the corridor shadows. He quickly dropped the croissant as if it were covered in worms, and then pulled himself up from the sectional.

Isabelle Minx was tall, five-foot-ten, I guessed, with long black hair worn straight as a razor. Her lips were plush and pink, and her eyes were almond-shaped and green as Colombian emeralds. She had high cheekbones, a somewhat square jaw, and a perfect nose. From where I was standing, the woman didn't have a single identifiable blemish or an ounce of fat. Her figure was a work of art (or a good plastic surgeon). Her suit was dark and tight and the skirt stopped two inches above the knee, revealing long slender legs and a perfect tan.

Bennett was in awe. "Shut your mouth," I said. "You look like a dweeb."

"I'm doing all the talking."

"Good luck."

Beautiful people seem to move in slow motion, as though they simply glide through life, no missteps or sudden spills. Isabelle Minx was one of those people, carrying herself like a model on a runway; each stride perfectly executed, with a confident upright posture.

All was lovely and pretty until the girl opened her mouth.

"What the fuck do you people want?" she demanded, flicking a long red nail in our direction.

"I'm Detective Bennett and I'd like to talk to you about Beth Valentine."

"She died, like, weeks ago."

"That's why I'm here," he snarled. "I'm running the case now and your name came up. Thought maybe you could spare a few minutes of your precious time."

Isabelle glanced around the lobby, caught the curious stare of the receptionist, and lowered her voice to a whisper. "I can't have cops coming to my work. We're straight and legal all the way, but it still makes the suits nervous. We don't exactly produce cartoons here."

"I don't care what you produce," Bennett said. "I just wanna ask you some questions so I can get the hell outta here."

She walked swiftly to the front door, pushed her way through the black glass, and sauntered into the parking lot. Bennett and I were close behind her. The sun was bright and hot, blinding my view until I could put on my shades. Isabelle kept walking until she reached a silver Porsche Boxster, at which point she stopped and leaned her buttocks against the shiny metal as if she were posing for *Playboy*. Her hand disappeared into the slim pocket of her suit and she removed a single cigarette and a sterling lighter. Her movements were slow and deliberate as she stuck the cigarette between perfect lips and ignited an orange flame. She knew she was beautiful, she knew how to work the system, and she *definitely* knew how to lie about her age.

Bennett's first question: "How old are you?"

"Twenty-two," she said with a straight face.

I couldn't help but laugh. "You were twenty-two back in 'ninety-five."

Her face grew tight and some of the raw beauty was lost to anger. "Who the hell are you," she asked, "to tell me I'm really, like, thirty-one?"

She looked away, sucking hard on the cigarette, probably hoping it would make her better at basic math. After several moments of huffing and puffing, her eyes found Bennett, just as he was starting to perspire beneath the hot glow of the sun. "I didn't know the girl that well, okay? We had a very shallow relationship."

"Define shallow?" Bennett wiped the faucet of sweat from his brow.

"We partied together." She brought the cigarette to her lips again. "Smoked some weed, drank some booze. That's it. We didn't sit around and talk about the meaning of life."

"Where did you score the dope?"

Isabelle bit down hard on her lower lip and I could see regret wash over her perfectly symmetrical face. She shrugged innocently. "Some guy in Venice."

"What guy?" Bennett reached into his pocket for a pen.

"Just some guy," she deflected, still chewing nervously on her lip.

"Does he have a name?" Bennett's face was red from the heat and shiny with sweat.

"Little Cambodian Man."

"What?"

"That's what Beth and I called him because we didn't know his name."

"You girls bought street drugs from a man whose name you didn't even know?" Bennett's voice was thick with fatherly concern.

"Drugs are drugs, honey," she said coolly, blowing smoke to the sky. "Who cares about names?"

"I do," he said. "Does Little Cambodian Man have an address?"

"Some apartment in Venice. He's a small-time dealer who doesn't sell anything heavier than ecstasy. Give the guy a break. We're not exactly talking Pablo Escobar here."

"Gimme the address."

She looked away again, tossed the hair, sighed a few times. It was tough for a girl to give up her dealer. I imagined it was like severing ties with a long-time hairdresser; you have no one to give you that quick fix and you're forced out onto the street to find a new guy, and then you have to experiment and build trust.

"Sea View Apartments," she said with remorse. "Fifth floor. Unit twenty. There's no elevator, so you'll have to walk up four flights of stairs. And please don't tell him I was the one who sold him out. He's a nobody and you're wasting your time if you think he might be a killer."

"You don't even know his name," Bennett said roughly, "so please spare me the psychological profile."

She flicked hot gray ashes into the wind and brought the cigarette back to her lips. "You're, like, really mean," she said to Bennett, flashing her green eyes at him. The sun hit her face at a picture-perfect angle, shaping her features and illuminating a glorious complexion.

Bennett remained strong despite the batting of her long, thick eyelashes and being told he was, like, really mean. "I wanna get this over with just as much as you do, honey."

She looked down at her watch. "I've got to get back to work."

"Are they doing a dildo-insert?" Bennett snorted.

"For your information, I'm not a porn star, and I have no interest in becoming one."

"Then what exactly are you?"

"I'm learning the business. Working with powerful producers and editors—because what I *really* want to do is direct."

"Of course."

"And Gardenia Productions is the best place to start," she huffed. "They make quality films with quality actors, and last year they made a profit of thirty million, and that's after taxes and operation costs."

"Impressive," Bennett said, "but we're not done here. I got more questions."

"Maybe later." She stood upright, pulling her buttocks from the silver metal. "A lot later."

Bennett wiped his round face with the back of his sleeve. "Listen, babe," he said in a deep monotone voice. "I can send my friends from Vice over here. Just for fun. They can mess things up pretty good, throw around a bunch of sex tapes, start asking those suits you work for a bunch of personal questions. Getting a search warrant would take less than an hour, and I'm pretty sure after my buddies tore this place apart, you wouldn't be allowed to *direct* traffic."

She tossed the cigarette to the ground and stomped out the remaining flame with a sharp heel. Her face was now slightly flushed from the sun's heat, and I was starting to get concerned about my own pale flesh, wondering if I remembered to put on sunscreen before I left the house.

Isabelle looked at her watch again and then let her eyes drift over to Bennett. "We can meet later," she said. "But I work a night job, too, so it'll have to be really late."

"That's fine."

"I dance on tables at Bella Donna Men's Club," she said proudly. "It's out by the airport. You could come by at around two o'clock and I'll meet you in the parking lot."

"That's fine," Bennett said again, unmoved.

I looked at both of them, and then turned to Bennett. "Two o'clock in the *morning?*" My head started to hurt. "Isn't that a little late? I mean can't we do brunch tomorrow?"

Bennett ignored me and walked to the car.

As we drove through Laurel Canyon, he made snide references

about Isabelle's tart attitude, and then chided me for suggesting a more convenient meeting time. "Always keep your mouth shut," he said, rolling down the window, "when I'm trying desperately to secure a meeting time."

"I read an article in *Ladies' Home Journal* that suggested getting at least eight hours of sleep every night."

"Stop reading."

12

The Sea View Apartments were old and ugly and showing signs of severe weather rot. Salt air had reduced the paint to dull beige and rusted the exterior pipes. Vagrants sat on the front porch making inappropriate gestures with their dirty hands and passing around a cheap bottle of booze. Ocean Front Walk was only a block from the building, with its million-dollar condominiums and movie-star residents, but the Sea View Apartments hadn't been renovated since the sixties, and neither had its tenants.

Los Angeles has some serious zoning problems and this is just an example of one of them. (I've already written two letters to Governor Arnold Schwarzenegger regarding this issue.)

We parked in the alley next to a blue Dumpster and made our way to the building. The air felt cool compared to the Valley, and the tranquil sound of the ocean drifted into my ears. Bennett pulled open the front door of the apartment complex and headed straight for the stairwell. The place stunk of marijuana, body odor, and stale whiskey. With each step, we were greeted by moaning derelicts and broken syringes. Bennett started to have an asthma attack, severe wheezing and gasping erupting from his mouth. When we reached the fifth floor, he had to stop and sit down. It was embarrassing.

"Detective," I said. "This is when good cardiovascular strength might come in handy."

"Screw off." After a minute or so, he pulled himself to his feet, walked into the corridor, and stood directly in front of unit 20.

Little Cambodian Man was small and wiry, with brown flesh and big yellow teeth. He was in his late thirties, with spiked black hair and nervous little eyes that darted back and forth when he opened the door. Poor guy took one look at Henry Bennett and knew there was trouble on the horizon. He didn't even put up a fight or make a run for the window.

"Yah?" he moaned, dropping his shoulders.

Bennett towered over him, casting a shadow across his face. The little man opened the door farther and the rich heady scent of cannabis drifted into the corridor. Bennett crinkled his nose and said, "I need to ask you some questions about Beth Valentine. You sold her some products."

"Yah," the man said, turning from the door. "Come in."

The apartment was a studio with bad lighting and no, uh, sea view. There was a brown kitchenette and a toilet against the south wall, and the air was thick with weed. Evidently, selling the small stuff didn't allow for the glamorous life.

Bennett pulled a notepad from his pocket. "What's your name?"

"Paul Chung Pow." He looked down at the floor. "PCP. My initials are PCP."

"That's very clever." Bennett removed a color photo of Beth Valentine and held it to the man's face.

"You remember her?"

"Yah."

"How long did she buy from you?"

"Two years, maybe."

"What, exactly, did she buy?"

"Mostly pot." He looked at the floor again. "Sometimes ecstasy."

"You know she's dead?"

"Yah," he said softly. "But not 'cause my stuff. Somebody cut her throat. Don't have notheeeng to do wit me. I sell solo, no other dealers work wit me. Nah. Not me. I work at restaurant at night mostly. Clean off tables. Sell grass fo' extra money to stay in United States."

"Uh-huh." Bennett nodded with the sympathy of an executioner.

"I wanna know who else she brought to this apartment? Who she got high with?"

"Usually herself," he said, "but sometime she came wit pretty dancer called Isabelle."

Bennett was not impressed with Paul Chung Pow's recollection. He put some heat on the little man.

"The airport is less than fifteen miles from this very apartment. We could get you a one-way ticket outta here, far from all the precious freedoms and crashing ocean waves."

"No. No. No airport. No plane. Let me think more. I have a bad memory, you see."

"Marijuana will do that to you," Bennett said.

Pow picked nervously at his chin, his little eyes darting back and forth across the room as he reached into the depths of his "selective" memory. "One boy wit her when she last came to buy grass."

"When was that?"

He shrugged. "Before she died. I know dat. Maybe a week before she died she come to visit me. And she had a guy wit her. That's all I know. I never seen him before and I never seen him again. But he's in a band."

"What did he look like?"

"He was white."

"That's a good start," Bennett said dryly. "Did he have a head? Did he have eyes and lips and a nose? C'mon. Wake the fuck up."

It was time for me to take part in this conversation, as we were getting nowhere with Bennett's threats.

"Listen," I said softly, taking a careful step toward Pow. "If the information you give us actually leads to the capture of a killer, then you'll be eligible for a green card. It's true. So think back real hard and picture that boy Beth brought and think of him as your key to the city, your ticket to a legitimate residency."

Bennett couldn't argue with me. Illegal citizens who provide valid information in a homicide case are often given residency without a heap of bureaucracy. (I left the part out about his having to go to prison for selling drugs.)

Paul Chung Pow clasped his small bony hands together. His eyes were bright with hope, and in a confident tone, he said, "White man, yes. Long blond hair. Lots of rings and things sticking out of his face. He talked 'bout music and had art on his arm."

How quickly the memory restores itself, I thought.

Bennett got excited and started writing down the details, kind of pushing me aside. He encouraged Pow's recollection. "Good. So he had multiple piercings? And a tattoo?"

"Yah." He brought his wiry fingers to the tip of his nose. "Piercing, yes. All over. Lips. Nose. Ears. And a big picture on his arm."

"Picture," Bennett said, tapping his pen against the notepad. "Of what?"

"Of another man," Pow said. "Another long hair like hisself."

"Was the man white or black?"

"White."

Bennett walked over to me, lowered his lips to my ear, and whispered the most horrifying words: "We're gonna take him back to the office."

"For *what?*" I felt sick. "He'll stink up the car and the Ethan Allen furniture. Can't you send a cab for him?"

"No. There's no guarantee he'll still be here when I walk out that door." Bennett waved a hand in the air. "He's a little nervous, might be a flight risk, and I want him to identify that tattoo."

The whispering made Paul Chung Pow even more nervous. His eyes glinted with fear. Bennett assured him that everything was okay and politely requested that he accompany us to our place of business. "We just want you to take a look at some tattoo books," Bennett said. "Can you do that for us?"

"Yah."

On the way to the office, Bennett told us some stories about flesh art, and how it's successfully been used to identify criminals, as well as nameless unidentified corpses. "The ME's office keeps a large collection of tattoo sketches on record for identifying purposes. Tattoos are like scars or physical deformities; they allow for witnesses to remember certain aspects about perps and sometimes they can even be traced. When I was on the force I knew every tattoo artist in the city. It was part of the job, working the beat. I have extensive artwork at the office, some of it dating back to the late sixties."

"Can't wait," I said, waving away the stench of our prisoner.

Back at the office, Bennett flipped open his three-hundred-page album containing colorful sketches and artwork, then located the section dedicated to Aging Rock Stars. We were looking for a tattoo of a white male with long hair, and Bennett was just guessing that the picture might be that of a famous musician. He set the album in front of Paul Chung Pow and started turning the pages. No such luck with guys like Keith Richards and Gene Simmons and Rod Stewart and Tommy Lee. Bennett skipped over to the section dedicated to Dead Rock Stars. After skimming through pictures of Jim Morrison and Sid Vicious and a variety of others, Pow finally made a move. He placed a nervous finger on the faded sketch of grunge musician Kurt Cobain.

"Dat's him," he said. "Dat's the guy on his arm."

"Are you sure?"

"Yah." He nodded. "I'm sure."

13

By the time the sun was lowering itself into the coastal waters, Chung Pow was back at his apartment, probably handing his products over to the LAPD Narcotics Division, and Bennett had talked to every tattoo artist from Sunset Boulevard to Sherman Oaks. He finally had a lead on the tattoo based on an artist's specialty.

I was mortified by all of this because grunge is *sooooo* over. And I don't need to relive it. Ever. Nevertheless I found myself sitting in a tattoo parlor in West Hollywood, watching some girl maim herself in the name of love. Bennett thought the process was kind of fascinating and told me how the needle punctures the flesh while pouring the ink . . . whatever, I forget.

A man named Morris Weaver owned the parlor and was responsible, as he put it, "for tattooing more rock stars than any other artist in town."

"You must be really proud," I said, after introducing myself.

"I am." He smiled, exposing two gold teeth. Pulling at his long black goatee, he politely escorted us back to his chair. He was tall and scrappy and wearing an old AC/DC shirt. His black boots were scuffed and dirty, but his hands were clean and so were his needles. "So," he said, looking at Detective Bennett. "What's the story? Lookin' for somebody with a Cobain tat?"

"Yep. White male with a lot of holes in his face and long blond hair. And he's in a band."

"Shit, man. That's like half of L.A. You got a photo of the dude?"

"No."

"Bummer. Most of the cops that come in here got a picture or drawing of who they're looking for."

"All I have right now is an eyewitness description."

"Man, that sucks."

Morris Weaver had a calm and collected way about him despite his Hell's Angels appearance. He was helpful and pretty darn organized. Reaching into a file cabinet beneath his ink collection, he pulled five or six folders from the bin. I almost fell over. "You actually keep files?" I inquired.

"Yes," he said. "Have to know what the client has had done in my shop. There's nothing worse than an unorganized tattoo parlor."

"I totally agree."

Flipping through the manila folders, Morris said, "These are the guys with both extensive facial piercing and a Cobain tat. I have a feeling the guy you're looking for is Pecker Talbott, if it's one of my dudes."

"Why's that?" Bennett asked.

"'Cause Pecker's the only guy in my files that has a band. The rest of them are junkies or in prison. Or they've gone totally straight and are in the process of getting the tat lasered off 'cause they wanna get married and have kids."

After looking through Pecker's file, he shook his head. "Shit," he moaned. "All I got are Polaroids of his arm. Don't have nuthin' with his face on it." He handed the photos to Bennett.

I could tell the good detective was disappointed.

"Sorry, man." Morris shrugged. "I usually keep good records. And Pecker had his face pierced here, too. But I ain't seen him around in a while. Grunge ain't that happenin' in L.A. right now."

"What's the name of his band?" Bennett asked.

"The Flaming Maggots."

"And they're not working the L.A. clubs?"

"Last I heard they took their show on the road 'cause they were getting booed off stage here."

Bennett tapped his finger on the Polaroid. "Can I keep one of these?"

"Sure, man."

"You wouldn't have an address for him, would you?"

"Nope. I ain't that organized. And Pecker moved around a lot. In fact, I don't even have a phone number for the dude. But I'm pretty sure his last name is Talbott. Guys that come in here don't exactly want me to have their contact information. You know, in case some cop comes lookin' for them."

"Right." Bennett shoved the Polaroid into his pocket.

Well, at least we had a name. But it didn't mean anything unless we could tie him to the victim, and right now he was just a one-in-a-million possibility who happened to have a Kurt Cobain tattoo and a lot of silver hanging from his face.

Bennett was quiet as we drove back to the office. His mind was probably thumbing through the information Morris Weaver had offered up. He pulled the Buick to a halt in front of my Mercedes. "You don't have to meet with Isabelle Minx tonight. I realize that two o'clock in the morning is the height of your REM sleep, and God forbid it's disrupted."

"I want to come," I said enthusiastically. "I'll take an Ambien when I get home so I can get in a good nap, and that way I won't be too cranky tonight."

"Yeah. You do that."

14

When my alarm buzzed at quarter to one, I pulled myself from the comfort of five-hundred-thread-count sheets and took a shower. I dressed in a pink Escada pantsuit with matching pink sling backs and a Harry Winston bracelet. I chose a purse that conveyed the look of someone who knew exactly what she was doing. It, too, was pink.

Bennett honked obnoxiously at one-thirty and I went flying from the house, trying to hush him by waving my hands frantically in the air. "This is Brentwood," I said, sliding into the car. "We don't honk our horns in the middle of the night. It's like writing a hot check to Neiman Marcus; you just don't do it."

Bennett didn't hear a word I was saying. He was too busy laughing at my outfit. "Did you raid Barbie's closet?" he snorted. "I haven't seen so much pink since Pepto-Bismol made its debut."

"Just drive," I said. "Let's get this over with."

Bella Donna's Men's Club could be seen from the 405 freeway, with its bright red lights and breast-shaped parking lot. Bennett edged the car up to the valet and killed the engine, waving away aggressive car attendants. We waited for Isabelle Minx in front of her strip club for what seemed like forever. I tapped my watch. "What time is it?" I asked Bennett.

"It's five minutes later than the last time you asked what time it is."

At two-thirty, Isabelle came sauntering out of the club wearing a tight red leather skirt and a halter that had to be flammable. She leaned down to Bennett's window like a hooker whispering her price. "Where we going?" she purred.

"Denny's," Bennett replied. "Two blocks from here."

"Yeah, I know where it is."

We watched as she slid into the silver Porsche that she had been leaning on hours earlier. Bennett groaned as he turned the key in his shitty, oxidized ignition. "She must make bank sellin' the booty on stage."

The customers at Denny's found Isabelle's outfit rather fascinating, and as we walked to a table they gawked and smiled. No one even noticed my elegant pink attire, and I felt somewhat disappointed since I put a great deal of effort into it.

Sliding into a brown leather booth, Isabelle tossed her leopard purse onto the table, and said, "I'm starving. My job is very physical and it takes a lot outta me. I get very dehydrated."

"That's so very interesting," I said cynically.

She flashed me those green eyes and pointed rudely in my face. "You're wearing enough pink to make Larry Flynt jealous."

"That's disgusting."

Bennett raised a hand and signaled the nearest waitress to the table. "I'd like the Hungry Man Breakfast with a side of sausage and extra pancakes, and gimme some biscuits, too."

I ordered a cup of black coffee and Isabelle ordered a vegetable omelet. Her first question to Bennett: "Did you guys bust my dealer?"

"Yep," Bennett said. "But we got some interesting information out of him first."

"Like what?"

"Like the last time Beth bought grass from him she brought along some grunge rocker with a face made of metal. Guy is white, with long blond hair and a tattoo of Kurt Cobain on his arm." Bennett reached into his pocket and removed the Polaroid of Pecker Talbott's arm. "You ever seen anything like this?" Bennett asked, shoving the photo across the table.

"No," she said. "Never. I thought grunge was, like, totally dead."

"It is," I said, inserting myself into the conversation. "It's soooo over."

"Anyway," Bennett said, giving me that look. "This guy is in a band and we talked to a tattoo artist today who dropped a name, someone that kind of matched our profile. Pecker Talbott."

She shook her head. "Nope. Never heard of him. But, listen, Beth had a lot of different guys hanging around. He sounds like another loser."

"Well," Bennett said, sliding the photo back into his pocket. "Whoever he is, he was one of the last guys seen with her before she was murdered. This is a possible lead I don't think the L.A.P.D. even had, and I'm going to pursue it."

"Good," she said numbly. "But I'd suggest checking out a guy named Victor Vartan. They call him Wicked Vic, and he's a total fucking sleazebag. You know, Beth started running errands for him like a month before she got the knife. I always thought it was a little odd."

"Victor Vartan," Bennett said, crinkling his brow. "His name was in the police reports, and he had an alibi tighter than Joan Rivers's face."

"Yeah, but, I still got a bad vibe about him."

"I'll keep that in mind," Bennett said. "He's a filmmaker, right?"

"Pornographer." She rolled her eyes. "He makes the worst crap on earth. Real down and dirty. Borderline illegal. But he's never been busted for anything; he stays right above the line. When Beth said she'd taken a job being his girl Friday I almost vomited. She must've really needed the cash. You couldn't pay me to step foot inside his office. I just don't think it's a coincidence that she died a month after taking the job. But Wicked Vic is sharp as a razor and he's all lawyered up because of his profession. You know, always spouting off about his First Amendment rights. I'm all for free speech since I'm in 'the business,' but his stuff is really tasteless. It's not even sexy or erotic. It's just gross."

Our food arrived and Bennett shoveled pancakes into his mouth as though he had just been released from a prison camp and was suffering from malnourishment. Talk about gross. Syrup dripped from his mouth onto his chin and then to the collar of his shirt. I sipped my coffee thinking about what the future was going to look like: an endless investigation into grunge music, and now further despair brought on by a pervy man making naughty films.

Bennett let out a huge belch. "What else?" he asked, looking at Isabelle.

"I wish I had more to tell you." Her eyes flickered with disappointment. "It's kind of sad that I knew her for years and don't have much to say. Guess I didn't know her that well. Like I said, we had a pretty shallow relationship. If I were you," she said, looking intently at Bennett, "I'd check out Victor Vartan. I'm telling you the cops totally overlooked him."

"Maybe that's because forty eyewitnesses provided him with a solid alibi."

"Yeah." She tossed the hair. "But the guy is a freak, and freaks are dangerous. I don't care how rich they are, how many lawyers they have, or how many people come to their parties. Vartan makes the Marquis de Sade look like Winnie the Pooh."

15

The next morning Detective Bennett and I were sitting in the lobby of Wicked Entertainment, which was located on the seamy end of Hollywood Boulevard and nestled between a Scientology bookstore and a topless joint. We were waiting to see Victor Vartan, the chairman of Wicked Entertainment and the man who had given Beth a job only a month before her death. His office was bizarre and ominous and, evidently, decorated by Satan. The sofas and chairs and desks were black as night, set against walls the color of dried blood. The lighting was sparse, the decor stark and demonic, and candles dripped hot yellow wax onto the floor. It was Martha Stewart's worst nightmare, and I had a chill from the vents blowing icy air into the room.

The receptionist finally signaled us to her desk. We arose from the sofa and made our way across the room. Her skin was milky white and done up in dramatic, stagy makeup. Her dark red lipstick looked like an open gash across her face. It was just awful.

"Mr. Vartan will see you now," she said, pointing to the dark corridor to our left.

Vartan's private office was no better, with black velvet drapes closing out any natural light, and artwork depicting ritualistic torture. Vartan kept us waiting in his office for twenty minutes, proving that even pornographers are fashionably late. Bennett was getting bored with the game. "This creep better be here in two seconds."

Speak of the devil and he appears.

Victor Vartan walked into the room wearing a polyester gray shirt and shiny brown leather pants. He was the ugliest man I had ever seen. Tall and gaunt with jet-black hair and strange discolored skin. His eyes were small and beady and looked glassy even in the dim light. He had an oily face flecked with blackheads and sores that seemed to be leaking. Bringing a black silk handkerchief to his face, he said, "Aaaah. I have company. The detective that phoned very early this morning." He talked as though we weren't even in the room.

"Right," Bennett said, extending a careful yet professional hand. "Henry Bennett."

Vartan's eyes rolled over to me, and in a smooth deep voice, he said, "And who's the chick?"

"She's my assistant," Bennett said, sitting back down.

"Very nice," he said, dabbing at his leaky face. "Very lovely."

I was getting the creepy-crawlies along the back of my neck. Victor Vartan was as sleazy as his work, and his sinister presence alone put a dark cloud over the room—but at least it matched the decor. He sat down in a black leather swivel chair and propped his feet up on the desk, totally inappropriate and overtly apathetic. "Soooo," he said in a whispery evil voice. "What's the deal? I already cleared my name in the Valentine investigation. Cops already came to my house and work and asked me all sorts of questions. I didn't even have to call my lawyers 'cause they didn't have shit on me. I wasn't involved in her death. Shame isn't it?" The glass eyes rolled over to me again. "She was such a pretty girl. And young. I even offered to put her in one of my films, but it wasn't up her . . . alley."

I slumped farther into the chair as his eyes glazed over and sank their wicked stare into my flesh.

"What about you?" he asked, pointing a skeleton finger at me. "You wanna be in movies?"

"No, thanks," I said.

Bennett cleared his throat and pulled out a copy of the police reports. "So," he began. "Beth was hired by you personally? And she worked three days a week for a month? And you paid her cash?"

"Yes, yes, and yes." Vartan was already bored with the interrogation, picking at his bizarre lumpy skin.

"People judge me based on the films I make. I'm sure that's why you're here asking me the same questions the police already asked. If I were a lawyer or a doctor, you'd be on your way, searching through the sewer of sleaze that runs through this city. But since I have illicit artistic interests, you're up my ass with all these boring questions."

"I'm not anywhere near your ass," Bennett snapped. "And, please do tell me about your films, since you're so proud of them. I have friends at Interpol who might be interested in your victims."

"Fuck Interpol," he said. "They don't have anything on me. Neither does the federal government. I got my rights. My films are dark and they're not for everybody, but I ain't going to prison. I write, direct, and produce gothic bondage films. There's a market for everything." His eyes were now level with mine. "And I mean *every*thing."

The room was ice cold and Bennett was still dripping with sweat, angry and red in the face. "Look, sleazebag," he snapped, "I could have this place tossed, and I'm willing to bet they'd find something on the other side of legal."

"No need to get nasty," Vartan hissed, jetting his tongue from purple lips. "That's my job." The tension in the room was oppressive and he was dabbing his face robotically with the black handkerchief. He turned his body in my direction and, in an almost embarrassed tone, said, "I have a terrible skin affliction."

"No *kidding*," I replied.

"I've had problems since I was a kid. Started with severe acne, which I picked at something fierce. Then I got eczema and strange little white sores. It's awful. I've been hiding behind this scarf for thirty years."

"Might I suggest a dermatologist?"

It was quiet in the room. Vartan apparently didn't know how to respond to such a difficult and confusing question.

I took the liberty of suggesting a specialist. "Joshua Wieder," I said. "UCLA Medical Plaza, seventh floor. He's excellent."

Vartan's eyes suddenly seemed full of fear, and his hand shook as he brought the fabric back to his face. "I can't," he said. "I'm weird about that kind of stuff. I can't have someone else touch my face."

"You make hardcore bondage movies and you can't have a facial?"

"No." He looked away, almost reduced to tears. "It's a phobia."

"You're a chicken," I said. "You like to inflict pain on others but can't take it yourself."

Bennett leaned his head back on the chair and looked at his watch. Time was melting away.

Victor Vartan had a low tolerance for pain but enjoyed inflicting it on others and selling it to international buyers. Total hypocrite.

"Look," he said coolly, trying to redeem his reputation. "I've had this affliction forever and it's not going to go away just 'cause I go to some fancy skin doc with an assortment of sharp instruments."

"You're a disgrace to your followers," I said, half joking.

Bennett rubbed his forehead. "Okay, enough already!"

It was quiet again and Vartan couldn't look at me. He went back to his stony evil tone. "I make explicit films," he said, totally shifting the conversation. "And if that's my only crime, then you people need to get the fuck out. I don't know who killed the blond little tart and I don't care. So what if she happened to run errands for me? Big deal. You ain't got nuthin' to go on and I think both of you should leave this office before I . . ." Vartan was leaking like a faucet now, neurotically patting his face with the wet handkerchief.

Bennett was no longer interested in having a street fight and pulled me up by the arm. Vartan opened the door and allowed for our swift exit, breathing his sour breath into my face as I walked past him.

"Don't forget," I said. "Joshua Wieder, UCLA Medical Plaza, seventh floor. He'll change your life. You won't have to wear that handkerchief around your face like you're Michael Jackson."

Vartan slammed the door. Moments later Bennett and I were walking along Hollywood Boulevard, passing vagrants and wide-eyed prostitutes with torn fishnets and broken high heels. Henry Bennett was really angry. In fact, I hadn't seen him this angry since . . . yesterday.

"Get in the car," he said, as we approached the Buick.

His hands gripped the steering wheel so hard his knuckles had gone white. "Claire," he said, taking deep breaths. "This is the kind of stuff that really annoys me. I'm in the middle of questioning this creep and you start giving him a cosmetic referral, basically insulting the hell out of him. He completely shut down. And kicked us out."

"The guy is a total wimp," I said. "He's making millions selling extreme S&M films and he can't handle a visit to the doctor. It's totally ridiculous and I thought I should call him on it."

He dismissed me for the day.

I went home and put on my running shoes, ran a mile, felt asthmatic, came home, and poured myself a stiff one.

16

All I wanted was just what everybody else wants, you know, to be loved.

—Rita Hayworth

Preparing for a date is very similar to performing an autopsy.

The entire process requires organization, concentration, good lighting, solitude, and vast knowledge of the human anatomy. The standard autopsy usually begins with a Y incision. The standard date usually begins with a *why* decision. *Why the hell am I doing this?*

It is estimated that a non-homicide-related autopsy takes about two hours to perform, and a non-homicide-related date takes about two hours to prepare for. Both activities involve scrubbing, cleaning, tweezing, and nerves of steel.

Glancing at the clock on my bathroom wall, I realized I had less than an hour to prepare for my romantic interlude with John Armstrong, and the biggest issue I faced was myself. My hair. My wardrobe. My nervous stomach. And my closet—which seemed like a sick maze, cramped and confusing. I felt like a trapped rat until I found the black Yves Saint Laurent pantsuit that would fit perfectly, given the proper underwear. I slid into devil-red silk La Perla panties and put on my black Victoria's Secret "Miracle" bra. Then I waited for the miracle. Nothing happened, so I continued dressing.

The doorbell rang exactly at eight o'clock. I snatched my Judith Leiber purse off the table and opened the front door as if I were modeling it. My date was dressed in a black pinstriped Valentino suit, white oxford dress shirt, gorgeous silver-blue tie, a stainless-steel Omega watch (Pierce Brosnan's choice), and Giorgio Armani dress shoes. Very Wall Street. Exceptionally conservative and dressy for L.A.

He dutifully escorted me to the black Navigator, his frame towering over me like a Valentino-clad Dirty Harry. My hands were moist with perspiration and I fought for words.

Once we were in the car he looked over at me with all sincerity and said, "You look lovely. Like Audrey Hepburn in *Breakfast at Tiffany's*. Just much taller." He smiled. Sort of.

It was all very weird and uncomfortable, and I suddenly realized why dating had escaped me all these months, years. I glanced over at his long legs in the pinstriped pants and appreciated the elegance of his clothing, along with the size and shape of his physique. I knew he had to be forty- or fifty-something, at least. But my insides were tingling. The butterflies. The elusive, mythical butterflies.

We drove to Geoffrey's in Malibu, passing through thick fog, the kind of dense, cloudy air that I had only ever seen in London and San Francisco. Mysterious. Romantic. Patches of white air. Moisture washing over the windshield.

Geoffrey's was nestled along Pacific Coast Highway, hidden behind a canopy of tropical trees and overlooking a glorious ocean. Due to the heavy fog, the shimmering blackness of the night sea could not even be seen. I didn't care.

We sat at a dimly lit table for two, surrounded by the elegant ambience of old Hollywood money and new technology money. John Armstrong ordered a bottle of Cristal champagne and looked me in the eye when he said, "You're very mysterious."

"So are you," I said.

"Private," he said, shrugging. "I'm just private. And, honestly, I haven't dated in quite some time."

"Me neither. It's been almost a year."

"That's about what it's been for me. I tend to bury myself in work."

"Gosh," I said, "I don't even know what you do for a living."

"Investment banking," he said flatly. "Mostly overseas. I travel a lot."

"For an investment banker, you sure do know *a lot* about night-vision goggles."

His lips parted, but he refrained from smiling. "My father was in the military, and I grew up with special toys. Other kids had bikes, I had specialized army equipment that my father kept in the garage."

"Okay," I said, shrugging.

The waiter arrived with the bottle of Cristal, and I found refuge in my first glass of champagne.

Armstrong reached across the table and took my hand, squeezing it gently. "Claire," he said firmly, "I really want to be here with you tonight. Don't be nervous. Don't be coy. Just be yourself."

I figured it took an enormous amount of effort to say those words to me. He wasn't exactly the warm-and-fuzzy type. My spirits lifted and I leaned over to him, placed a gentle kiss on his lips. From that moment forward, the night was sexy, fluid, and easily conversational. I don't even remember what I ordered for dinner, but I do remember putting my hand beneath the table and onto his muscular leg. I also remember him kissing my hand repeatedly, loosening his tie. Watching my mouth when I talked. Smiling at my sudden spills and occasional choking—the typical date mishaps, only perfected by Claire Fontaine.

He asked me what I did for a living as if he really didn't care. I responded with an enthusiastic, "I work for a homicide detective."

"Really?" he said, surprised.

"I'm assisting him on a case."

His eyes studied me, contemplatively, and he mumbled, "What's the case?"

"Can't really discuss it, if you don't mind. It's classified."

"I understand." He nodded. "Completely understand."

This was a man with secrets, I suspected.

Armstrong seemed to appreciate me, and in a town occupied by the vampires of insincerity, this was a rare and noble experience. We sat at Geoffrey's for at least two hours, eating, drinking, pretending we actually enjoyed talking about ourselves, and then began the drive home. The fog had only worsened by eleven and he drove exceptionally slowly through the whiteness. The stillness of it all seemed surreal.

I realized that in our time together I had learned very little about him, not even his age. He walked me to my front door and, awkwardly, leaned down to kiss me. His hands were big and strong as they caressed my back, and his kiss was deep enough to weaken me at the knees.

And then he was gone.

Man of mystery takes flight. Leaves lonely girl gasping for air.

17

The background check on Pecker Talbott produced some interesting information. He had two prior convictions for possession of an illegal substance (marijuana), and his last known address was a trailer in Oxnard, California. His phone was disconnected and we had to drive to the residence to see if he still lived there. We were doubtful, but the drive was only forty-five minutes and we took the coast route.

Pecker Talbott's trailer was located in the most remote part of the RV park. There was an old Harley-Davidson motorcycle leaning against the trailer and a broken-down military vehicle sitting in front of a crumbling wooden shed. Several mangy abandoned dogs were picking at scraps along the dirt road and looked as if they weren't opposed to eating people. Bennett killed the engine and we just watched the place.

"Can't imagine someone actually lives there," I said, stroking the soft suede of my boots.

Bennett opened his door, stepped out, and started walking toward the trailer, leaving me in the car. Watching the rabid dogs tear apart chicken bones, I decided I was better off in the trailer and hurried after him.

The man who answered the door seemed too old to be our guy, and he didn't have a single piercing. He was in his early fifties and had a fat greasy face that merged with a fat greasy neck. His fatigues were too tight for his round belly, and the tanktop he was wearing hadn't seen detergent in three or four months. He tossed an empty Budweiser can to the side and watched Henry Bennett with distrustful eyes.

"You with the ATF?" he asked, getting in Bennett's face.

"No."

"Then who you with?" the man grunted.

"I'm a private detective from Los Angeles," he said. "I'm looking for Pecker Talbott."

"Whad he do now?"

"Nothing," Bennett said. "Just like to ask him some questions."

"But you ain't with the ATF?"

"Correct."

The man pushed the screen door open farther and let us inside.

It were as though hell had come up through the ground and settled in this rotting trailer.

Flies buzzed over dirty paper plates, ants carried small pieces of bread across the floor, and roaches had their own sink. Trash was piled high, almost to the roof, and the place stunk like sulfur and smoke. But the gun rack was polished clean and contained an extensive collection of firearms.

Pulling at his fatigues, the man offered us a place to sit, while pushing fried pork rinds onto the floor. I decided to stand, kicking the ants from my boot. "Pecker in trouble?" he asked while lifting the lid on another can of beer.

"Not yet," Bennett said. "Do you know where we might find him?"

"He's my son," he said. "My name is Willie Talbott and I've been livin' here for a few years. Pecker used to stay here, but now he's on the road with his band and he ain't around much."

"Right." Bennett yawned. "But do you know where we can find him?"

"Shit. He's up and down the Pacific Northwest. The only time I ever hear from him is when he needs money."

"Considering you don't have a phone, I would imagine . . . that's never."

"Shit. Pecker writes me letters and puts a return address on the envelope hoping I'll write back and send some dough. Does it look like I got a savings account? But the kid still writes and I still try to read his letters. Lemme find his last letter. He just sent one last week." Willie Talbott started going through the mountains of trash scattered throughout his trailer. "Here it is," he said, wiping anchovies off the envelope. "Looks like he's in Seattle right now, livin' in a motel and playing gigs at night. Still holding on to the grunge thing. He's gotta tattoo of Kurt Cobain on his arm."

"We know," I said, swatting at the flies. "Did he ever mention a girl in L.A.? Maybe someone he dated? Or someone he killed?"

Bennett snapped his fingers at me and switched on his serious detective voice. "Mr. Talbott," he said warmly. "We're looking into the death of a young girl. Your son fits a description of a man seen with her a week prior to her death. And we just wanted to see if maybe he knew the victim, or had any pertinent information regarding her murder. Simple as that. No one's in any kind of trouble."

"Oh. Shit. Pecker wouldn't hurt nobody except himself. He's one of them poetic musicians, and sometimes it makes me crazy. I told him when he was twelve years old that as long as he wudn't no fag he could do as he pleased."

The insects were getting restless and so was I. The heat in the trailer was making the stench worse and I felt nauseated. "Can I see that envelope?" I said, extending a moisturized hand.

He recoiled uncomfortably. "No. I'm not giving up my son to a couple of flakes from L.A."

"What if I said I could get you into the Southern California Gun League, free of charge," I said. "You could show up at the meetings, meet some new friends with similar interests. Maybe obtain a few more rifles. Expand your hobby."

"You could do that?" he whispered.

"I've got the right connections. I'll send you the information."

He threw the envelope at me. "Here. You can keep it if ya want."

"Thanks."

Talbott was staying at the Avalon Motel in Seattle. I imagined it was one of those places that rented by the hour and had vibrating beds. He had written a heartfelt letter to his father that read something like this:

Dad,
I need monie. Pleeze send whut you can to the return adress.
Luv, Pecker

Bennett snatched the letter from my hand and gave it a read. He looked up at Willie and asked, "How long will he be at this address?"

"Don't know," he grunted. "He's usually shacked up somewhere for a month or two. Unless the band gets kicked out of the joint. They get pretty rowdy, those boys. The Flaming Maggots. They can really bust up some good equipment. But some people still come to see their show."

We spent the next ten minutes listening to Willie Talbott complain about the Bureau of Alcohol, Tobacco, and Firearms. Evidently he had been busted for selling illegal fireworks several years ago, and he'd been delusional about being persecuted ever since. "Don't trust anybody that wants to take your gun away," he said defiantly, raising one hairy arm into the air. "Or stop you from having a good Fourth of July. The second amendment is more important than the first, and I don't know the rest of 'em, but I'm sure it's a bunch of lib'ral muck."

"Well," I said, pulling at the back of Bennett's shirt, "isn't that so very interesting?"

We kicked dirt up as we peeled out of the trailer park and cruised back down the coast. Bennett edged the car along the side of the road and we walked a block to eat fish tacos and drink iced tea. Having a good laugh over Willie Talbott, Bennett said, "Hard to imagine his offspring pulling off a clean homicide."

"Hard to imagine his offspring doing anything clean."

Bennett crunched on a taco, letting the shell fall to pieces over his plate and shirt. I handed him a napkin and explained how it was to be used. Then I inquired about a possible trip. "Are we going to Seattle?"

"No," he said. "Not yet. I gotta do some more legwork before I jump on a plane. And you'd probably stay here anyway. I don't need any extra baggage when I travel."

"That's too bad," I said, "because I have a five-piece Gucci luggage set."

"I'm sure you do."

18

The next morning I started making some phone calls inquiring about the Flaming Maggots. Most people just hung up on me, others laughed, and a couple of people stayed on the phone long enough to say, "They fucking suck." One man at a record label on Sunset said the Flaming Maggots were the worst band he'd ever heard. He confirmed that they were probably up in Seattle, jamming out tunes for people on heroin or methadone. But then he said, "Rumor is they're headed to Amsterdam."

"Amsterdam?"

"Yeah," he said. "There are so many junkies and potheads in Amsterdam, the Flaming Maggots actually have a pretty good following there." He went back to his critique. "Oh, not only are they bad musicians, but they're also ugly. And ugly doesn't sell records. Good-looking people who can sing sell records. Those guys will never have a deal. Never."

When I got off the phone I walked into Bennett's office and plopped down in the chair in front of his desk.

"Just got off the phone with some A&R guy. He said the Flaming Maggots are headed to Amsterdam."

"When?"

"Soon," I said. "But no exact date."

He paced the room. "Shit," he sighed. "I'm going to have to ask Nina for travel money."

"Travel money? What are you, *six?*"

"It's part of the deal."

"The woman can't afford a makeover and you're going to try to get air and hotel expenses out of her? Puh-lease. I'll put it on my black American Express card if you let me come with you."

"You have a black American Express card?"

"I don't leave home without it."

Bennett didn't give it a thought. "No," he said. "I'll pay my own way. And I'll call Nina and tell her about the trip. I'll cover my own expenses. We'll travel as cheap as possible. I mean *really* low-ball it."

On the drive home, I was haunted by words like *cheap* and *low-ball*. As soon as I arrived, I started packing, almost dreading what should have been a joyous occasion.

It took me several hours to decide what to bring, and when I finally got everything loaded into the proper compartments it was close to midnight.

I hadn't heard from Armstrong, and my imagination was starting to wander again. A wife. Kids. Two wives, maybe. Ten kids. A long rap sheet detailing his fraudulent activities, embezzlement, identity theft.

That night I dreamt about Claus von Bülow, secret societies, the Illuminati, and double-crossing, fast-talking bastards who looked good in a tailored suit.

19

I stepped off the plane wearing a Burberry raincoat, totally prepared for Seattle weather. Bennett was carrying an overnight bag that looked like it was thrown around in Vietnam. My two pieces of luggage were waiting in baggage claim when we arrived.

"We're not going to be here twenty-four hours and you've got *two* fucking suitcases," he said, still pissed off.

"Hey, I'm prepared."

"You're ridiculous."

"You're gonna wear the same pair of underwear and the same pair of socks for an entire day."

"So?"

"I'm not like that."

The cab ride to the Holiday Inn was marred with tension and bitterness. It's amazing what two suitcases can do to a man. It sent him into an inarticulate rage and forced me to rethink that extra pair of shoes. We were both miserable, and the rain was cold and gray, darkening the sky like nightfall.

When we got to our motel I unpacked my suitcases, requested that my jewels be kept in the hotel safe, and searched desperately for the minibar. The Holiday Inn is not known for fancy amenities, but it was cheap (like Bennett) and had clean sheets. So it was fine for the night.

Wearing a black turtleneck and charcoal-gray slacks, I met Bennett in the lobby and we took another cab ride, this time to the Avalon Motel. It was a one-story structure and looked like a halfway house, with its crumbling brick and dirty windows.

We walked into the lobby and noticed a hotel clerk bent over a comic book and drinking a beer. Bennett tapped on the counter to get his attention. The man looked up. "Yeah?" he muttered.

"I'm looking for someone that might be staying here," Bennett said. "His name is Pecker Talbott and he's with a group called the Flaming Maggots."

"They fucking suck," he said. "And their drummer wets the bed every night and has ruined four of our mattresses."

"I don't care," Bennett said. "Where are they?"

"They're probably at a club called Xanex." He yawned. "It's about two miles from here on Colbert Street."

It was raining hard now and darkness had settled over the city. The air smelled clean and cold, until we stepped into club Xanex. It was a small place with a long narrow bar and concrete floors. The stage was old and some hippie group was playing their tunes for a rather stoned audience. Bennett walked up to the bartender and asked about Pecker and the Flaming Maggots. The next thing I knew we were backstage stepping over sound equipment and rubbing shoulders with chain-smoking rockers.

Bennett walked as though he knew exactly where he was going, and I followed him, impressed by his confidence and sense of direction. There was a man in his late twenties leaning against the wall, thumbing at a guitar, a cigarette dangling from his lip. He was six feet maybe, with long blond hair and a face made of metal; silver and gold rings hung grotesquely from his nostrils lips, eyebrows, ears, and chin. He had on dirty brown jeans and a torn flannel shirt, strumming away to his own sad poetic tune.

Bennett wasted no time. "You Pecker Talbott?"

"Who wants to know?" he asked, putting the guitar down.

"Me."

"Who are you?" He smiled, rearranging the silver on his face.

"I'm Henry Bennett."

"You look like a cop," the man said, removing the cigarette as ashes floated down to his shirt.

"You're mighty perceptive," Bennett said. "Stop wasting my time."

"Yeah," he said. "I'm Pecker Talbott. What's goin' on?"

Bennett removed a color photo of the victim in her death pose and handed it to him.

Pecker's eyes widened. "Shit," he moaned. "That's Beth Valentine."

"Yes," Bennett said. "It is."

"She looks dead."

"She *is* dead."

Pecker slid his body down the wall, leaning his buttocks back on his heels. "Why the hell—"

"That's why we're here," Bennett said. "Thought maybe you might know why or how or who."

"Meeee?" He looked up, desperation washing over his grungy face. "I don't know. We had a thing back in the day and that was it. It was like a marriage 'cause we were together forever."

"Forever?"

"Like three weeks or some shit like that," he said, tossing the cigarette. "God, man, I can't believe she's dead. She was so totally hot. I mean she spread like butta but she seemed pretty cool, sorta nice and all."

"Yeah." Bennett shoved the photo back into his pocket. "I'd love to know where you were on the night of August twenty-seventh."

"Man, that was a long time ago."

"Think hard."

"We went on tour in August," he said. "Right around that time. I think we were in Oregon. But I wudn't in L.A., I know that."

"Can you prove it?"

"I think so," he said. "My drummer keeps our calendar."

I cleared my throat. "He also wets the bed over at the Avalon Motel," I whispered.

"What?" His eyes were level with mine.

"You heard me." I leaned down to him. "The hotel clerk complained about some ruined mattresses."

A few minutes later I had the pleasure of meeting the rest of the maggots. The Flaming Maggots. They were an intense group of grunge artists who lived and breathed Nirvana, even now, more than ten years after their poetic idol took his own life. It was kind of sad—they were lost kids who had become lost adults, still trying to relive an old era that had long gone to pop rock. Bennett and I must have spent two hours with them, going through their tour schedule, getting statements, and listening to their new lyrics. Fortunately for Pecker Talbott, he had a solid alibi as to his whereabouts the night of Beth's murder. He was onstage in Oregon, and five others testified to this, as well as the club owner in Oregon.

Unfortunately for us, the trip now seemed wasteful and we were back to walking along a trail that had grown cold. And the Flaming Maggots were about to get onstage and play their set. They had invited us to stay for the show and we accepted.

It was midnight when Bennett considered himself off duty and ordered a whiskey from the bartender.

I attempted to order a cosmopolitan but was met with an unfriendly face who poured me a shot of vodka.

"There," he said, pushing the shot glass in my direction. "That's our version of a cosmopolitan."

"I'll just take a glass of water, smarty pants."

After their last song, Pecker walked off the stage, wiping his face with a towel and loosening his flannel shirt. He sat down next to us at the bar and tossed back three shots of tequila. "Whad you guys think of our show?"

"It was . . . different," I said, nudging Bennett for help.

Bennett nodded. "Yeah. You guys are pretty interesting. And very loud."

Pecker furrowed his brow. "Hey, how'd you guys find me, anyway?"

"We went to your place in Oxnard," Bennett said. "Talked to your father."

"Oh. Yeah." He tossed back another shot. "How's he doing? Did he send some money my way?"

"No." Bennett looked at his watch.

"Honey," I said, leaning into Pecker. "The trailer looks terrible. Don't ever go back, or you'll get typhus or something. He's totally let the place go and there's trash everywhere. And he's got an arsenal of weapons that would make even the NRA nervous."

"That's my pop," he said smiling.

Bennett paid the tab and practically shoved me out of the bar.

I waved to Pecker and thanked him for his time, as useless as it was. The night air was refreshing. Until I was stuck in the back of the cab with Bennett, who was grumpy as hell, bitching about his eardrums and how this trip had cost him at least three hundred dollars. And how Pecker Talbott wasn't capable of killing a rodent much less a girl that "spread like butta" and was a good person, too.

Back at the Holiday Inn, I showered off the residual grunge and crawled into a bed that smelled like mothballs.

20

We arrived the next day at LAX, clear blue skies, no rain in the forecast. I could tell Bennett was ready to ditch me. He'd had enough of all my luggage and lace. And I had to admit, I was fairly tired of smelling his three-day-old socks and looking at that disgusting duffel bag he carried around with such pride, like it was some medal he'd earned in the military.

We took separate cabs from the terminal and I immediately went home to unpack, make sure all my jewels were still intact. Rosa was sitting in the kitchen, doing a crossword puzzle and drinking hot tea.

"I'm back," I said.

"No chit."

"Better be nice or I'll call immigration."

"That rodent of yours, Claire . . ." She finally looked up at me, her face twisted with malice. "Would be considered a delicacy in parts of Mexico."

"If anything ever happens to that rabbit, Rosa, you're toast. El finished and el fired."

She swayed back in the chair, hands raised like an innocent. "I do nutheeng. I'm just saying. Given the right amount of oven heat, I'd say around 450 degrees, and a touch of truffle oil, and a sprinkle of sage, it would be an excellent meal. Lots of protein, very tender."

I had become nauseated listening to her give me a recipe for Sergeant's death. "I'm outta here," I said. "Going upstairs to unpack."

"By the way." She raised an eyebrow. "The handsome neighbor came by to see you today."

"When?"

"About an hour ago. Just thought you should know that someone out there might actually be interested in your—"

"Stop."

"Nice man." She resumed working on the crossword puzzle. "Probably too old for you."

I didn't stick around for Rosa's advice on my love life. Instead I brushed my teeth and skipped over to Armstrong's place. I found it a little odd that an investment banker was home in the middle of the day, walking around in khaki shorts and tennis shoes.

He didn't invite me inside, but rather, we stood on the front porch like strangers. This was agitating because I wanted to have a look around his place, see how he lived. It was impossible. He'd built a wall around himself and no one was getting over it, or through it.

"Listen," he said, arms crossed. "I wanted to invite you to an auction tonight. I know it's late notice and all, but I have some free time and thought maybe you'd find the items of interest."

"I accept," I said. "What's being auctioned?"

"Guns."

I tried not to look stunned. "Oh, I'm so glad you thought of *me*."

"It's a military auction," he said. "The Pentagon is selling off some of the great weaponry from the past hundred years. We're talking sniper bullets from World War I. Air force and naval equipment from World War II. And semiautomatics, rifles, and machine guns from Vietnam."

"You *really* know how to make a girl melt," I said.

"I just thought with your job, being in law enforcement, this might be something of interest."

I let out a laugh. "Clearly, if I were going to be stockpiling firearms, I really should've gone into investment banking."

He looked down, shrugged. "You don't have to go. We could have dinner another time."

"No. No. I want to go, John. I'd like to be, you know. With you."

He blushed as much as a man of his stature could. The wall was still impenetrable, and I could not even get a glimpse of his foyer. "Great," he said. "The event starts at eight. I've got a conference call at midnight so I'll have to be home by then."

A conference call at midnight.

"That's fine," I replied. "Need my beauty sleep."

"No you don't."

That was his idea of a compliment.

21

I had never been to a military auction and certainly never imagined that I'd be sitting right behind five-star General Frank Nichols while he ambitiously bid on a survival kit valued at forty thousand dollars.

Armstrong was so intrigued by all the weapons and the war heroes, he barely noticed when I took my jacket off and gave the world a glimpse of my own grenades.

By the time they got around to the WWII body armor, I was ready for a drink.

The balcony of the Huntington Museum overlooked ten acres of sprawling land, manicured gardens, and a variety of statuesque trees that swayed in the wind. It was a balmy California night, and I felt like I had stepped into another world, standing there in a red-white-and-blue ball gown, drinking warm champagne on the veranda of an exquisite historic mansion. As I lost myself in visions of the Old South, a strikingly handsome man stepped into my territory, looked down at me with cobalt eyes.

"I missed you," he said.

"You mean you actually noticed that I was gone?"

"Yeah." He shrugged. "Right after they auctioned off the shoulder-fired missile to Rumsfeld."

"That's so flattering."

He took my hand and we moved through the museum, rubbing shoulders with tuxedo-clad veterans.

"I hate to cut the evening short, but . . ."

"You've got a conference call at midnight," I said.

"That's right."

When we got back to the neighborhood, he parked in front, walked me to my door, and kissed me. This time it was different, a little deeper, more passionate. I didn't bother inviting him inside for a nightcap because he had work to do, business to conduct, and I imagined it involved a multitude of shadowy participants, with code names and call signs. Totally annoying.

I changed into Dana Buckman casual wear and decided that, although it was late, I, too, had business to conduct.

22

Nina Valentine's house was dark, the Pontiac missing from the driveway. I rolled down the window and listened to the ceramic chimes; they had their own story to tell. The train graveyard loomed in the distance beneath the jagged glare of a partial moon. The wind swept along my neck, a dog barked in the distance, leaves circled on the dark pavement. A feeling of sadness washed over me as I sat there, Mercedes idling, staring at a dark and desperate house. I wondered what the walls would say if they could talk. And then I realized the only thing that could cure the sudden melancholy was to find the owner.

Mercy Hospital was three stories of old brick, a rectangle of sixties architecture, with a revolving door that was spotted with more fingerprints than AFIS. I found Nina sitting behind a nurse's station, her head buried in a romance novel. Her white uniform was snug, blond-gray hair pulled back into a bun. A slash of red lipstick across her mouth. She looked up when she heard my footsteps, her eyes bloodshot from the endless nights, the insomnia, the face in the window. . . .

"Claire." She bounced from the chair. "Ohmygoodness."

I felt guilty for not having good news, any news. I wanted to make something up. "Thought I'd come by and pay you a visit."

"I'm thrilled." She moved in for a hug. "The graveyard shift is lonely. Eleven to four. All my patients are out cold, no visitors. Guess I like it that way, for now. Don't have much to say anyway."

She offered me a stale cup of coffee and I gladly accepted, sat down across from the station, crossed my legs uneasily. Those eyes looked at me with a glimmer of hope and it about killed me.

"Do you have any news on my baby?" she asked. "Did Seattle turn out to be a success?"

"We talked to some people, Nina. That's it."

"Oh." Her face crumbled in disappointment.

"Seems like the rocker is innocent, kind of a moron, too. You should've seen his old man's place. Never seen anything like it. Anyway, I just wanted to check in with you, that's all. I'm sorry I got your hopes up. I thought maybe we could sit and talk, pass the time. I don't sleep that well anymore, either. We could be insomniacs together."

She was amused by this, a little flattered as well. "I like that," she said. "You're a nice kid, Claire. A little fancy for my taste, but you got heart."

"I'm not a kid, and I'm not that fancy anymore. Bennett has totally ruined my style. Really done a doozy on my threads. But, yeah, I do have heart. Wouldn't be sitting here at midnight if I didn't."

"Do you ever see things at night?" Her tone got serious, eyes glinted with fear. "Things you know aren't real. Like hallucinations or something."

"The face in the window."

"I told you about that?" She frowned. "Don't remember."

I nodded. "You'd had a generous amount of booze."

"Of course. My memory is shot from the stuff."

"You said he comes to you in the night, at the window, and he doesn't really have a face."

"Yes, that's true. He's still there. Every night. I used to see him in my dreams, that's why I stopped sleeping. Now I just see him all the time, in my own strange reality."

"My goal, Nina, is to make that face go away."

"Don't think you can."

"I know it'll be difficult, but I want to try to make it happen. I'll do whatever it takes. Someday you'll sleep again."

A single tear rolled down her left cheek. She brushed it away quickly. "You have the heart of a boxer." Another tear, then another. "My daughter was like that."

23

I couldn't sleep that night, so I pulled myself out of bed and decided to go on a drive. I edged the Mercedes along a lonely stretch of Wilshire Boulevard and then cut through Beverly Hills. The air was cool and scented with fresh flowers and money. It was then that I noticed a car trailing me, white headlights glowing in the distance, following my every twist and turn. I made a right on Sunset and drove another twelve miles or so, the same headlights still a block behind me. I wondered if maybe I was paranoid from lack of sleep or if maybe the combination of various psychotropic medications was causing some kind of delusional side effect. When I reached Western Avenue, I made a sharp right and pulled into the parking lot of Home Depot. A feeling of relief fluttered through me, as I knew shopping would calm my nerves. The Home Depot on Western Avenue is open until three A.M., which is helpful to those being stalked in the night, as well as those who desperately need to paint their kitchen. I walked the aisles, looking at silver doorknobs and potted plants. It was closing time when I bought a gardening magazine and left the store.

As I walked to my car, I could hear the distant hum of an engine approaching me slowly from behind. I picked up my pace and fumbled with my keys, but the car pulled up on my right side; a long black stretch limousine with tinted windows. I kept walking, face down, pepper spray now in hand. The back window rolled down and at first I could only see darkness, until an ominous pale face emerged from the shadows. It was that freak, Victor Vartan, still hiding behind a handkerchief, and whispering something wicked.

Vartan told his driver to stop the car, and then he leaned his head out the window, attempting to make eye contact with me. "Hey," he said, like we were old friends. "Get in the car."

"You must be on crack." I showed him the pepper spray.

"Get in the car," he said, his black beady eyes glowing from the chemicals. "I'm not going to hurt you."

The parking lot was empty, the street lamps weren't as bright as they should've been, and Victor Vartan had me all to himself. "I've got a secret," he said, "and I want to tell it to you. I owe you."

"You don't owe me anything," I said. "Really. Have a pleasant night. I'll be going now."

Without much warning he stepped out of the limo. His face hung like a sliver of moon against the night sky. He pulled the handkerchief from his face like a magician revealing the final stage of his trick, waving the black fabric in the night air. "I went to see the dermis doctor," he said proudly. "It wasn't that bad after all. The eczema has pretty much cleared up and those strange white sores, the ones that leak, are drying out. But I've got a long way to go before I'm normal."

"I'll say," I said, lowering the pepper spray, somewhat amazed by his much-improved complexion. "I told you. The guy can work miracles and you needed one. I'd suggest a chemical peel or laser therapy, once you build up the courage."

"I owe you for what you've done for me," he said, briefly patting his face. "So I'm going to tell you a secret."

"That's really not necessary," I said, waving away his acidic coke breath. "Did you follow me all the way from Brentwood?"

"Yeah. I'm all piped up about my new face, and I really wanted to reward you with something nice, something that would help you out."

"Oh," I said, still feeling isolated in a rather empty parking lot in the worst part of town. "Maybe we could do this another time, in a very public place with excellent lighting?"

"Whatever you want." He ran his skinny pale hands through his jet-black mane. "What did you have in mind?"

There's really not a more public place than the Santa Monica Pier. I suggested tomorrow at noon in front of the taffy shop. As he was getting back into the limo, he swung his head in my direction. "Leave the fat man at home," he said, referring to Detective Bennett.

"Why?"

"Because I hate cops," he hissed. "I don't trust 'em and I don't help 'em out when they come asking questions about dead girls or anything else, for that matter. If you wanna hear my secret, which I would imagine you'd find quite fascinating, leave the heat behind."

"Okay."

"And wear something really tight and sexy that hugs your body like a glove." Those were his last words to me before completely disappearing behind tinted windows and driving away.

I sat in my car for twenty minutes thinking about Wicked Vic and his secret, his promise of interesting news. I had to take the bait simply because he was one of Beth's last contacts, the elusive man who paid her in cash to run his sleazy errands. I decided I would tell Bennett I was going to be late to the office because I was having an emergency pedicure.

When I got home I noticed most of Armstrong's lights were on inside his house, and I made it a point to slam my car door, several times, in hopes he would hear the commotion.

And he did. I noticed his frame at the window. It looked like he was holding a cell phone to his ear. The next thing I knew we were standing on my front lawn, chatting like old friends. I think he was curious as to why I was coming home in the middle of the night. "You have another date?"

"Business," I said, formally. "Like you."

"My conference call is over." He was attempting to flirt.

"I see that." Biting my lower lip. "Would you like to come over for a drink?"

"That would be nice."

After two martinis and a shot of Bailey's, I had enough confidence to pin him against the wall. His hand slid down my back and fumbled, almost clumsily, at my bra. His tongue buried deep inside my mouth, while his body tensed and felt hard against mine.

We made love like lonely people.

Wanting it to last forever, I lost myself in the touch of another human being.

But just before dawn, I awoke to an empty bed. And the romance suddenly seemed lost, not so innocent and fanciful, knowing that my lover had slipped out during the night.

24

Still flushed with passion and pleased with my post-coitus glow, I dressed in a red Tahari suit and drove to the Santa Monica Pier. It was the perfect place to meet a deformed sleazebag who was probably withholding important information about a homicide. The wooden pier was flanked with novelty shops and filled with plenty of tourists and locals. I saw Victor Vartan standing across from the taffy shop, his hand on the metal rail, sunglasses hiding his eyes.

I walked right up to him, not wasting time on pleasantries. "Okay," I said coldly. "I'm here. What's the big secret?"

Vartan removed the dark shades, revealing bloodshot eyes and arched villain eyebrows. "You're not wearing something tight and sexy," he said. "I'm very disappointed."

"That's too bad. I'm not one of your bimbos."

The sun was warm against my face and brought to my attention the fact that I had forgotten to wear sunscreen. I could literally feel the sunspots forming, dark brown circles playing connect-the-dots all over my face. I felt panicked and my eyes scanned the pier for an appropriate plan of relief. Noticing a beach shop down the way, I asked Vartan if he would excuse me so I could go and buy sun protection. A few moments later, I emerged wearing a tan, wide-rimmed hat that provided coverage to both face and neck.

"Can we get on with it?" Vartan's voice thick with agitation. "I ain't got all day. I'm in the middle of editing some fetish films for the Latin trade, and later I'm auditioning some girls that have—"

"That's okay," I said, raising a hand. "I don't need to know."

His skin was looking better, even in the harsh glow of natural light. I complimented him on the improvement and noticed he wasn't using the handkerchief as a face diaper or a mask. But he was still freaky as hell and I wanted to get out of there, exfoliate, do something nice for myself.

"I really like you," he said. "I know it sounds strange and shit, but you kind of changed my life. I hate that you work for a cop and all, but whatever." He shrugged. "What I'm going to tell you might help you with the investigation, and I haven't told anybody. I'd rather have a colonoscopy than help the LAPD or your fat boss."

"Okay."

"And you gotta promise me that you won't ever tell n'body that you heard this from me. Got it?"

"Fine."

"No. I'm serious. I don't want any shit blowing my way. I've had enough legal issues because I make gothic porn. If someone turns up at my office asking me questions about this, I'll make life hell for you. I've got a contact at the DMV—that's how I knew where you lived, what kind of car you drove. If you betray me, I'll leave dead squirrels on your doorstep."

"That's just gross," I said. "And as someone who cares about animals, I find it very offensive and cruel that you'd do that. But you got my attention and I won't, uh, betray you."

"Good."

We walked to the end of the pier, where poor men were casting fishing lines into the sea in hopes of catching their dinner. Vartan leaned coolly against the rail, popping his right leg out, and raising his face to the sun. "It's nice," he said. "To be standing here like a normal person, catching some rays, and exposing my flesh. I really owe you."

"I'm waiting."

"The little slut hung around this club called Babylon," he began angrily. "It's a high-end joint in a bad neighborhood, underground, loaded with a rich clientele that don't got nothing better to do than smoke-out and drink Stoli straight outta the bottle."

"Babylon," I said.

"Yeah. It's gonna be tough to get past the bouncers 'cause the place is prime for celebrities. It's tight. I been there once, as someone's guest, and not a single chick would talk to me. It ain't my style, but Beth liked it. Probably made her feel like she was screwing uptown, you know. 'Cause she was kind of downtown."

"Yeah. That's nice."

"You have to be a member to get in on a regular basis," he said. "One of them hoity-toity places. Total rip. High-society crapola. I'm not sure the police ever checked out the place, probably couldn't get in anyway. One of them black box joints with lots of security and velvet-rope action. Somebody over at the club must've liked the little cherry, 'cause she sure couldn't pay the tab herself, know what I mean?"

"Guess so. She had a big fancy daddy at the club?"

"Don't know if he was big or fancy," he said, licking his worm lips. "But he had to have some cash on hand to pay for that overpriced, overrated country club."

"Thanks," I said, jotting down some notes, really looking official.

"Anytime, baaaby. I mean. *Any*time."

"Eww. No. Stop."

He parted his lips and flashed the weird toothy grin. Then he walked away, strutting down the pier like a lonely sailor in search of a good time. I watched him depart and finally step into the back of his black stretch.

25

Bennett was sitting at his desk eating stuffed-crust pizza when I arrived. He wasn't that happy to see me. "You must've had a *really* chipped toenail," he groaned. "It's damn near two o'clock in the afternoon."

I walked into his office, removed my wide-rimmed hat, and slumped down into the chair across from his desk. "It's been quite a day," I said with a sigh.

"Whut?" He shrugged. "Were they out of your favorite color at the nail salon?" Smart ass.

"I just met with Victor Vartan at the Santa Monica Pier," I said. "He followed me to Home Depot last night and chased me down in his big fancy limo."

He dropped the pizza, his face turning white. Feeling the harsh gaze fall upon me, I decided it was best to just keep talking.

"Vartan's skin is looking better because he went to see my *guy*," I continued. "Anyway, he said he had a secret to tell me, something that might help with the case. But he made me promise to leave the fat man behind—that would be you. I agreed and we decided to meet on the pier."

Bennett's eyes narrowed sharply. "You met with Vartan alone?" The fury in his voice was alarming. "Don't ever do anything like that again. Ever. Or you'll be fired. I don't wanna be responsible for something happening to you, or get sued by your old man. Vartan is a sicko. You should've known better. And what's this shit about him following you to Home Depot? You shoulda called me right then and there, put a stop to it."

I slumped farther into the chair. "But he gave me information, Bennett. I think it might be a lead. Like totally. Just hear me out."

"You got ten seconds."

"Babylon."

He shrugged. "Five seconds left."

"Vartan said our victim was a member of Babylon, some private club downtown. Somebody had to be paying the tab, 'cause she wouldn't have been able to. Place is outrageously expensive. This is good stuff, Detective. He didn't bother telling it to the police when he should've. Guy liked me enough to give me a break."

"The guy's a freak," he said. "And if you ever, and I mean ev-er, pull a stunt like this again, you're out of here. Back to shopping malls and charity balls."

"Yes, sir."

He straightened his torso a little, which took every muscle in his back. "Other than that, nice work."

"Really?" I wanted to soak up every moment.

"Yes."

"Do you want to make me a partner?"

"No."

"Are you sure?"

"Yes. Very. In fact, I've never been more sure about anything in my entire life."

26

Armstrong picked me up at eight o'clock for dinner.

"You didn't even leave me a note," I said. "Last night, when you snuck out of my house."

"I didn't sneak out," he said. "I wake up early with the stock market. I've got a job to do regardless of where I fall asleep."

"I've got a heart," I said. "Regardless of who I fall asleep *with*."

"Poetic," he said, edging the car toward Beverly Hills. "Maybe I'm too old for you."

"Don't try to sabotage this with the age issue."

"I'm not sabotaging anything."

We had dinner at the Polo Lounge in the Beverly Hills Hotel. We spent a good hour talking about Cialis, Levitra, and Viagra. In an effort to calm my nerves I drank too much and probably made a fool out of myself. After dinner, we slipped into the bar and watched gaudy call girls pick up rich johns with bad toupees and sheepish grins. I studied Armstrong's hands, his face, the way his clothes fit his body. It was awful how attracted I was to this man, physically, emotionally, and mentally. Suddenly I felt so vulnerable, fearing that one day he might move or just disappear into the strange world of espionage.

When we got back to my house, I invited him inside for a nightcap and was surprised when he declined. "I can't stay over," he said. "I've got an early flight in the morning—five o'clock."

"Oh. You're leaving?"

"Business trip," he said. "And I wouldn't want to abandon you again after madly seducing you."

Phony laugh on my part. "Where are you going?"

"Bangkok," he said. "I'll be back soon. We'll pick up right where we left off."

He kissed me.

And, then, of course, he left me standing in my own doorway. Heart pounding. Eyes watering. Hips swaggering. *Had I already succumbed to this man? What was happening to me?* I thought.

I slipped off my clothes, left them on the floor, and crawled into bed. As I lay there, full of ennui and doubt, I started to wonder if John Armstrong was married; living a double life that stretched across several continents. I'd seen this sort of thing on the Lifetime channel, and it was not entirely impossible.

I could spend hours and days obsessing over the wife and children that didn't exist, over the phony identity that was conjured up by my exorbitant imagination. I closed my eyes, felt the tears crawl down my face, and decided it was best to stick to reality. Even though it seemed destined to bring me pain.

Sergeant kept me awake for an hour as he chewed into the comforter at the end of the bed. I could hear the seams coming apart as he worked his way down to the sheet. Finally, and I must say, embarrassingly, I slipped a Vicodin inside a carrot and fed it to him.

27

The morning air was cold and damp when Bennett and I left the office at eight-thirty.

On the way to Babylon, we had to first sit in the drive-thru lane at Burger King so he could get his lard-filled breakfast. Bennett steered the car with his right hand while the left worked at stuffing his face with sausage and eggs and doughy biscuits. I drank black coffee from a Styrofoam cup and looked out the window at the passing cars, waving off the stench of animal fat that drifted in my general direction.

"I bet your cholesterol level is four-fifty," I said flippantly.

"I bet your I.Q is forty-five," he grunted back at me, spitting white biscuit particles into the air.

Babylon sat on the edge of downtown among the abandoned warehouses, vacant parking lots, and auto-repair shops. It was not what I expected, given the price of a membership and the highfalutin clientele. Bennett pulled the car to the curb, the engine still humming, and leaned across the seat to have a better look at the place. Square in shape, black in color, ominous in spirit. "Looks like a dump to me," he said.

"I guess that's the point. No sign out front. No glitz and glamour on the outside. It's a perfect disguise for a place that caters to the rich and infamous. And with annual membership going for fifty grand, there's going to be a lot happening on the inside. It's trendy, new money."

Bennett rolled down his window and the cool air tickled my nose.

We watched the place for about ten minutes, sitting there in the hazy morning sunlight, skyscrapers towering in the distance, bulky brown Dumpsters lining the street as if they were dropped from the sky. It was a bad area. A section of town meant for brick and mortar, sulfurous air, and vagrants looking for a place to be invisible. A place to curl up and die. But I felt too visible, sitting there in a car with all of its hubcaps, my Chanel bracelet twinkling in the sunlight, my purse held close to my side. I asked Bennett to roll up his window.

Babylon was remote, desolate, uninviting.

To someone on the outside it wasn't even worth a look, a moment of passing curiosity. The exterior was perfunctory, dull as a prison cell. It was bleak and black and square as a box. But to someone on the inside, to a member who seeks solace and privacy, it was the perfect place. A disguise. No parents. No paparazzi. No pedestrians.

Just as I was on the edge of boredom and reaching for my nail file, a wine-colored Jaguar pulled onto the street, slowly coming to a halt in front of the club. The woman that emerged from the car was six feet tall, with a figure meant for a runway and tailored clothes meant for *Vogue.* Her hair was long, blond, razor straight, laying flat against a youthful face. She moved swiftly toward the front door as if she knew she was being watched. As her right hand disappeared into a Gucci clutch, Bennett said, "Looks like we've got company."

"Amazon."

"Whatever." His left hand was on the door handle, his eyes followed her movements, calculated, predatory.

"She's got money," I said.

"Then the two of you will get along."

She disappeared into the darkness of the club, her blond hair fading into the shadows. "She's going to be a tough one," Bennett said. "I can already tell. She's got more attitude than, say, you. It's gonna be a bitch to get access to this place. They got cement walls for a reason. Place is out here in the middle of nowhere, buried between warehouses and sweatshops and power plants. It's strategic on their part. They don't want nobody snooping around, no press, no private investigators. It's obvious by the black paint on the walls they want nothing more than to be invisible. If they wanted company and publicity, they would've opened their doors in Beverly Hills or Malibu."

"You're not threatened by a little black paint, are you?" I said in a girly voice.

"It's not the paint that bothers me," he said. "It's the locale. The despair that surrounds this place. There's something about it. Like a beast lives within those walls, taking lives, cutting up girls. I got that feeling."

Bennett's jaw was tight, set solidly in a grimace that only a glazed doughnut could fracture.

We opened our doors and stepped into the light. The pavement felt hydrous and cheap and worn down to a thread by steel trucks and heavy workmen's boots. Bennett rang the bell next to the front door, and the sound reverberated like pipes rolling over in the basement. The blonde appeared in the doorway, statuesque, illuminated by sunlight, the smile on her face fading fast. "Oh," she said. "I thought you were the cleaning people."

"Nope," Bennett said. "Just here to ask you some questions about the club."

She inched the door closed, partially shadowing the beauty of her face. "We are closed." Her voice was like ice rattling inside a glass. "If you want to take a look around you can come back this afternoon, at five o'clock. One of my hostesses will gladly be of assistance. At that time, you can review our membership policy, our annual fees, and the facility." She began to close the door in our face. Bennett raised his hand, the palm pressing against the metal.

"Ex-cuse me," she said harshly. "I'll call the police if you don't leave this instant."

"I *am* the police."

"Well." She tossed her blond hair in a huff. "Do you have a warrant?"

"Do I need one?"

"Yes, you do." She swung the door open wide enough for me to get a glimpse of the Italian marble laid out behind her. "This is a private club and we go to great lengths to protect our members."

"Oh, really?" Bennett's voice was laced with cynicism as he pushed Valentine's gruesome photo into her perfectly chiseled face. "Did you protect *her?*"

The blonde withdrew, flushed, looking down at the floor. "What do you want from me?"

"I want some answers," Bennett said, stepping into the doorway, blocking the sunlight. "Do you rec'nize this girl?"

"Maybe." Her eyes locked on the photograph long enough to make out the details. "I don't know. There's so much blood it's hard to tell."

"She was a member here," Bennett said. "Least that's what we heard."

"I don't think so." She folded her arms. "She might have been a guest."

"Her name's Beth Valentine," Bennett said. "Maybe you could check your records for us. Set things straight. And if you insist I come back with a warrant, I'll do so. And I'll also bring a reporter from the *Los Angeles Times*. He'd love to do an exposé on this place."

"Come on in," she said. "I'm expecting the cleaning crew, that's why I was so quick to open the door. They're always here at nine-thirty sharp." She pushed the door closed and set the alarm. And then she introduced herself with the forced politeness of a corporate travel agent. "I'm Tiffany Beckam," she said in a robot's voice. "Head of member services here at the club."

"Detective Bennett." They shook hands awkwardly. "And this is my associate, Claire Fontaine."

Our eyes met.

A cold and distrustful gaze, steely, unflinching. I could beat her to death with my purse and she knew it. My designer shoes and manicured nails and Harry Winston accoutrements told their own story. I was no cop. No street sleuth walking the beat. No Dumpster-diving chump in plain clothes hiding out in alleys and parking lots waiting for some perp to make a mistake. I could tell by the look on her face she thought it odd that someone as impervious and impeccable as myself was keeping company with such a disheveled and stained creature as Henry Bennett. But I made no sudden attempt to relieve the girl of her curiosity and I kept my nose in the air, my eyes straight ahead, slightly gazing past her left shoulder as if the coat rack in the distance was far more attractive than her bone structure.

Trepidation flooded her face as she turned to lead us into the main room. Bennett had put her in a compromising situation. She could either face the press and risk the secrecy of the club, or answer a few of our questions. The floor, white and green marble, needed a sweep down, as numerous piles of cigarette butts lined the edges, along with discarded matchbooks and half-eaten olives. We sat down at the mahogany bar and I caught my reflection in the mirror behind the rows of exotic liquor. The lighting seemed fluorescent, the air blue and hazy.

All three of us looked dead, and I wondered if maybe we were. This black square box of a nightclub harbored a secret. Tiffany Beckam was probably clueless—she sure looked it. But within these walls was the answer and I knew it. I wondered if Bennett felt the same thing. The oppressive darkness of a place with no soul.

He watched the girl intently. He had a poker face if I ever saw one, a stiff upper lip, flat and emotionless. She offered us coffee like she didn't have any and Bennett shrugged her off.

"I would love a list of your members," he said, tapping the mahogany with his fingers.

She laughed. "People in hell would love ice water."

"I *know* people in hell," he said. "And they don't give a shit about water."

"There's no way, Mr. Bennett." She brushed her blond hair away from her cheek, seductive, purposeful. "I want to help you out, I really do. But our business is based on confidentiality, and handing out a list of names and addresses, well, that would go against everything we stand for. I'm doing you and your friend"—her eyes rolled over to me—"a favor."

I looked at my reflection again. The blue light brought out my wrinkles, and my features seemed severe and asymmetrical. No one would look good in this lighting. And I mean no one.

"The lighting in here is terrible," I said straight to her face.

She lowered her chin, her eyes squinting. "What?"

"You heard me," I said.

Bennett had become invisible.

The war had begun.

"How dare you," she snapped. "Waltz in here, at what, nine o'clock in the morning, and insult my lighting."

"It's dreadful."

"Is not," she hissed.

"Is too."

"Is *noooot.*"

"Is *tooooo.*"

This could have continued all day but the good detective put his hand into the mysterious cloudy air and said, "Stop!"

Tiffany's index finger came at me like a knife in a butcher shop. "I'll have you know, this is the hottest private club in town."

"I don't care if it's the Playboy Mansion on acid," I said. "Your lighting sucks. And when the lighting sucks, people look bad. And old. How anyone gets 'picked up' in this funeral parlor I have no idea. Look at yourself."

Her eyes followed mine to the mirror and she lost herself in the gray and lifeless face staring back at her. It took her several moments to pull away, to adjust herself and shake off the horror. "Oh." Her voice sounded remote. "You're right. It's. Bad. My. Gawd."

"Yes." I nodded. "Eventually, you'll lose business because people will start noticing their reflections, and if they're sober, it will come as a bitter shock. It'll take five shots of eighty-proof just to get them to talk to someone else. Bad lighting is bad for business. I know of four-star restaurants that have closed their doors because no one wanted to be exposed like a corpse for the sake of good foie gras."

Bennett's breathing had gotten deep, almost a growl. "I don't give a shit about lighting. Both of you can walk around under a candlestick if it makes ya feel better. What I want are answers, and names, and information about this girl." He slid the photo across the bar.

Tiffany dropped her head and stared at it blankly, then raised her eyes to mine. "You really think the lighting is thaaaat bad?" Her voice still seemed distant. "I'm going to lose business because of it?"

"Yes. Trust me. If enough people sit where I'm sitting and have to face their own reflection without so much as a painkiller, they'll leave Prada dust in your face on the way out the door."

Bennett's fist pounded the black-and-white photo. "Goddamn it," he said, flushed with anger. "I'm going to knock the daylights out of both of you. And no matter what kind of lighting you're sittin' under, you'll look like you've been beaten to a pulp with a garden rake. Now listen up. I ain't got all day to talk about bad lighting. And shit. This is serious business and I'll take it to a judge and come back with a court order and a few friends that would love to make copies of your little membership book." His eyes locked on Tiffany. "You think lighting is bad for business, wait until I go knocking on your clients' doors, asking questions about a dead girl."

Bennett's anger filled the room, and the blue haze now looked purple. Tiffany Beckam's cheeks were moist with what I would characterize as "crocodile tears," and her Pilates posture had folded into the fetal position. A ball of nerves wilted the amazon into a lesser being.

"Let's go down to my office," she said in a mortuary whisper. "I'll go through my records and maybe we can come up with something."

It sounded like a compromise, and by the time her feet hit the marble floor Bennett was standing over her, saying something like, "I want names. I want to know who paid this girl's tab. 'Cause she sure couldn't afford it."

She pretended not to hear him, and we were leaving the main room when the front door buzzed, reminding me again of pipes beneath concrete turning over in their rusted sleep. "The cleaning people," she said, almost sounding relieved. "They're here."

As Tiffany clicked off the alarm and pulled open the door, harsh sunlight flooded the marble floor and three men pushed their way inside, carrying heavy equipment and plastic buckets. "Morning," one of them said in a faint Spanish accent. We left them to do their routine chores and walked to a silver elevator that looked like a cigarette case.

"The cleaning people," she said in a voice laced with judgment. "Maybe you should check them out. Check their criminal records or whatever. They're an unsavory group of men, let me tell you. And they're in this place every single morning, know each and every crevice like the back of their own brown hands."

Blame the help.

Bennett shook his head in disgust. "I'm not looking for illegals who clean your floor after the party, lady. I could care less who sets foot inside this stinkhole before midnight. The guy I'm looking for is nocturnal. He ain't up at nine in the A.M. rubbing Pine-Sol on your bar. He ain't on his hands and knees sweeping cigarette butts into the trash. So don't give me that rich-girl bullshit about running a check on the cleaning crew."

The elevator smelled like an expensive department store, and the peculiar blue haze didn't follow us inside. We descended into the ground, a slow and easy hum accompanying our ride, and I wondered how far into the bowels of the earth we would have to go in order to find answers. Bennett was quiet for a time, and so was Tiffany, with her arms crossed like pretzels in front of her chest. The elevator came to a stop with a slight thump. We had hit rock bottom. The doors rolled open and there was a long narrow corridor in front of us, walls painted stark white, floors clean as an operating room, glamorous black-and-white photography hanging from the walls. It was another world unto itself, where the actual business of Babylon took place. Dead actresses like Veronica Lake and Joan Crawford stared back at me from the photographs. The air was completely devoid of smoke and bad cologne and booze. It was a nice change, and Bennett cleared his throat in appreciation, swallowed the phlegm.

"No one comes down here," she said. "It's off-limits. All the financials are kept locked up. We've got cash on hand, about two hundred grand. There's a double lock and an alarm in the elevator so during operating hours no one can wander down here, all liquored up, looking for a private place to do whatever. I like it clean and sparse. Keeps me focused."

Beckam's office was large and well lit. A coffee table centered the room nicely along with white leather furniture that looked as though it had never been used, entirely for looks. Her desk was octagonal, metal, the kind purchased from an expensive catalog. Her computer was retro, Apple, and the color of torn plums. I felt a knot of envy in my stomach. (Note to self: Update home equipment. More pastels. Maybe a pink printer.)

"Let's see," she said, sliding into her leather chair. "Beth Valentine." Her fingers hit the keys as she ran the girl's name through the computer system. Her face lit up when the results came back. Blinking at Bennett, almost humbly, she said, "You're right. She was a member."

"Who paid for it?"

She looked back at the screen and ran her index finger down the glass. Then she held it there, at the bottom of the page, shaking her head as the expression on her face turned sour and grim. "Oh," she said, looking back up at Bennett. "I should've known. Total sleazoid. We booted him from the club about six months ago because he was, well, in some legal trouble. Haven't seen him around since then. I called him the Ghoul. He always had a lot of cash on hand, touchy-feely type. He was one of our oldest members. Pushing sixty years old, I'd say. One foot in the grave."

Blame the old.

"What kind of legal trouble are we talking about?" Bennett said, leaning his hip onto the desk.

"The Ghoul was a suspect in an ongoing murder investigation. That's pretty much when we gave him the boot here at Babylon. You know the old saying 'All publicity is good publicity,' well, that's not the case when you're talking murder and mutilation. We want our clients to feel safe here and we didn't want the LAPD hanging around outside. And we certainly didn't want Vice hanging around inside. We politely asked him to *never* come back again. Made my skin crawl."

"Gotta name?"

"Quince Stanfield," she said. "I don't recall the exact detail of the crimes he was questioned about. I do remember the victims were prostitutes. A string of them were murdered, maybe six months ago, and this Quince Stanfield, he was on the suspect list." Her eyes drifted beyond my shoulder. "He always liked the pretty girls at the club. The young girls. Like your victim. Beneath all the Armani he was nothing but a dirty old man and I was relieved when he never showed his face in this place again. We all were. At least those of us with breasts. I can't believe I didn't think of him straight away when you showed me her picture. Seems like another era when he was part of the decor. Thankfully we've cleaned house and thrown out the trash."

Bennett seemed pleased with the information. "Did the Ghoul purchase other memberships for any other pretty girls?"

"Yes, as a matter of fact," she said, looking back at the screen. "Two other single white females. I suppose you're going to want their names?"

"Correct."

She wrote them down on her personalized stationery and

handed the piece of paper to Bennett. "You didn't get this from me," she said tartly. "Far as I know, both these girls are still alive. But I'd check up on Quince Stanfield. That man is trouble waiting to happen and he's gray as a ghost. You'll see." It sounded like a warning.

Bennett almost laughed. "You've been a real help," he said to the girl. "Hopefully the rest of your clients will not meet such a gruesome fate."

"Yes. Hopefully not. Would be terrible for business."

Blame death.

On the ride back up the elevator I noticed Bennett had retreated to his own private place. His eyes cast a frozen glare straight ahead and I knew he was thinking about Quince Stanfield and those dead hookers from months ago. Tiffany walked us through the lobby, the sound of our heels clicking numbly across the marble. When she held the door open for us and the sunlight danced across her face, I could see the relief in her eyes, the soft manner in which her features seemed to relish our departure. She shook Bennett's hand as if she had just sold him a Mercedes and then forced herself to smile in my direction.

"Thanks for the lighting advice," she said.

"You're welcome."

I felt as though I had just stepped out of a dungeon.

The smog outside was an improvement from the blue haze of pollution that lingered inside the club like thick smoke left over from a house fire. My lungs felt like they were full of cotton, and daylight hurt my retinas.

Bennett was moving fast toward the car.

Something dark and bulky disappeared behind a blue Dumpster in the distance, only to stick its head out and look both ways. A street person, dressed in garbage, seeking solace, a place to hide from the life he no longer had. But his furtive, shadowy movements reminded me of how strangers lurked in the night, often presenting themselves at inopportune times. Shapeless silhouettes that floated through the black air and followed us at a stalker's distance. And then took the form of a beast when it got hungry for blood.

He likes to see terror in the eyes of the innocent. He likes to hear the screams and bloodcurdling shrieks of women taking flight.

Death owned the night, I thought.

He was nocturnal, a creature of flesh and blood, but passing and fading like a hallucination.

28

We had a possible lead. Quince Stanfield.

Bennett revved the engine without saying much and when we hit the 101 freeway, I asked, "Where are we going?"

"Hollywood division."

"Is that a police station?"

He looked over at me, wincing a bit, like I was the dumbest person in L.A. "Yep. That's a police station. The Hollywood division, just like the name."

Dare I ask. "What're we going to do there?"

"*'We,'*" he said, forming invisible quotation marks with his fingers, "aren't going to do anything. *I* am going to talk with some of the Homicide guys about this old pervert, run his name past the working stiffs, and see if he's really a threat to society or if Tiffany Beckam just didn't like the old guy, created some superficial story about him being a suspect, and blah, blah, blah. Phoniest broad I ever met."

A few moments of silence passed, and then I said, "So I'm just going to sit in this hot stinky car while you go inside, enjoy the air-conditioned atmosphere, and chat up your old buddies? I don't think so." Diva snap with my left index and thumb.

Another glib look from the fat man. He hissed, "I ain't waltzing you into Homicide like we're partners working the beat. I might not be with the brass anymore, but I got a reputation to uphold. If I walk into the department with you on my arm, they'll laugh their asses off."

"Who said anything about being on your arm? Wasn't planning on any body contact with you. Ev-er."

"You know what I mean."

"No, I really don't, Detective. All I'm hearing from you is this crap about me sitting in the car while you get to do the legwork and reminisce with your old pals from the division. I'm not here to decorate your front seat, although I do a damn good job of it."

"It won't take me but five minutes," he said. "I'm just going to run in and make a copy of the guy's file, if he's even got one. You won't even notice I'm gone."

I noticed.

Five minutes turned into ten, then fifteen. I was so bored I put another dent in the dashboard with my Louboutin heel and then reapplied my makeup in the rearview mirror. Making my way toward the brick building that housed an army of detectives and uniforms and administrative bureaucrats, I wondered how it might look, someone such as myself showing up, uninvited, swinging a blue suede purse with intimidating authority.

A bored-looking woman with a face meant for a construction site stared back at me as I pushed through the glass doors. Unamused and billowing with distaste for the feminine, she asked, "Can I help you?"

"I'm looking for Detective Henry Bennett," I said, drifting closer to the front desk. "He walked into this building about six hours ago, leaving me sitting in his hot stinky car."

"Six hours ago," she moaned, rolling eyes the color of coffee. "Try ten minutes ago. He's down the hall, right past the shotgun case. And *your* name is?"

"Claire Fontaine. I'm his partner." My voice cracked.

She studied my expensive threads. "His *partner*," she guffawed. "You must be joking."

"Do I look like I'm laughing?"

"No, but you do look hys-ter-i-cal. You workin' undercover with the detective? Can't imagine him trolling the streets with the likes of you, 'less it was for some underground operation. You being all dolled up like a call girl and all."

I swung my feet and my purse in the direction of the hallway and walked furiously past the gun rack hanging on the wall. I could hear Bennett's voice in the distance, thick with confidence and authority. Papers were being rustled, an old copier was humming, and phones were ringing. It was a noisy place, somewhat confusing to a civilian, and the lighting was bright enough to raise the dead. Burned coffee was still brewing from at least five A.M., and before I made eye contact with Bennett, I noticed the blank stares peering at me. Men in starched uniforms with polished shoes and cadet postures. The police department came to a standstill upon my arrival, no longer hectic and frayed, the office noises dying down to a single fax machine in the back of the room. I felt as if a spotlight was shining on me.

Bennett's face turned white as a hospital sheet. "Claire," he said, "didn't I tell you to wait in the car?"

"I'm not a dog," I said, feeling no bigger than the ant that was crawling across the floor. "I'm working this case, too. And you know I'm a big help, mister. So don't stand there in your bad clothes and order me around like I'm some brainless doll."

It was so quiet in the place you could hear a badge drop.

The fax machine had churned out the last of its paper, and all eyes were on me. The silence hurt my head and my shoes felt too small, inappropriate, overpriced. I suddenly felt ashamed. The uniforms and detectives had stopped their duties and had gathered around for the show. They had faces bent into smiles, eyes twinkling with interest, and certainly better things to do. Bennett walked around from the desk he was standing over and looked down at me. "You've done a fine job, yes. Now get back in the car. This is not a shopping mall. You can't just waltz in here like you're buyin' shoes and take a look around. These fine men and women have a job to do."

"I don't see a single woman," I said defiant.

"She's out front, at the reception desk."

"If that's a woman, I've got two percent body fat."

Several of the officers snickered in the back, attracting Bennett's cold harsh gaze. The show had taken on a humorous tone and most of the men seemed tickled pink at my presence, something feminine and frivolous. Bennett's face looked like a ripe turnip about to open at the ends. When one of the uniforms reached out a friendly hand and introduced himself to me, it was pretty clear who had won this battle. They would never let him live it down if he sent me off to the car without so much as an introduction. One of the detectives wearing a plaid shirt handed me his card and invited me for a beer after his shift. Making friends. Taking names.

Bennett gave the audience an obligatory nod. "Okay, folks, calm down. I think we've all seen what a woman looks like. No need to get all rambunctious about it. Her name is Claire Fontaine and she's a royal pain in my flabby ass. And, yeah, she's sorta helping me out on the Unsolved from August. She's far from being my partner. . . ."

Bennett ordered me to have a seat behind an empty desk and keep my mouth shut. He warned the brass to keep away from me, gave some bullshit spiel about sexual harassment within the LAPD and how the mayor's office was cracking down on slick willies that wore the uniform and carried a badge. It was nonsense, and we all knew it. But I found my way behind the desk, and everything spun back into a whirlwind of noise and movement and fluorescent light. I got an occasional glance from one or two of the rookies, but the rest had resumed filing, taking calls, telling dirty jokes.

Bennett was standing ten feet away from me, but I felt in arm's reach, and I was certain I could smell his feet. The man sitting at the desk in front of him was wearing a gray suit, cream-colored shirt, and an unfashionably wide tie. They were looking at an assortment of black-and-whites, and from what I could decipher, the photos were far more gruesome than Valentine's. I could see twisted limbs, pale naked flesh decorated with blood. Dead women. And a lot of them. Bennett caught me trying to steal a glance at the photos and let out a big sigh. "You wanna take a look?" he asked uneasily.

"Yeah."

"Fine. But don't blame me for your nightmares, hear me?"

"Yes."

I moved cautiously toward the desk, my eyes drifting down to the photos that had been displayed like a sick, unsolved puzzle that only the devil could piece together. I swallowed deeply when the first photograph was brought to my attention. Bennett studied me for a reaction. I tried not to give him one, but my eyes blinked back mysterious moisture that shone like diamonds beneath the office lights. I felt hot around the neck, as if the sweaty hand of death was trying to asphyxiate me right there in the middle of the squad room.

"This was his first victim," he said, showing me the headshot, "in a string of prostitute killings that began about six months ago."

"Quince Stanfield?" I asked. "He did that?" Head tilted, mild confusion.

"No," Bennett said numbly. "But he was questioned at length, many times, and he failed the first polygraph test. But in the end he was cleared. There were five girls that got tore up by some monster, all at night, all east of Vine. We're talking real rough stuff, butchery, mutilation. And this monster did five different girls within a two-week period."

"And they never caught the guy?" I said in a voice full of dread.

"No. And the killings just stopped. Guy did five girls in two weeks. And then just disappeared."

"Isn't that unusual?"

The detective sitting behind the desk answered. "Yes. Very. Most of these guys accelerate and the pattern of rage only intensifies. This lunatic went crazy on these women, bloodthirsty, misogynistic. He was either arrested for a different crime and is currently incarcerated, or he's dead, or he's moved on to another state."

"Oh."

He reached out his hand. "I'm Detective Hank Neilson. Bennett and I go way back."

"Pleasure," I said. "You were handling the case?"

"Yeah. Until it got closed. Department didn't want to spend any more man hours on dead hookers since the perp seemed to have vanished. It was one of the most difficult cases for me, given the number of victims and the manner in which they died. You never really get used to the brutality, even after years of working sex crimes and homicide."

There was a faint air of depression in his voice. He had the face and hands of a boxer, but I wondered if the dead filled his dreams and kept him awake at night. He handed me another photo, almost tentatively, looking at Bennett for permission. "This was his fifth victim," he said. "The monster really went to work on her. There wasn't much left to put back together and the coroner had his work cut out for him. We didn't have any prints, trace evidence, or decent witnesses to go on, so I figured the guy was organized enough to use gloves and take the murder weapon with him. Obviously he was into knives. Everybody is into knives these days. Almost makes me miss the nineties, when everybody was into guns. Less mess to clean up."

"And this Quince Stanfield character," I said. "You thought he might've been the—"

"Not entirely. He was a possibility. Unstable and violent. The fifth victim was seen getting into a car that was just like Stanfield's shiny black Caddy. And the girls down on the boulevard had less than positive things to say about the guy. For one, he had started getting sadistic. Slapping girls around, biting, hair pulling. We saw him as a man that was escalating, experimenting, and he bit a girl named LaDonna Jackson, sent her straight to emergency, and she needed sixty-something stitches in her arm. He was a regular john to these girls for years, with no priors. And they said he had a nice car and, despite his being a dirty old man, they generally liked him. Until he went insane. Rumor is he started carrying a knife in the car, flashing it around like a lunatic. Then he got rough with a few of the girls, which changed his reputation on the street, and they started to think of him as a potential threat. Dangerous. Volatile. He was no longer just a dirty old man—he was now a dirty old man with a knife and a black car and enough money to buy himself a fancy defense attorney. Which he did. He failed the poly so we had enough dirt to keep on the guy, but I never really thought he was capable of pulling off these particular acts of rage. We're talking about someone who is smart and sane and strong enough to break bones and clean up after himself. Stanfield didn't fit the profile."

"Because he was sixty?"

"Yes." Hank handed me another picture. It was Stanfield's mug shot. He looked like a homeless man that hadn't bathed in weeks, greasy and dirty, wild gray hair twisted into knots, hollow eyes, skinny drawn face. "He looks crazy because he is. And he failed the psych test, and our department shrink thought him too insane to be organized and methodical. He was also too scrawny, too weak to take control of a street girl. But we watched him for a long time, because the prosties were scared shitless of him and his car fit the description. And, well, he was biting people."

"He's a free man, then?"

"Not entirely." He smiled. "We ran some tests on the old geezer and it turns out he's sick as a Thailand concubine."

"Huh?"

Bennett kind of snorted and then lifted a Styrofoam cup to his lips. Hank looked at me with the kind of eyes that saw right through people.

"Advanced syphilis," he said, almost sounding amused. "Evidently, Stanfield had been a carrier for years, didn't have symptoms, and eventually and quietly *it* invaded his body. And mind. It had spread to the brain tissue. Neurosyphilis. He literally went insane. Explained his erratic behavior. We just handed him over to the Health Department. If he's not dead by now, he's living in a bungalow in West Hollywood."

I felt a little overwhelmed by the squad room, the pictures of dead girls, the stories of incurable insanity and pervasive illness, and knowing that whoever killed those prostitutes was probably still out there, taking lives, roaming, watching the innocent. Bennett could tell I was ready to leave and take what I had learned about the world and file it away in the darkest part of my mind.

"Well," he said, slapping Hank on the back. "It's good to see ya, my old friend."

Hank stood up and I noticed he had the same shapeless physique as Bennett. And the same daunting size and stare of an old cop who probably hadn't had a good night's sleep since he joined the force.

He shook my hand gently. "It was a pleasure to meet you, Claire. Hope I didn't scare you off by showing you what goes on in the real world."

"No. I'm fine. I've learned a great deal today. Thank you."

I walked out of the room waving to the uniforms and wondering how I would digest the photos.

When we got into the car Bennett didn't give me a moment of grief. "You okay?" he asked.

"Yeah. I'm fine."

"Hank's a great guy," he said. "And a great cop. He handles the worst of the worst. I'm sorry if you were exposed to elements of the job that—"

"I'm fine," I interrupted. "I made the decision to waltz into that room and take on whatever was thrown my way. And I'm open to learning, and if that means seeing and hearing things that will cause me to double my Prozac dosage, then so be it."

"Great attitude," he said. "I got Quince Stanfield's address. We're gonna pay him a visit."

"Oh, goodie." My stomach felt tight. "The CDC won't even touch this guy and we're going to his house. Lovely."

29

Quince Stanfield's West Hollywood bungalow, salmon pink, one story, would probably sell for half a million on the market. His yard was pristine and ornate, billowing with roses and tulips and ceramic bunnies that were dressed in gardening hats and flowered dresses that reminded me of Easter. Bennett pulled in behind the burgundy Seville that was sitting in the driveway and took a long hard look at the place. "This guy must be a fag," he said. "He's got the frilly WeHo address, topped off with plastic bunnies that're dressed better than me."

"*Every*one is dressed better than you," I said. "And that includes yard art."

"Pipe down or I'll make you ride in the backseat with the backwash and hash browns from yesterday's breakfast."

I knew he wasn't kidding, given the anger I had aroused in him back at the police station.

I kept my mouth shut when we got out of the car, retreating into my own private world, tracing the edge of the sparkling green lawn and taking in the scent of fresh-cut gardenias and peach-flavored tea. Bennett stopped at one of the ceramic bunnies, looked down, shook his head in disgust, and mumbled something that sounded like "fairy"—and then he proceeded to step heavily onto the porch. Unfortunately, when his weight, in its entirety, was pressed firmly into the white wooden floor panels, alarming sounds erupted from beneath his feet. The wood seemed to splinter, maybe even crack into pieces, unseen but not unheard.

As he rang the bell, chimes went off for at least fifteen seconds, flooding the quiet air with loud clatter that seemed to distract the tranquillity of the neighborhood. The man that answered the door was hardly sixty years in age, hardly a disheveled madman who had been ravaged by illness. Mid-twenties, wavy hair the color of cornflakes, azure eyes, shirtless with an enviable six-pack, skin bronzed and shiny with oil.

"Yes?" he asked pleasantly, wiping his manicured hands on yellow Juicy Couture sweats.

"Looking for Quince Stanfield," Bennett said. "He still live here?"

We both knew the answer.

"Not anymore." The man's face didn't seem as youthful when he stepped into the sunlight, and I realized the year-round effort to keep his skin the color of terra-cotta had taken its toll on his neck and forehead and cheeks. "What's going on?" he asked in an effeminate tone, still full of warmth.

"I'd like to ask him some questions," Bennett said.

"You with the Health Department?"

"No. I'm a private investigator."

"Oh." He stepped back into the house, bit his lower lip. "I'm his nephew."

"You gotta name?"

He reached a nervous hand out to Bennett. "I'm Royce."

"Henry Bennett." They shook hands clumsily, different worlds colliding uneasily, and a little too much oil for the detective. He wiped his palm on his trousers and invited himself inside. I got a meek introduction to Stanfield's nephew in a half-assed attempt on Bennett's part to be inclusive. It was hardly acceptable and far from polite. But Royce was nice enough to offer us just-brewed peach tea, and the inside of the house was bright with flowers in bloom and Andy Warhol artwork and polished teak furniture. Bennett didn't touch his glass of iced tea and didn't waste much time with small talk. He interrupted me as I was complimenting Royce on his collection of rare and antiquated pop art.

"Is your uncle still alive?" Bennett said as though asking the time of day.

Royce cleared his throat. "Yes." We took a seat in the living room and I noticed the tasteful decor and the thick coffee-table books dedicated to blue oceans and Mediterranean sand castles. "He lives up north."

"Where up north?" Bennett removed his notepad from his pocket. I followed his lead, pulling out a monogrammed leather steno and a Mont Blanc pen. I'm sure we looked like a vaudeville act, and Bennett stared at me in harsh silence until I shoved the pad back into my purse. His eyes rolled over to Royce. "You got an address for your uncle?"

It was quiet for at least a minute.

Bennett farted.

I daydreamed about a Ralph Lauren world.

Royce let out a defeated sigh. "Is this about those dead hookers?" he asked, eyes to the floor.

"Maybe." Bennett's voice sounded like a sonic boom, disruptive, intimidating.

"Because if that's the case, you're looking in the wrong direction. My uncle, Quince, he's not a killer. The only reason he was a suspect in those murders is 'cause he liked prostitutes and happened to know the workin' girls down on the boulevard. It's the oldest business in the book. And Quince took advantage of the . . . opportunities. But it got him into trouble. I mean. Now he's sick as a dog, caught something years ago and it spread to his brain and spinal cord."

"We know," Bennett said. "Doesn't make him innocent. LAPD tailed the guy for weeks after the murders, meaning they had a hunch he might've been their perp. And they usually got good instincts. And your uncle . . . well . . . we heard he has a violent side. Some of the girls ID'd him in a lineup, said he was a regular john, and known to be a biter and a hair puller. But girls always got into his car 'cause he flashed the cash."

"A biter and a hair puller?" Royce's eyes flickered nervously. "I heard he had a kinky side, that's all. Maybe he was just experimenting, being wild and raunchy."

"He chewed on a girl's arm so bad she needed more than sixty stitches. If that's your idea of experimenting, you got bigger problems than your uncle."

"I never knew the details," he said, looking away. "Quince was always generous with me. But he lived up to his dirty-old-man reputation after dark, behind closed doors. I didn't exactly ask him about it, and he never nosed around in my private life either. I'm sure he knows I'm gay, queer as a three-dollar bill and proud of it. But we never talked sex. Growing up, I heard stories about him. Then six months ago his life fell apart because of those murders. Even though he walked and no official charges were pressed, the guy became a social pariah, and the illness was starting to take its toll on him, physically and mentally. That's why he left the city entirely, moved up to Big Sur. Don't even think he has a phone. Basically, he gave me this house when he moved, and I was smart enough to redecorate, using beach colors and teak."

"It looks very nice," I said. "You've done wonders with the place."

"Why, thank you." His eyes seemed moist in the new light that was drifting through the window, and when he pulled himself from the chair his movements seemed stiff and painful. He opened a window and said, "It's getting hot and stuffy in here. I'm sweating like a fag at a Janet Jackson concert."

I let out a little laugh. When he sat back down, Bennett started into him again, wanting an address for Quince and information about other women in his life. And about Babylon.

Royce wiped the stream of sweat from his chest and shook his head in disgust. "Babylon," he said bitterly. "What a waste of space. Been there once as a guest. It was total hetero. And I was so bored. Bunch of rich kids doing dope and drinking like sailors. Completely distasteful. And my uncle paid out the wazoo for a membership, thinking he was some thirty-year-old 'cause young girls would flirt with him, compliment him on his silk suits and diamond Rolexes while they drained his wallet. Every chick in that place was out to find a daddy, young or old, sugar or not. The music was dreadful. Oh . . . and the lighting. My *Gawd!* It was the worst. I looked ancient."

"That's exactly what I said." My eyes lit up and at that moment we bonded over bad lighting. Bennett ignored both of us, scribbling on his pad.

The wind started blowing and I could hear the sound of leaves gathering on the back porch, circling and dancing among themselves, and then finally settling into silence. Bennett stretched his shoulders and looked over at Royce. "You ever meet any of Quince's lovers?"

"No."

"Never?"

"Never." He folded his slender hands in his lap. "Quince didn't have girlfriends, per se. He had sex. And I think it was one-nighter stuff. Girls from Hollywood Boulevard. They'd do whatever he wanted, and evidently, according to your records, that was *a lot.* This is L.A. No pretty girl with a life and a bank account wants a sixty-year-old perv. He may have lived uptown, but he had to shop downtown for the romance, if you know what I mean."

"And it was always like that?"

"Yeah. Thirty years of skanks and streetwalkers and syphilis. I think he was an addict. You know, once they started hounding him about those murders, Babylon ditched him. Everyone did. No matter how much money you have, a murder rap isn't something you can buy your way out of. Even though he didn't do anything—never charged, never incarcerated—public marked him as a guilty sleazoid with a hard-on for corner trash. Doesn't fly too well in this area. So now he's holed up in a cabin in the middle of nowhere, living out the rest of his miserable life in isolation. Like a freak."

"Where exactly is this cabin?"

Royce got up, walked over to an antique desk the color of Caribbean sand, and pulled open the top drawer. Flipping through an address book thick as a python, he rambled off Quince Stanfield's current digits and reminded us that it wasn't the kind of place that would be easy to find. "Off the beaten path," he said, shrugging. "Sent me a letter once, described his place as desolate and safe and hidden beneath a dark forest, something like that."

Bennett noted the address, put the pad away, and pulled himself to his feet. "Quince ever mention a girl named Beth Valentine?"

Royce sat back down, crossed his legs, and picked a piece of lint from his Juicy Couture. "Not that I can recall. But, like I said, he never mentioned specifics. There were lots of women in and out of his life, a revolving door of girls that were too young for him. Why? Who's this Beth girl?"

"She's a dead girl," Bennett said.

"And you think my uncle might've . . ."

"We're just checking every possible lead."

"How old was she?"

"Twenty-two."

"How'd she . . ." His eyes drifted off, distant, trancelike.

"Knife."

"Same as the hookers from the boulevard?"

"Not really," Bennett said. "This vic got off easy compared to the prosties."

Royce sat up in the teak, flooded with new energy. "I hate to do this to my uncle," he said, "but I gave you his address and I think you should pay him a visit. Take a look at him. I hardly doubt you'd find him capable of killing anyone. Only person he ever hurt in his life was himself."

"Tell that to LaDonna Jackson."

"Who's LaDonna Jackson?"

"The girl Quince chewed on last year," Bennett said roughly. "Took a hungry-man bite out of her right arm. Doubtful your uncle is as angelic as you think."

"Just pay him a visit," Royce said calmly. "I think you'll understand why the police never arrested him. Granted, he's deteriorated substantially in the past six months. But even back then, when the cops were snooping around, tailing him like he was some kind of monster, he already had the shakes and didn't weigh more than one hundred and forty pounds. And he's sixty. Looks like a grandfather, skin and bones."

"Age doesn't count as an alibi," Bennett said. "Plenty of older men have committed heinous crimes."

"I figured you'd say that, Detective." Royce was still calm. His eyes hadn't boiled over like the other witnesses we'd come across. It was a nice change of pace and I felt at ease, almost tranquil, surrounded by beach colors and handcrafted furniture and coffee-table books filled with fanciful photographs. And the peach tea reminded me of my Southern upbringing. I didn't really want to leave, but duty called and Bennett was making his way toward the front door, a little too hastily for my style. He did his obligatory wave and said "Thanks" in Royce's direction. Then he was out the door and sunlight flooded the foyer, casting a harsh glare on the silkscreen.

"Thank you," I said, turning to Royce as he walked me out.

"You're welcome."

"Sorry for barging in here and bringing up bad memories for you. Detective Bennett isn't exactly known for his manners."

"That's okay," he said. "He's got a job to do. And dead girls all over the city need his help. And, honestly, I never knew my uncle bit someone. I knew . . . he was into working girls and all the action they could provide. But, frankly, I'm shocked about the biting and hair pulling. Guess you never really know anyone in this life."

I thought of Armstrong.

"Very true," I said. "It was a pleasure to meet you, thanks for the peach tea, and once again you did an excellent job with this place."

"Thanks."

Just as my feet hit the porch that had been handicapped by Bennett's weight, the bastard started honking, waving his hands about in the Buick. Royce closed the door and I picked up my pace, diving into the front seat.

Bennett sneered. "I'm not interested in sitting around while you make friends with the pink mafia."

"Don't be such a homophobe."

"When I'm ready to split," he said, shaking a finger at me, "I'm ready to split. Say your good-byes like a normal person and follow my lead. I don't need you lingering around while I'm riding shotgun, ready to leave."

"I do not linger." I tossed my purse onto the floorboard. "He was a nice guy with a nice house and I felt your exit was rude and haughty and I was embarrassed."

He rolled down the window as we headed toward Sunset. I pointed out Marilyn Monroe's first apartment on the right side of the street, and even that didn't diminish the tension.

We ended up at DuPars for a late lunch, and I watched Bennett eat a chiliburger topped with American cheese and onions. I was dreading the next two hours in the car, knowing the background music that was likely to erupt from his bowels. Not to mention the stink. I picked at a Cobb salad, thinking about those prostitutes and all their body parts. And how horrific their last moments must have been. Beth Valentine seemed like a distant memory to me, submerged beneath new visions that were far more gruesome. I couldn't shake the images, and food seemed irrelevant.

Bennett was digging into a piece of chocolate cake when he said, "We're gonna go talk to LaDonna Jackson after lunch."

"The hooker that Quince bit in the arm?"

"Yes, Sherlock. Her."

Bennett paid the bill and tipped the waitress at least fifty percent. I noticed when we were leaving the place, she gave him a wink and they had a "moment." We got into the car, and even with the windows rolled down, the air felt hot and moist and full of toxins.

"What was that action back there?" I jerked my thumb at the restaurant.

"What action?" Playing dumb.

"With the waitress," I said, agitated. "The hefty tip, the wink, the look on her face as she watched you leave. Not your ordinary exchange at the local diner."

He explored his gums with a toothpick while looking in the rearview mirror, smirking like a frat boy at a strip club. "We had a thing," he said. "Years ago. No big deal. Cops and waitresses. They go hand and hand."

The visual of Henry Bennett rolling around in bed with the fleshy redhead brought bile to the back of my throat, but when it settled and I could swallow, I thought it was kind of sweet, old-fashioned in a way that I would never know. And even though I had never imagined Bennett in a romantic sense (thank Gawd), it was nice to know he hadn't been entirely isolated by the job, rejected, and forced to spend endless nights alone, with the bottle, sitting in the dark thinking about missing persons and domestic disturbances.

"Have there been many?" I asked, looking over at him.

He smiled the widest grin I'd ever seen on his face. One hand dangled out the window, the other on the steering wheel. His eyes were on the road, but I knew he wasn't paying any attention to the car in front of us. His mind was crowded with seductive memories, the smile frozen across his face.

"Maybe," he said, shrugging. "This isn't something I want to discuss with you."

I was slightly insulted. Slumping against the warm leather, I said, "Oh, but you'll talk endlessly and freely about your intestinal issues, bowel movements, and explosive diarrhea."

"That's different," he said. "I'm not going to bring my personal life to the job. Farting isn't personal. It's just a part of my life."

"Well, unfortunately, it's become a part of my life, too. And I'm hardly grateful."

"You'll live."

I couldn't leave it alone. "Have they all been waitresses?"

The smile again. "No." His eyes were still on the road but too reflective and immobile to be watching for brake lights and stop signs. "A couple of stewardesses. A manicurist. Dental hygienist. Paralegal. A secretary in the D.A.'s office. And some more waitresses."

"You've been a very busy man," I said.

He waved a dismissive hand at me. "That was a long time ago, before I packed on thirty pounds and started drinking Mylanta for dinner. When I was younger and on the force, things were different. Women were a part of the job, the life. And some of them just liked being around the uniform. We called 'em cop-groupies. None of these relationships blossomed into anything long-term. Never married, and I like it that way. I'm a loner."

As we drove east along Hollywood Boulevard, the sun was lowering itself behind us and I could see the gold and purple colors of twilight descending like a curtain over the city. I didn't push Bennett further for details surrounding his elusive and fleeting romances, and he didn't offer up any more information. It was quiet for a long time. His clown smile had faded but his eyes still had a youthful twinkle in them. But I knew by the time we reached LaDonna Jackson's apartment that twinkle would be gone, vanished, and replaced by something dark and cold and unforgiving. The cop-stare would be in full force, unrelenting. The smile would seem like a hallucination conjured up for my own amusement, and his lips would be tight, unsympathetic. Bennett would be back to his old self and nothing would seem frivolous or carefree, and memories of his youthful female admirers would be as distant and foreign as China.

30

LaDonna Jackson lived two blocks west of the boulevard in a two-story apartment building that looked like a fleabag motel—one of those seedy places that rented by the hour and came equipped with yellow sheets and coin-operated televisions. Bennett climbed the stairs two at a time, I raced to keep up with him. When we reached the second floor I could smell hash being smoked from behind closed doors.

Our feet trod uneasily along concrete that was broken and cracked and didn't seem sturdy enough to hold the two of us.

Bennett knocked twice on apartment 9.

We were met by a disheveled woman. Toothless, skin like a saddlebag, a half-empty bottle of Southern Comfort in her right hand, and a cigarette dangling from her left. The hollow, lifeless eyes and sunken cheeks suggested addiction, a hard life, and a ravaged youth. "Yeah?" she asked bitterly. Her breath was acrid and lingered in the violent air for what seemed like forever.

"I'm looking for LaDonna Jackson," Bennett said.

"So." She brought the cigarette to chalky white lips and took a drag. "Everybody lookin' for LaDonna Jackson—'specially men like youself." Her eyes were floating in bile and she refused to acknowledge me.

"I'm a detective," Bennett said, "and I need to ask her some questions."

"*You* a detective," she laughed, the breath acidic and sour. "Well, maybe LaDonna give you the LAPD discount, honey."

"I'm not looking for any deals," he said roughly. "And I'm not here to bust her for hookin', so just tell me where I can find her, if she's not in there."

The woman jerked her head in the direction of the strip. "She sells wigs during the day. And at night she sells more than that. Some dump called Little Shop of Whores. Get it? It's a spin on *Little Shop of Horrors.* But this place she work at, they got hairpieces and leather boots. She's a model citizen, really. Been trying to go straight for years, Detective, so don't be too hard on her."

"Like I said, she's not in any trouble. It's just routine."

"That's what they all say." She took another drag on the cigarette and then closed the door in our face.

We headed back down the stairs, and as we slid into the car, I said, "That lady needs an Altoid."

"She needs a lot more than that, kid."

It took us only two minutes to get to Little Shop of Whores. It was located directly off of the boulevard, decorated in pink neon, and tucked between a liquor store and a cheap clothing outlet that was probably a front for drug dealers. When we stepped inside I noticed the large and colorful selection of wigs that were nailed to the south wall. The other three walls were dedicated to spiked stiletto boots and leather lingerie and S&M couture. Real classy joint that reeked of cheap cologne and a tasteless clientele. I immediately recognized LaDonna Jackson from the photograph Bennett showed me. She was standing behind a counter made of glass, wearing a red plastic bustier and a metal choker around her neck. She was much prettier in person, with plush brown skin and a mouth full of teeth. Her lips were pouty and painted Merlot, her eyes were green as pine, and her curvaceous figure had not yet been ravaged by illness or addiction.

LaDonna watched Bennett like a hawk. Her eyes never left his as we approached the counter. I figured she sensed the heat and thought he was a cop. Her fleshy shoulders tensed and she folded her hands in front of her as if she were standing in church, possibly a subconscious attempt to seem proper and maybe even disguise the red plastic that draped her body like a glove.

"LaDonna Jackson?" Bennett said, sounding as though he was about to arrest her.

"Yes," she said softly.

"I'm Detective Henry Bennett," he said, shaking her hand. "And this is my . . . associate."

She looked over his shoulder and gave me an unfriendly nod, probably thought she was being doubled-up on and I was there to oversee the shakedown.

"What's going on?" she asked, looking to the floor for answers.

"Here to talk to you about a former client," Bennett said.

"Oh." Her head jerked upright, and she looked into his face. "You gonna charge me with solicitation?"

"No."

"Oooh." Her eyes lit up and she unfolded her hands. Propriety fell away as her breasts tumbled forward and the extra twenty pounds she was carrying seemed carnal and forbidden. Bennett did his best to keep his eyes on the girl's face despite her attempts to shuffle her cleavage. LaDonna was working him, shifting in the red plastic, fingering the auburn curls that rested on her Latin skin.

Bennett didn't play her game and tossed Quince Stanfield's mug shot onto the counter. She looked down at it, and all the warmth and color seemed to drain from her face. The tawdry movements disappeared as if rigor had set in, and her eyes no longer held the gleam of promise. "I know him," she said, looking up at Bennett. "Mister Q. He was a regular of mine for years. Until the mutha-fucka bit me."

She turned and showed us the backside of her right arm. There was a sizeable scar surrounding an indentation in the flesh, discolored with jagged edges. "He pulled a Mike Tyson on me."

"That's what we heard," Bennett said. "What else can you tell us about him?"

"He's pretty much insane. Been cruising the boulevard long as I can remember. All the girls worked him. He paid us good money, never tried to skip out on the bill. It was about a year ago that he started turning, gettin' all crazy and shit. That's when he took a bite out of me. Shoulda seen his face, like a madman. I ran out of that motel stark naked and went straight to emergency. They was kind enough to stitch me up for free. Sixty-something stitches. I've had some awful things happen to me in this business, but that was one of the worst. Mr. Q ain't right in the head. And about six months ago when some of the girls around here started getting killed, the police suspected him. Five women that worked the boulevard got sliced up like hamburger meat. It was awful. You couldn't find a workin' girl in this area for least a week. Couple of girls even went straight and moved home. I just laid low until the murders stopped and then we kind of teamed up on the street. No one got into a car alone till it seemed safe again." She laughed to herself, shook her auburn curls. "Safe. It's never really safe out there, at night, on the streets and in the back of cars and tucked into motels. Who am I kidding? Thing is, we all got to make a living. And I'm saving my money so I don't have to work this gig forever. Work here during the day, eight bucks an hour. Then there's my *reeel* profession. I'm savin' my money, swear to God." She glanced over at me with reflective eyes and a face that seemed lost in the horror of it all. Trying to convince us she was bent on retiring, knowing full well she was probably a "lifer" like most of them. "My roommate is a crackhead and I don't want to end up like her. I'm too smart for that. And I've even got a savings account. I got plans. Big plans."

Bennett nodded. "That's good to hear, LaDonna. Would hate for you to end up like those five girls. They were young like you. And not half as pretty."

Her smile brightened her entire face. "You really think I'm pretty?" she asked in a teenager's voice.

"Yes. Absolutely."

I couldn't help but think of Bennett's youthful days on the force, and all of a sudden he had the charm of James Bond, standing in a wig shop making a seasoned prostitute blush like a virgin. I longed to roll my eyes, but I didn't want to ruin LaDonna's rare moment of confidence.

"That's a very nice thing to say, Detective. Don't hear it a lot in my line of work, and when I do it's usually followed by a foul act. So thanks."

"You're welcome," he said, shifting back to business. "Ever hear about Quince Stanfield biting anyone else? Getting rough with some of the other girls?"

"Sorta." She shuffled her doughy cleavage again. "There was some talk about him on the street, even before the murders. He was a regular john in the area and most of my, uh, peers did bizness with him. He was always kinda pervy, you know, with his big black Cadillac and greasy gray hair. And he liked to play dirty in the sack. But none of us cared 'cause that's our job—doing what the wives and girlfriends refuse to do. And Mister Q liked to spend money and that's what was most important." She looked at the mug shot again. "But then he started getting violent. I heard a rumor a few months ago that he had some freakin' disease that tore apart his mind. Haven't seen him in these parts for a long time."

Bennett removed the photo from the counter, sensing the girl no longer wanted to look at it.

"What did he do now?" she asked in a timid voice. "I'm assuming he's in trouble again, or you folks wouldn't be standing in a place called Little Shop of Whores."

"That's true," I interjected. "He's a suspect in a case we're working on."

Bennett gave me that look and took over from there. Total pig. "Let's just say, he's a person of interest."

"He's interesting aw'right."

"I'm just following up on a possible lead. Seems Mister Q was mighty generous with the ladies. And it's true about a certain disease ravaging his brain. Figured I'd come talk to you about him, get a better profile of the guy and how he works before I go driving up the coast to find him."

It was quiet in the shop. I could hear the clock on the wall.

After a moment, LaDonna shrugged her shoulders. "I'm surprised he's still alive."

"Well, unfortunately, he is," Bennett said. "But living far from the city."

"Good," she said. "One less creepoid to worry about tonight."

As we were leaving the shop, Bennett looked back at the girl and she waved to him. "Detective," she said, wearing a seductive smile. "Thanks. You ever want to go get a coffee, you just drop by and we'll go have ourselves . . . some coffee."

Bennett blushed and said, "I'll keep that in mind."

I pulled open the glass door and stepped onto Hollywood Boulevard. The sky was dark and cloudless and still. Bennett revved the engine and we headed west. He was silent and I imagined his head was full of thoughts and ideas. Something brilliant was being tossed around in that thick skull of his. He was sizing up the enemy, devising a game plan, and on the brink of investigative genius.

"I want a taco," he said, looking over at me.

"What?"

"I want a taco," he repeated. "Maybe a green chili burrito."

"That's what you're thinking about right now?" I rolled down the window.

"Yeah."

"I'm so disappointed. I took one look at you, sitting over there in silence, face hard as stone. And I just knew you were lost in thought, ingenious and productive, about to break this case wide open."

He slumped farther into the seat, the leather farting beneath his movements. "I was just thinking about dinner," he said.

"How original."

31

My house was too quiet. A deafening silence, a painfully stoic surrounding, as if no one really lived there. I almost felt like an intruder, familiarizing myself with the place as I made myself a drink and found my way to the sofa.

I thought about Armstrong and his sudden absences, quick and furtive attempts to escape, skirting the issue of romance and longevity. With a Stoli martini in my right hand, the booze settling nicely in my veins, I walked across the front lawn and onto his doorstep. The house was dark, an ink-black silhouette set awkwardly against the night. The rest of the neighborhood was bright. Lights were burning inside homes, families were sitting down to dinner, couples were engaging in romance, bulimic actresses were barfing up their last meal. The charm and eloquence of Brentwood, California.

All the curtains were drawn, successfully shutting me out. I couldn't even get a glimpse of his world, and I figured that was how he wanted it. As I was checking to see if the screen could be popped out, I heard the sound of an engine in the distance. Headlights blinked.

I went still.

The car edged to the curb and a corpulent woman emerged, brown grocery bag in her right arm. I sighed in relief when Rosa started walking to my front door. Finishing off the drink, I headed back across the lawn.

She was fumbling for her keys when I said, "It's already open."

Her face was full of alarm when she turned to face me. "Claire," she grunted. "What you doing, standing out here in the dark, drinking like a sailor?"

"Just the usual," I said.

"Stalking the neighbor?" She pushed open the door.

"Checking things out."

"You get arrested for that kind of stuff."

"I haven't done anything," I said. *"Yet."*

She unloaded the groceries.

I made myself another drink.

"How about a nice healthy dinner?" she asked. "Soak up some of that toxic alcohol."

I plopped down on the sofa again, this time stretching my feet out, head against the cushion. "Rosa," I called from the living room. "Please come in here." A sporadic wave of energy pulled at my insides.

A moment later she was standing in front of me, a sour look on her face. "Yes?"

"I think it's time I see his house." I jerked my thumb toward Armstrong's place.

"Maybe someday he invite you over."

"I don't have that kind of time."

Walking away, she said, "You're impatient and young. Gets you into trouble."

"Wait."

She stopped. "I have dinner to prepare. Don't care to have this ridiculous conversation."

"I'm going to ask a favor."

Her shoulders dropped. "I knew this was coming."

"I was thinking about maybe . . . getting inside, taking a look around, that's all. Completely harmless."

"Breaking and entering," she groaned. "You call that completely harmless?"

"No one will ever know."

"I will."

I went below the belt. "Remember how I helped you with that visa application?"

"You'll never let me forget."

"I think it's time you do *me* a favor."

"You mean, cleaning your toilet isn't enough?" She rolled her eyes. "Fine. I do this for you. And you don't ask me for nothing else. Nothing illegal. No more nonsense."

"That's a deal," I replied, slipping on my night-vision goggles.

Moving stealthily like a cat, and confident I could desensor his alarm system within six seconds, I slipped across the lawn. When Rosa caught up with me, I popped off the window screen. Using a Yorkshire blade I had picked up in London a few years back, I carefully separated the latch just enough to raise the glass. Of course, the alarm sounded, as I knew it would. Resonant and sharp buzzing filtered through the stagnant air. I climbed into the house and headed for the alarm box. Rosa followed close behind, moaning and groaning about getting a new job.

Sweating like some kind of farm animal, I detached the red MegaZ 45L wire from the blue MegaP 76J wire. I wasn't sure what to do with the yellow wire. But it was pretty. I once thought about painting my bathroom that color.

The harrowing buzz went dead.

Confident that we had just completed a successful break-in, I pulled off the night-vision goggles and turned on the foyer light.

"I have a baaaad feeling about this," Rosa said, but let out a sigh of relief.

John Armstrong's house was bigger than mine but almost sterile in comparison. Masculine and sparse, and definitely missing the touch of a woman. There were no pictures of friends, family, or pets. I thought it odd, and by the time I reached the second floor, I realized everything about his house was cold and impersonal and strangely detached, very much like the man himself.

Just as we were stepping into his walk-in closet, I heard the front door open and the sound of heavy footsteps climbing the stairs. Rosa's face dissolved into shock. "I told you, Claaaaire!" she cried. "We're going away for a long time. To a place with bad lighting and orange jumpsuits!"

My heart sank further. "I look awful in orange. It totally washes me out."

"Just wait until they put you in a cell with some chick that looks like Gertrude Stein. Talk about washed out."

I was holding Armstrong's belt when the closet door flew open, almost torn from the hinges.

Standing before us were three men of considerable size and stature and wearing black uniforms. The leader flipped on the light, tore the belt from my hand, and said, "Get out. Put your hands in the air."

It didn't take long to realize these boys weren't from the neighborhood-watch unit. They were highly trained government officials and had the finest night-vision goggles I had ever seen. Armstrong must be into some heavy-duty stuff, and I was numb from the thought. The men patted us down for weapons and then started asking us the tough questions: "What's your name? Social security number? Date of birth?"

"Listen," I said. "This is all a big, big, big mistake. My name is Claire Fontaine and I live next door. John Armstrong is my, well, lover. And I don't think he'd be too happy if he knew what was going down here."

They laughed at my expense.

Then the leader clicked on his cell phone and took a few steps backward. He mumbled and grunted and I heard my name whispered. The corners of his mouth were drawn up when he walked back over to me. "You're free to go," he said stoically. "There won't be any charges filed against you. Or your friend."

"Who says?"

"Armstrong."

"Did he say anything else?"

"Get out," the man replied. "Don't come back. You've broken rule number one, lady. Way to go."

"Oh, and, what rule is that?"

"The trust rule."

I could feel the pain edging its way into my chest, the ache of rejection, the certain solitude that was bound to come my way.

And just when I thought it couldn't get any worse, Rosa snatched her purse and keys and looked at me as though I had just run over her dog. "I am so disappointed in you. This madness. I can no longer work for you."

"You're quitting?"

"Yes. Yes, I am." She wanted to sound convincing.

"Please don't leave me now."

"I can't go on like this without, you know, a little extra compensation."

"So, basically, you're using this tragic and embarrassing experience to get a raise?"

"Yes. Yes, I am." She was convincing.

"This is pathetic."

"No." She waved a finger. "Standing in your neighbor's closet, after climbing in through the window . . . now, that's pathetic."

"How much?"

"Extra hundred dollars a week?"

I gasped. "That's an additional four hundred dollars a month!"

"Good help is hard to find. Take it or leave it."

"I'll take it," I moaned. "Until I can find better help."

I slept poorly, unable to stop thinking about Armstrong and how angry he must have been, and about the way those men in black just stood there, laughing at me, with those eyes of steel.

32

Bennett picked me up early for the drive up north. It was time to face the mysterious Mister Q and his assortment of blisters and . . .

The area known as Big Sur is about ninety miles in length, just north of San Simeon and south of Carmel. An exotic stretch of land blessed with seaside cliffs, unpolluted air, foliage, it is considered to be one of the most scenic locales in California, and also one of the most secluded. After a while, Bennett pulled the tired old Buick onto an unpaved road and we soon found ourselves sitting in front of a lone cabin, high above the coastline and hidden by a canopy of redwoods.

"What a nightmare," I said, reaching for my lipgloss.

It was almost three o'clock when the hermit slithered out of his house.

The Ghoul reminded me of a cinematic vampire. Something out of *Nosferatu* or *Salem's Lot.* He had an egg-shaped head, gray and thinning hair. His flesh was so stark, white, and lifeless, he appeared to be covered in flour. Stanfield was lurking on his front porch, staring out at us with beady unblinking eyes. The green gown that hung from his bones was likely taken from a hospital, and it blew listlessly in the wind, giving life to a rather dead and emaciated man. He was waiting for us to make a move, and I had a feeling he would stand there all day, threatening us with his black stare and sickly appearance.

Bennett turned to me, slowly, not wanting to disturb the environment outside. "Okay," he said. "Time to talk to this freak. I'm not sure what he's going to do. Looks crazier than a shithouse rat, but he's too skinny to take either of us. Stay close behind. Keep your mouth shut. Don't rouse the monster. He's dangerous, you know. And he's a biter. I'm certain you don't want his disease, so keep your distance, don't get too comfortable. He's volatile. Like LaDonna Jackson said, he's gone *nuts* in the past year."

"Understood." Bennett got no argument from me. This wasn't the kind of situation I fancied myself to be in, and the thought of this guy infecting me with neuro-whatever made my stomach curl.

Bennett pushed open his door, and then so did I.

Stanfield hadn't moved from the frozen position he'd taken moments earlier. His eyes were fixed on us, unflinching, dark as the earth. The gown rustled in the wind, his arms and legs poking out like dry chicken bones. He was really gross, and when I got close enough to see him in his entirety, he seemed almost otherworldly. He still hadn't moved and Bennett was stepping onto the porch. I wondered if possibly the man had died and his body just hadn't hit the floor yet. A standing corpse.

And then the Ghoul turned his head. Blinked once. Made a guttural sound.

Bennett spoke softly. "Mr. Stanfield."

"That's me. What do you people want, been sitting in front of my house all day. You with the Health Department?"

"No."

"You reporters?"

"No."

"You with law enforcement?"

Bennett reached his hand out to the man, but he refused the shake. "I'm a private investigator."

"Who's the *guurrl*?" Stanfield's eyes floated over to me and he gave me a look-down. Still the pervy old man, even in death. Chills ran down my spine and settled into my lower back. He licked his gray lips with a tongue that was red as pig's blood and then made a rather unpleasant gesture with his right hand.

Bennett took a hard step forward and cleared his throat, shifting back into his usual curt and crass manner. "Listen, Gramps, we're not here so you can get your rocks off. The *guurrl* is my associate and she deserves some respect."

The Ghoul showed his teeth. "Fine. What do you want with me? I'm a very sick man and I don't like visitors. And unless you're with the Health Department, I probably don't have anything to say."

"Can you just give us a moment?" Bennett asked nicely, the phony act coming to life again.

Stanfield shrugged. "Yeah. I guess. I ain't got nothing better to do. But die."

He turned and walked into the cabin, inviting us inside. "Excuse the smell," he began as we stepped into his house, the aged wood creaking beneath our feet. "I have to swallow ten pills a day and I use a lot of skin ointments, topical steroids, and camphor. The boils have become infected, you know. And it stinks like a dang hospital in here."

The Ghoul hadn't lost his sense of smell. My nostrils were greeted with an assortment of aromas. Menthol. Anti-infectants. Band-Aids. Hydrogen peroxide.

Bennett and I looked around the place. A moment of silence between the three of us as Quince Stanfield lowered his skeletal physique onto the bed that had been placed in the center of the living room. Furniture was sparse and conventional and gray. The heat was on full blast, exacerbating the hospice odors and moistening my neck and hands. The curtains were dark purple and pulled shut, preventing any natural light within the house and forcing Stanfield to live in perpetual evening. No phone. No television. A single stack of pornographic magazines was next to his deathbed and oddly placed between a bottle of penicillin and a tube of Vaseline.

I tried hard not to breathe, fearing the illness might be lingering in the heated air, searching for a new host to invade. Stanfield crossed his chicken legs and sipped from a Styrofoam cup. "Don't worry, dear," he said in a creepy voice. "You can't *catch* it. Not unless you want to."

I ignored his stare, and Bennett was brave enough to sit down in a chair. Stanfield set the cup on the table next to his bed. "What's this about?" he sighed. "Them girls that died a few months ago?"

"Not entirely," Bennett responded. "But I am here because a girl died. Someone you knew, and knew quite well."

Stanfield's face twisted in confusion. "Who?"

Bennett removed the victim's death photo, walked over to the bed, and handed it directly to the Ghoul. His eyes fixed on the girl. His hands shook badly, Parkinsonian shivers, the picture vibrating between his fingers. The confusion on his face transformed into sadness and he set the photo on his nightstand, almost knocking over a bottle of Lubriderm. "Beth," he said softly. "I'm in shock."

"Why's that?" Bennett said.

"'Cause she was a nice kid. And so very beautiful. We spent time together at this famous club—"

"Babylon," Bennett interrupted. "Yeah. We know. And management asked you not to come back after you got yourself into trouble."

"True," he said. "Snobs. Of course, they had no problem taking my money. But since they pride themselves on discretion and cherish their unlisted address, I got booted. Didn't bother me that much because I had bigger things to deal with, like beating a murder rap and getting out of town and keeping myself alive. The world came crashing down on me after those girls got butchered. Can you believe the police *actually* thought I might've done those awful things?"

"Yes," Bennett groaned. "I can. You don't exactly have a choirboy's record, Mr. Stanfield. Years of soliciting hookers for cheap sex, a known john in the area, biting and hair pulling. Talked to one of your favorites from the boulevard. She said you had gone nuts."

The eyes were fixed on Bennett now, hard and black like marbles. "I'm hardly a predator. The disease was starting to 'infect' my mind. It had spread to my spine and brain and it's irreversible. I am nuts, you see. It's true. Doctors said it was called organic dementia, and that syphilis was the underlying cause of the illness. I never knew I had it 'cause I didn't show symptoms, but over the years it festered and spread. Once it gets this far there's no turning back and I'm just waiting to die. My brain is a useless pile of mush, and, well, as you can see, my body is no better. I'm down to one hundred and twenty pounds and the sores never go away." He pulled up his hospital gown and revealed the pink rubbery spots on his left leg. Not a pretty sight. I looked away as he edged the gown farther up his leg, taunting us with the promise of indecent exposure.

"Enough," Bennett said roughly.

Stanfield smiled and his face went still and flat, reflective. I assumed he was thinking of the good ol' days when he was not so flaccid—and entirely capable of picking up cheap women in his shiny black Cadillac so he could whisper sour somethings into their ear, cop a feel, hand out fifty-dollar bills like they were candy.

"Organic dementia," Bennett said, breaking the awkward silence as he rolled his eyes.

"Yes." Stanfield's smile disappeared as he came back to reality. "Organic dementia brought on by neurosyphilis. You see, Detective, the reason the Hollywood division cut me loose is because they thought me too insane to have committed those murders. And I was, by their standards, too old and sickly to inflict such wounds."

"But you did bite a girl," Bennett said. "She needed more than sixty stitches, and the scar on her arm is very evident."

"Aaaah. LaDonna Jackson." The reflective gaze again, thinking about good times and a plush Latin woman with a great smile.

"Yeah, her. And from what I hear, there were more incidences. Girls on the street were talking about your madness, exchanging stories of abuse. You became quite a threat to them, and your fancy car started to look more like a hearse."

He waved a dismissive skeleton hand at Bennett. "I admit there were several unpleasant acts on my part. Some slapping, hair pulling, groping. A little nibble here and there. Nothing these girls aren't used to. I had a ladies'-man reputation for thirty years, Detective. Any girl standing on any corner would jump at the chance to do business with Mister Q. I was generous with the cash, and it bought me a willing stable of flesh. But then I started changing, getting sick in the head, couldn't control my outbursts, and some of the girls got frightened. Guess I don't blame them, but I'm certainly no serial killer that gets his kicks dissecting women."

"I hear you also bought Beth Valentine?" Bennett asked bluntly.

The Ghoul tilted his head. "What?"

"You paid Beth's membership at Babylon."

"True," he said, shrugging. "I did that for a couple of girls. Beautiful girls."

"But they're not dead," Bennett pointed out. "Like Beth Valentine."

Stanfield's eyes drifted down to the crime-scene photo on his nightstand. He picked it up with trembling hands and suddenly he seemed ancient, life passing with each tainted breath, fatigued by the incurable plague that had invaded him years earlier. "So beautiful," he sighed. "Hard to believe someone would do such a thing. I guess I, you know, paid the fee for her because I wanted her around. Not that she would spend the night with an old troll like myself. In fact, none of the girls at Babylon would touch me with a ten-foot pole."

"Doesn't sound like you were very popular," Bennett said. "Why spend so much time and money on girls that wouldn't give you the time of day?"

The Ghoul half-smiled. "Because I wanted to be around beautiful things. I might've had money in my pocket and nice clothes, but it never did much for me in the romance department. I'm not exactly Paul Newman. Even before the illness took over, I was hardly considered handsome. That's why I've been 'paying for sex' my entire life.

Everyone at Babylon, including the elitist amazon who runs the place, had me pegged the moment I stepped foot in the joint: *The letch*. The wolf in sheep's clothing. Gramps. Viagra-in-a-suit. Leftovers from Studio 54."

I almost started to feel sorry for Stanfield, and then I remembered how he had left his teeth in LaDonna Jackson's arm long enough to cause extensive bleeding. I was feeling hot, bored, and tired of standing in a room filled with white gauze and blue pills. "Mr. Stanfield?" I asked politely. His head thrust upright as if he were a puppet on strings. The black eyes were fixed on me, interested, amused.

"The *guurrl,*" he whispered. "So nice. Yes, my dear?"

"You and Beth Valentine ever have any disagreements?"

"Heavens, no," he said. "We were friends, if you can even call it that. She was more of an acquaintance, and probably tolerated me, like most of the girls at the club." His eyes drifted down to the photo. "I'm still in shock. Never imagined something like this would ever happen to her. So beautiful."

"We heard she lived a wild life."

"A lot of girls in this town live a wild life. It's part of the Hollywood culture—live fast, die young, all that bullshit. But somehow the beautiful girls seem to survive."

"Beth didn't."

"That's what shocks me," he said, fingering the photograph. "The death of beauty."

"Beautiful girls get murdered all the time, Mr. Stanfield. It's not a freak incident or anything."

"Rarely," he said, shaking his head, "does beauty get the knife."

Bennett was slumped in the chair, rubbing his face with listless and bloated hands. Stanfield pulled himself from the mattress and walked over to a dust-covered armoire. His gaunt arm disappeared inside and he removed an envelope. It was clearly aged, stained. "I wrote a poem many years ago," he said, taking the envelope over to the bed and sitting down with a sigh. "About beautiful girls."

He dumped the contents onto the bed. I could see a few color Polaroids that seemed meant for a skin magazine, and he shuffled through them without an ounce of shame, reflective again, smiling. "Good times," he said. "Back then. Lots of girls. But not the pretty ones."

Bennett stood abruptly from the chair, groaning about the drive back to the city and how he wasn't interested in listening to poetry and looking at Stanfield's personal photography collection.

"You're certainly welcome to leave," said the Ghoul. "The *guurrl* can stay."

Bennett paced the room, further disturbing the acrid odors and dust particles and shadowy light.

"Just let the man read his poem," I said defensively.

Bennett looked at his watch, shook his head, and slumped back down into the chair.

Stanfield pulled out a single piece of paper that was heavily lined with creases, torn at the top right edge, and aged the color of dijon mustard. "Here it is," he said, flooded with emotion. "It's called 'The Myth of Beautiful Girls.' "

Bennett let out a long dramatic yawn. The Ghoul shot him a look, then returned his eyes to the piece of paper.

"Go on," I prompted, like a teacher encouraging the bashful student. "Read it."

Stanfield shifted, the clavicle bones were exposed again. " 'The Myth of Beautiful Girls,' " he began.

Darkness falls over a crescent city and the dreary take flight.
Man and earth collide as day turns to night.
All the pretty faces come out to play.
But only evil is allowed to stay.
Whilst their whimsical beauty dances through the air,
The threat of dawn only brings despair.
With their glorious features and satin curls,
so begins the myth of beautiful girls."

Bennett yawned again. "Not sure what all this means."

"I wrote it years ago, when I still had my mind and my senses." He folded the paper. "Don't you understand, Detective? We live in a make-believe world. And we assume, even in the shadow of night, that the beautiful are safe. Above the rest of us. Lucky. Blessed by the graceful hand of God. But as you can see, it's only a myth."

Stanfield suddenly tossed the paper aside and inched his gown toward his neck. "I've grown very tired," he said, wilting like a dead flower.

"That was a lovely poem." I put two hands together. "I don't think I'll ever forget it."

"That's nice." His eyes closed.

Bennett pulled himself from the chair with a grunt. "Well, if you have no other information and no other poetry to recite, we'll be on our way."

The Ghoul sat up on his elbows. "One more thing." It sounded like a threat.

"What?"

"Mark Astor."

Bennett pulled out his notebook. "Who is Mark Astor?"

"He's someone Beth associated with at the club. Late twenties. Rich kid. Looks like Conan the Barbarian. I never liked him. But then again, I never really liked anyone."

"So, she's got a history with this Mark character?"

"I don't know if I'd call it 'history,'" he said, "but they seemed pretty tight."

"We'll check it out."

Stanfield dropped from his elbows, eyes closed, mouth open. I thought I could hear him snoring by the time we left the cabin. Bennett seemed pleased with a new name, a possible suspect, anything. "Mark Astor," he said as if those two words held a secret. "Didn't see his name in the police reports. Gonna have to check that sucker out."

It was almost one in the morning before I crawled into bed.

The sheets felt like shards of ice against my skin, and the wind outside seemed to have a story to tell. While I lay there, solitary and silent,

I thought of Quince Stanfield and his strange and eloquent words. And as I reached for them in my mind, they came to me in a haunting rhythm.

Darkness falls over a crescent city and the dreary take flight.
Man and earth collide as day turns to night.
All the pretty faces come out to play.
But only evil is allowed to stay.
Whilst their whimsical beauty dances through the air,
The threat of dawn only brings despair.
With their glorious features and satin curls,
So begins the myth of beautiful girls. . . .

33

We got a hit on Mark Astor's background check.

"The guy was busted for grabbing itty-bitty-titty," Bennett snorted. "But the charges were dropped because the girl refused to testify against him."

"How old was the girl?"

"Fifteen," he said. "At the time of the assault, Mark was twenty-five. That's statutory rape in any state. He's been off the radar for three years, no arrests, no nothing."

The current home address listed for Mark Astor was in Bel Air, and by the time Bennett and I arrived at the estate, I was car sick from all the sharp twists and turns in the road. We had to be buzzed in at the gate, which took a little maneuvering on Bennett's part, because the rich don't like cops showing up before their attorneys do. The woman's voice coming through the white speaker was breathy and hesitant. "I'm not exactly sure who you are," she said. "Or why I should let you on my property."

"I'm not with the L.A.P.D.," Bennett said. "I'm just a P.I. and this has nothing to do with you, ma'am."

"Pardon me," she said in a huff. "But this is *my* home, so it has everything to do with me."

"I'm looking for the *man* of the house." Sounded like a total chauvinist.

"He's dead." A moment of silence. "Died last year. Had a massive coronary. Blake Astor. My husband of thirty-five years. He was found in bed at the It'll Do Motel down on Fairfax Boulevard. The coroner said he had so much Viagra in his system it caused the capillaries to—"

"Ma'am," Bennett interrupted. "We're looking for Mark Astor. He's twenty-eight."

"Oh. You're talking about my son. He's far from being the *man* of the house." She let out an enormous sigh that turned into static on our end. "He's not here. But I'll buzz you in."

The gate rolled open and Bennett edged the car along a road that seemed to take its form from a snake. The landscape was lush and manicured and populated with statues and tennis courts and guesthouses. The circular drive was stacked with expensive German automobiles, and the house was enormous, at least ten thousand square feet, a Mediterranean villa taken from the pages of *Condé Nast Traveler* and dropped on an acre in Bel Air. The color of the house reminded me of how dawn unfolds along the coast: salmon pink, effervescent. It was breathtaking and intimidating, not exactly what I was expecting, given the seedy reputation of our lead.

The front door opened as if it were being operated by a technician, and the woman standing before me was just as lovely as the voice that emanated from the speaker. She reached out a tan hand that glittered with diamonds. "I'm Suzanne Astor," she said coolly. "No relation to the East Coast Astors." Her green eyes rolled over to Bennett and she was less than enthused to meet his acquaintance. She invited us inside and I realized half of the walls were constructed of glass, most of the furniture was Oscar de la Renta, and that Suzanne Astor had more money than God. Bennett and I followed her into the living room, which was the size of my entire house. She had state-of-the-art electronics, his and her Picassos, and an extensive collection of Baccarat figurines. I had a terrible case of house-envy. And Bennett was so in awe his jaw was set in shock.

Suzanne touched a button on the coffee table and a wet bar floated out of the wall, with promises of champagne and vodka and brandy. Twinkling like stars in the sky were Vega glasses and handcrafted flutes. "Mark Astor is my son," she said. "Would anyone care for a drink?" She said it as though the mere mention of her son's name forced her to empty an entire bottle of Grey Goose in sixty seconds flat.

Bennett shook his head. "No thanks. We don't want to take up too much of your time," he said in his phony voice. "We would really like to talk to Mark. Do you know where we might find him?"

She walked behind the bar and removed a martini glass.

But her eyes never left Bennett.

Suzanne Astor was sixty years old, I guessed, but her face and figure never left fifty. She wasn't one of those overprocessed wives, with a frozen forehead and swollen lips. I could see the loneliness in her face but it hadn't worn her down. And I could hear traces of icy cynicism in her voice, but deep down she had a heart that still pumped, and a tummy that hadn't been tucked. Still looking directly at Bennett, she made herself a martini like she had been tending bar at some raucous tavern for twenty years. "What is it you want with my son, Detective?"

"We just want to ask him some questions," Bennett replied. "About a girl he used to hang out with."

"How old is she?" Her voice hissed from across the room.

"She was twenty-two."

"At least this one is legal." She poured her cocktail into the glass. "What do you mean *was* twenty-two?" It got very still in the room and I watched her green eyes change color in the light. "Is she dead?"

"That's correct," Bennett said, sounding like a math teacher. "Please understand, we're not here to arrest your son. He might have information about her that we've yet to uncover. It's just routine questioning."

"But he's not in trouble?"

"Not yet," Bennett said. "We don't have any evidence suggesting he did anything wrong, Mrs. Astor."

"Call me Suzanne." It was an order. She sipped the drink while looking out the enormous panoramic window that faced the pool. "Let's go outside. It's getting hot in here."

She picked up her Chanel sunglasses from the coffee table, and we followed her out the door, down a flight of stairs, and onto a glorious sun deck with partial views of the city. The rock pool cascaded like a waterfall into a bubbling hot tub that reminded me of a spa treatment I once had in Palm Springs.

"It's so peaceful out here," she said, sitting down in a padded white chair and inviting us to do the same.

The water lapped at the edges, foamed and circled, and then tumbled into the heated spa. Suzanne leaned her head back and invited the sun to warm her face. There was a slight breeze that carried with it the scent of gardenias. "I have to protect my son," she said, sliding the glasses up her nose.

"From what?" Bennett asked.

"From himself."

"Is he dangerous?"

"No," she said. "But he is dumb."

"How dumb?"

"Very. Sometimes I wonder if one drunken night, twenty-eight years ago, I might've slept with my own brother. That dumb."

Bennett almost smiled.

"I can't just allow private investigators to go sniffing around his new home without first asking their motives."

"New home?" Bennett's voice was thick with disappointment. "He doesn't live here?"

"No." She bit her lower lip. "He's in a hospital."

"Which one?"

"Trinity Rehabilitation Center," she said. "In Pasadena."

"What's being rehabilitated?"

"His mind."

It was a long time before anyone spoke at the table. The sun shifted its angle and a gray shadow was cast upon us. "Trinity is good for him," she continued. "Medical professionals monitor his actions and activities, and his addictions aren't allowed. He's surrounded by people that can take care of him, make sure he stays out of trouble. I'm too tired and old to babysit."

"He's twenty-eight," I said flatly. Bennett shot me a tough-guy look.

"Yes, dear. But a dumb twenty-eight. And he's volatile and crude and not the same person I gave birth to. He's been abusing steroids for years, the kind bought on the black market. It's been a nightmare. And then there was the incident that almost sent him to prison."

"The fifteen-year-old?" Bennett prompted.

She removed her glasses and I could see the surprise on her face. "You did your homework," she said glibly. "Yes, the fifteen-year-old. Her name was Paulette something. And she was from Simi Valley, and white trash if I ever saw it. But, according to Mark, they were in love. Well, her father didn't take to the idea of his daughter being shanked by a grown man with more muscles than a professional wrestler. There was no rape involved. It was entirely consensual. Her father disapproved, the police showed up, Mark got charged with statutory rape. The entire thing was such an embarrassment. And, of course, the father came sniffing around and realized there could be a big payday for him—and there was. I wrote a big fat check and the whole thing went away, just disappeared. So the fifteen-year-old cost me about thirty grand. Two weeks later, I brought the girl's name up to Mark and he didn't even remember who she was. Things got worse from there. His temper, his moods. Something just snapped inside him. And I never got the real Mark back. When his father died, it didn't even seem to faze him. He shrugged his shoulders and said, 'Yeah, well, shit happens. I gotta go work out.' "

Bennett and I looked at each other. The sun rolled back into view, and Suzanne put her glasses on. She finished off the martini with a sigh. "What happens to people?" she said in a whisper. "Do they just lose their minds?"

"Some do," Bennett said. "I think the steroids probably messed him up."

"No kidding. It's been like living with the devil. And, unfortunately, he's like his father in the romance department, with an appetite for the young. The forty-dollar hooker that showed my husband the fastest way to a heart attack was barely twenty. If I didn't have so much money, I'd be a pariah in this ridiculous neighborhood."

Bennett's collar was damp and oily with sweat. "Did Mark ever mention a girl, Beth Valentine?"

"Not that I can remember," she said. "He didn't talk too much about his social life with me because he knew I would disapprove. I do know that prior to sending him to Trinity, he spent a lot of time at that silly nightclub, Babylon."

Bennett nodded. "Mark knew our victim from his late nights at the club. I'd like to pay him a visit. What's their rule on visitors?"

"I'll call ahead and make sure your name is on the list," she said. "You know how it is living in L.A. It's all about being on *the* list. But I've got pull since I pay the tab. It runs me about five thousand dollars a month."

"Sure hope he's being *rehabilitated*." Bennett was obviously bored and antsy, glancing furtively down at his watch. "Can't thank you enough for your time."

Suzanne pulled herself from the chair. Looking down at both of us, she said, "I'd like to show you something, if you have a moment?"

"Sure." Bennett shrugged.

She left us sitting at the table, soaking up the sun.

Bennett shook his head, frustrated. "I hate when people get all liquored up, and then I have to hear about all their fuckin' problems. The only reason I'm here is to find out where that little shit is living. I could give a crap about Miss Knots Landing and her neighbors and her dead cheating husband."

"That's a terrible thing to say," I replied. "She opened up to us. That's what you wanted, isn't it? She gave us enough information to find the dude. Give it a rest, and give the poor lady a break."

"Poor?" He rolled his eyes. "She's got a wet bar that comes to her when she calls it."

We heard the back door close and our conversation quickly ended. Suzanne approached the table holding a leather-bound photo album. She sat down at the table and opened it to the first sheet. "This is one of our family albums," she said.

Bennett let out an enormous sigh.

I hunched forward and took immediate interest in the pretty color glossies that once represented her life as a wife and a mother. "This picture was taken many, many years ago," she said, pushing the album over to me. It was one of those family-vacation photographs with a blue ocean in the background and a happy smiling threesome; a mother, a father, and a son. All of which were thin and tan and wearing Ralph Lauren white.

She tapped her fingernail on Mark's face. "This was him in St. Barts," she said. "Look how handsome he was. The shape of his face, the color of his skin."

"He's very attractive," I said agreeably.

Bennett nodded like a robot.

Suzanne wiped fresh tears from her cheeks. "Mark doesn't look like that anymore," she said, shaking her head and sniffling.

"What does he look like now?" My stomach felt tight, full of dread.

She didn't answer for a long time. Sitting there beneath the sun, I could see the immense pain in her face. "Different," she whispered. "He looks different."

Mark was a kid when the picture had been taken. He had a full head of sandy hair and bright green eyes, his cheekbones were high, and his mouth was wide. He was tall, slender, and still boyish in looks. His father (now dead from the forty-dollar hooker) was an older version, handsome and rugged, well preserved.

"We were so happy back then," she said. "Or maybe I was in such denial about things . . . that it didn't matter what went on behind the veil of happiness."

"Those are lovely photos, Mrs. Astor." Bennett pushed his chair from the table. "But if we're gonna get in to see your son today, we'd better get going."

"Oh. So soon?" She seemed wounded by Bennett's desire to leave. "I'm just getting started. I've got thirty or forty photo albums, Detective."

Gasp.

Another gasp.

"Not today," he said, smiling. "But I'll come back real soon. I promise."

We left the house so fast I don't even remember saying good-bye to the woman, and soon Bennett was speeding down the sinuous road like a madman. It didn't take long before I could taste my breakfast in the back of my throat, as my head swung violently with each sharp turn. The Buick was almost on two wheels as we took the last curve at sixty miles an hour. I sort of remember Bennett looking over at me and saying something like, "Thirty or forty photo albums! She must be on crack."

"Please. Slow. Down."

"No."

Twenty minutes later we were parked at a Shell station and I was wiping off the seat and window with a monogrammed silk handkerchief. "Told you to slow down," I said. "Now it's going to smell like bagel and lox for the duration of our trip."

"Whatever. Just get in the car. Let's go."

We sat on the freeway for at least an hour, windows rolled down, static on the radio. The air was warm and humid, laced with the smell of exhaust fumes, worn rubber, and lox. It was not a pretty drive, and I could see the heat rising off the metal in front of us.

"Look at all these people going to Pasadena," Bennett said. "You'd think the Rose Bowl was today."

"Maybe they're all going to Trinity Rehabilitation Center."

"Yeah. With my luck . . ."

He pulled off the freeway and snaked the car through an industrial area lined with automotive repair shops, packing plants, and desolate warehouses that were streaked with grime and mineral deposits. Trinity sat at the base of the San Gabriel Mountains, and it looked like a gray cloud that had dropped from the sky. From a distance I could see the chain-link fence and barbed wire. I wasn't amused.

"It looks like a prison," I said.

"Probably is to some of the people inside."

"Do you think they're dangerous?" I wondered aloud. "These people inside."

"If they were a serious threat to society," he said, "they'd be in San Quentin or Folsom." I could tell by the sound of his voice he didn't want to talk about it. And I was certain in the last few minutes of our drive, he farted. And on purpose. He held his face close to the window, the breeze cutting through his wispy hair, diluting his own stink. I said nothing of the incident, and when we arrived at Trinity, and he stepped from the car, I quickly sprayed Chanel No. 5 on his seat and then joined him in the parking lot.

34

Trinity Rehabilitation Center—a three-story block of concrete, gray as winter, slab-faced with a flat roof. It reminded me of pollution, or charcoal smoke rising up from the earth and taking shape. There was a guard at the entrance wearing a blue uniform and sitting behind a wall of glass with a small speaker cut into the center. "Can I help you?" he asked in a disinterested voice.

"I'm Detective Henry Bennett and this is my associate. We're here to see Mark Astor."

He ran his rubbery finger down a clipboard and nodded. "You're on the list." He buzzed the glass double doors that needed a shine, they rolled open, and we stepped into the lobby. Another unfriendly drab face was sitting behind a nurse's station. She told us Mark Astor was in room 24 on the second floor, and that visiting hours ended at six P.M. We took the elevator up, and when we stepped into the hallway I noticed the sparse decor, the white walls, and linoleum floor. The air was cold and scented with antiseptic, but it couldn't mask the quiet rage behind the walls. My shoes made too much noise, and I suddenly became conscious of every step I took, the clatter and clank of Manolo Blahnik. Bennett looked down at me with disapproval and shook his head.

Room 24 was spacious and clean as a marine barracks. Two twin beds on opposite ends of the room, crisp white sheets with hospital corners, a television mounted to the wall, a bathroom with a metal sink and a glass shower. There was an elderly man in one of the beds, shoeless, gaunt as a skeleton. His greasy-gray hair rested on angular shoulders and his long, sinewy fingers clutched a Bible. Bennett cleared his throat, and the man leaned up on his elbows, curious eyes settling upon my shape.

"Yes?" he said in a broken voice.

"We're here to see Mark Astor," Bennett said. "Who are you?"

"I'm Bob." He tossed the Bible onto the bed. "I'm here to save your soul. Don't you realize Armageddon is days away—the burning of the earth, the locusts, the seven seals."

"Okay." Bennett nodded. "But where's Mark?"

"Mark's a sinner," he said. "An enormous, pulsating, cruel, and emasculating sinner. He's in the Yard with the rest of the musclemen, pumping that ridiculous iron. I don't go outdoors. Ever. I stay in here, where it's safe, with Jesus."

"How do we get to the Yard?"

"Go down to the first floor, make a hard right, go straight through the metal door. Then you'll be outside with all them zombies."

"Thanks."

As we turned to leave, the old man made a wet sound with his tongue and said the word "tribulations." The entire place was creepy. I couldn't wait to set foot outside and feel the warmth of the sun, escape the stench of bleach and the silent dread that waited behind closed doors. We did as the crazy prophet said and found ourselves walking along a narrow concrete path toward a metal gate that was already open for our arrival. Bennett and I stood there, beneath the smoggy haze of Pasadena, eyeing the patients of Trinity as they roamed about the Yard, a small patch of dry land with brown shrubs, surrounded by a daunting chain-link fence and barbed wire. I looked over at Bennett and said, "What a dump. Suzanne Astor didn't wait long enough for her change. Five grand a month for her son to be locked up with a crazy old loon and have this stained patch of earth as his playground. For heaven's sake, he doesn't even get his own bathroom."

"Put a lid on it," he said, making his move toward the weight lifters.

My eyes caught the cold, harsh glare of a woman whose life had been drained by something potent and addictive. Her green jumpsuit hung on her bones as she smoked unfiltered Lucky Strike cigarettes and hissed in my direction. She looked old and wasted. I wanted to move quickly past her, catch up with Bennett, but my heels were digging into the earth, sinking with every step. I finally broke down and took them off, carrying them in my right hand.

The men lifting weights reminded me of inmates—incarcerated, grizzled, towering. Bennett mumbled something to one of them and he nodded in the opposite direction. If Mark Astor was here, he didn't look anything like his picture anymore, because my eyes searched the place and found no man who could have possibly once been the boy in the photos. Then I heard Bennett introduce himself, and the man sitting in front of him said, "Yeah. That's me. What do you want?"

Mark Astor's sandy hair had receded back to reveal most of his skull. His head was as misshapen as a tumor, and his cheeks were so swollen his eyes had become mere slits in his face. His neck was pitted with acne scars, and his arms were the size of canned hams. His white tank top was yellow beneath the pits, and his tan was dark and oily; self-tanner had stained his palms orange. When he stood up, he was taller than Henry Bennett, and his legs were thick and meaty.

"What's this about?" he asked in a deep husky voice that sounded as though it was conjured up from the darkest corners of hell.

"I'm investigating the murder of Beth Valentine," Bennett said. "We thought maybe you might have some information about her."

"Like what?"

"I don't know," Bennett replied. "Seems the two of you were quite close. Least that's what I've been hearing from the folks over at Babylon."

"How'd you find me?" The voice again, sending a slight shiver down my spine.

"Your mother."

Mark looked around at his fellow iron men and then back at us. "Let's go someplace else," he said. We followed him across the yard, through the cigarette smoke that drifted like fog, and past a group of men with overactive tongues. Mark sat down on a wooden bench close to the chain-link fence, testosterone posture, hands like baseball mitts. Bennett and I remained standing, looking down on him as if he were some kind of circus freak.

"What's the story?" Bennett said, already looking at this watch.

"Do I *look* like someone with a story?"

"Yes, you do."

I sat down next to the giant. He didn't move. The odor he gave off was manly, hormonal. I felt uncomfortable sitting there, in his shadow, wondering what he was thinking.

Bennett kicked at the dirt and rubbed his face. "How well did you know the girl?"

"Not that well, I guess."

"Were you ever lovers?"

The giant laughed. "No way, man. You see, I've been on the 'roids so long that I'm not good in that department. My body is all fucked up, out of whack. I started using back in high school. Thought it would turn me into a man, and instead it turned me into this. Lost half my hair. And my neck is permanently scarred from an outbreak of acne that was then exposed to staph, a bacteria that ate away at the skin."

Bennett knew I was dying to give him a reference to a dermatologist, but his sharp gaze prevented me from opening my mouth.

"That's terrible," Bennett said, devoid of emotion. "Now tell me about your relationship with the victim."

"She was a nice girl. We were friends and that's it. Hung out at the club, did some dope. I guess I dug her company cause she wasn't into me for my money or my family's money. She was cool like that, not some phony broad with fake tits and a motive."

"Speaking of motive," Bennett said, "know why someone would kill her the way they did?"

Mark lowered his head and folded his hands. "No, man. It's, like, so out there. Beth didn't strut around with attitude like the rest of the girls. And she never asked me for anything. In this town, everybody always wants something. But not Beth. She was cool that way. A regular girl just looking to have a good time."

"That's what worries me," Bennett said. "I think that 'good time' may have gotten her killed."

"Look," he said. "I'm out of the loop. I've been in here for six weeks and I don't have any plans of leaving, long as my old lady keeps paying the rent here. Trinity is a good place for me to be. And my mother seems happy to be rid of me. Things haven't been easy at the house for a long time. We've had our differences since I was, like, born. And my father died a year ago. Did she tell you about that?"

"Yes."

Mark let out a shriek of laughter. "He overdosed on Viagra. The guy had an erection at his own funeral!"

It was quiet for a moment, as Bennett studied the subject before him. "You seem pretty callous about your own father's death."

"The guy was banging a hooker in some motel down on Fairfax. Cry me a river."

"You've been tough on your mom," Bennett said flatly. "The fifteen-year-old cost her a fortune."

"Oh. Are you big buddies with Suzanne Astor now?" His voice sounded like glass breaking into a hundred pieces. "Gimme a break. Thirty grand is pocket change to that fuckin' bitch."

We had struck a chord in Mark Astor, and it was one of anger and resentment. His eyes became slits of rage, tucked beneath a red pulsating forehead. The giant breathed heavily, looked over at me, and in a rather mocking tone asked, "What's the story?"

"Do I *look* like someone with a story?" I said dryly.

"Yes, you do," he groaned. "Why're you carrying your shoes?"

"Because the heels kept sinking into the soil."

"Oh."

Bennett rolled his eyes and shoved his hands down into his pockets. "Let's talk about all this rage you got toward your own family, kid."

"I ain't no kid," he said. "And it's not rage. It's just . . . you know . . . hate."

"Same thing. I don't like a man that talks about his mother that way, and laughs at his own father's death. Makes me suspicious about his character, his state of mind."

"I don't have much of a mind left."

"Won't argue with that."

"Look." Mark picked at his neck. "I'm in a mental hygiene facility for a reason. And I choose to stay here. I could walk out the door today. But I don't. My van is sitting idle in the parking lot and has been for six weeks. I just pray to God my mother keeps sending Trinity money so I can stay here where it's safe."

"Safe?" Bennett shifted his weight onto his right foot.

"Yeah. Safe. I want to die in this place."

His testosterone posture seemed broken, and I wondered if his sudden vulnerability was all an act.

"Are you in danger?" Bennett asked.

"Not now." He rubbed his orange palms together. "But, you see, when I was on the outside, I was dopin' and I couldn't stop. Everybody's always holding something—steroids, coke, whatever. Temptation was too great. I could've never cracked the habit if I had stayed on the outside."

Bennett and I looked at each other. The Yard seemed to fall away and it was just the three of us, in the strange silence, beneath a gray sun.

"Why do you drive a van?" I asked.

"What?" His lip curled.

"You heard me. Why do you drive a van?"

He shrugged. "'Cause I outgrew the Porsche. Couldn't fit into the seat anymore, head hit the roof. I feel more comfortable in a van. What's the big deal? You with the car police?"

"No, no. It's just unusual."

"Well, if you haven't noticed, I'm unusual."

"Noted."

Mark pulled himself to his feet and threw an enormous shadow on the ground. Bennett was looking up at him, not backing down. "We ain't quite finished, so sit down."

A guttural noise came from deep inside him, sounding like an animal dying. "Look, buddy," he said. "I'm not your guy. And my flunkies over there are starting to stare. We lift together at four o'clock, and I gotta work on my tan. It's part of my recovery. Fun in the sun. Mother pays the bill. I'm safe. With my homeys. And Bob brings Jesus to the dinner table."

"Sounds like paradise," Bennett said. "But I don't like your attitude. And I wanna know where you were on the night of August twenty-seventh."

"You gotta be kidding." He sat back down dejectedly. "Do I really look like somebody who could kill a person?"

Bennett nodded. "You look like somebody who could kill five persons."

"Yeah. Well, I didn't touch the girl. She was my friend. Ask those morons at the club. If you want an alibi, I don't know if I have one 'cause I don't remember the month of August. If you want to search my van, have at it. Front door is unlocked. It's the gray Dodge in the back row. You can even ask my mother, she'll tell you I'm *no* killer. And she despises me." Mark stood up and gave Bennett the finger. "See ya. Wouldn't wanna be ya."

"I could have you sent up on obstruction charges, kid. You'd do time for that, in a real fuckin' prison with guys that bench press your weight."

"I'm not obstructing anything. I'm trying to be helpful here, offering up my vehicle for inspection. You could probably go back to my house and look through my room without no court order. My mother would like the company. Did she try and show you our family photo albums?"

Bennett was quiet. So was I.

"I'm sure she did," Mark continued. "She's a lonely old bag. And she drinks Nyquil just for the alcohol."

"Hey," I said defensively. "Don't knock it till you've tried it."

The sun disappeared behind a thick patch of smog and Mark looked up at the sky. "There goes my tan."

"What a shame," Bennett muttered.

As the giant walked away, I could smell the pungent odor of his sweat. He swung his thick head back in the direction of Henry Bennett, and in a voice meant for Dante's Inferno, he said, "Give my love to Mommy Dearest."

"Keep on walking," Bennett said roughly.

We left the place in a hurry, as if we had committed a crime and wanted to escape the property. The parking lot was hot, almost steamy, and the building was behind us now, sitting there like a storm in the middle of a desert. Bennett slid across the front seat and fired up the engine. "Smells like perfume in here." He made a gagging sound.

"Aren't we going to inspect his van?"

"No. He offered it up knowing it's clean. And, besides, I need luminol and a magna light to pick up anything relevant, like bloodstains."

I reached into my Gucci clutch. "I've got luminol in my purse," I said, "but you're on your own with the magna."

He turned to me, his mouth wide, frozen in awe. "You have luminol in your purse?"

"Yeah."

His obnoxious laughter followed. "Shoulda left you back at the mental ward."

35

You're beautiful when you're angry.
—Clark Gable to Lana Turner in
Betrayed, 1954

John Armstrong was back in town.

He knocked on my door at half past eight, wearing a grim, stony face and speaking in a very, very, very unforgiving tone. "You broke into my house," he said, stepping cautiously into the foyer. "I don't trust you."

I let out a shriek of cruel laughter. "Oh, you don't trust *me?* What a joke that is. You're the one living the secret double life; jet-setting across the world under this phony investment-banker facade. For all I know, you're really married with kids. That's why I broke into your place, to learn more about you because I sure can't get any answers straight from the horse's mouth."

"I'm not married," he said. "I can tell you that."

"What else can you tell me?"

"I was born in Chicago."

"John Armstrong your real name?"

"For the most part."

"Does Delta Force always watch your house when you're away?"

"For the most part." He looked contemplative about further discussion.

"That's some heavy-duty security. You must be a secret agent, or an assassin, or a high-level CIA operative."

"I can't discuss that part of my life," he said. "That's just the way it is. I took a vow years ago, and I can't break it for you or any other woman. It's my life. There's not a lot of room for discussion when it comes to my profession. And I can't have people breaking into my house. Ever."

"Well. I can't give myself to someone like you. It's a waste of time. You're completely closed off from the rest of the world. Everything is an illusion in this town, and that includes you."

"That's fine," he said. "I came to tell you it's over, and it's for the best, and you'll find someone else; someone better at dating, and playing the game, and younger than me."

"You're *dumping* me?" I said, feeling the weight of my heart as it sank into my stomach.

"I hate the word 'dump.' It's crass and juvenile. Think of it as a mutual split."

There was nothing mutual about it.

Armstrong was making the decision and trying to sugarcoat it with benign words like "mutual" and "split."

I was only bluffing, trying to act tough. "Wait a minute," I said. "This is so sudden. I'm not psychologically prepared for it."

"In the same regard, Claire, I wasn't prepared to have my house broken into."

He was out the door and across the yard. I could hardly move, paralyzed by the loss of something so real and honest and tangible.

And, even worse, Sergeant had taken all the Ambien and I was forced to lie in bed for hours, twisted with insomnia, thinking about how quickly our relationship had ended, how my futile antics had ruined a perfectly good romance.

And when sleep finally came to me, I dreamed about Virginia Woolf and Sylvia Plath, chronic self-loathing, distilled whiskey, and double-barrel shotguns.

36

A storm woke me up at dawn and there was no hope of falling back to sleep.

Lightning lit up the purple sky like a sliver of glass cutting through the night, and rain pulsated and pounded against the windows. Thunder exploded in the distance every few minutes, vibrating the walls of the house and rattling the overpriced art that was hanging on them. Ennui flooded through my veins like a bad virus, slowing my morning routine to a weary crawl. It took an exorbitant amount of effort to make a pot of coffee, and when I opened my closet doors, all six of them, it wasn't as enthralling as it used to be. I pulled the closest Gucci suit from the rack and slid into it with robotic and tired movements. Despite a healthy dose of blush and lipstick and eye shadow, I still looked like a broken doll that couldn't be fixed.

I got to the office before Bennett and tried again to make coffee.

It was peaceful as I sat at my desk thumbing through autopsy reports and photographs. And then he arrived, disturbing the tranquillity.

"Morning," he said. "Believe this storm? Gutters are already full. You're up early. That thunder is like a bomb going off."

I just sat there, dejected and bitter.

"What's wrong?" he asked, pouring himself a cup of coffee.

"I had a *bad* night."

"Awe, man, me too. About broke the porcelain with explosive diarrhea. Ate one of them hot dogs they sell from those sidewalk stands. Hit me like a ton of bricks."

"I can top that," I said. "The other day I broke into my neighbor's house and got busted by some secret commando team. This particular neighbor also happened to be my lover, and also happened to be employed by some federal agency. I'm certain I've been flagged. And I'm certain I've been dumped."

"Man, that is bad. You win." He walked into his office.

I couldn't believe the lack of empathy coming from this man, knowing what trauma I had just been through. "Is that all you have to say?"

Bennett tore into a chocolate glazed Dunkin Donut and shrugged. "Yeah. What'd you expect?"

"A little compassion." I threw my hands into air. "Sympathy. A pep talk."

"A pep talk," he choked. "You gotta be shittin' me. I ain't a therapist, honey, and I ain't the right guy to talk to about relationship problems . . . seeing as I, you know, don't have them. Relationships, I mean. I can't give you advice, not even a shoulder to cry on. As for sympathy, I've spent a lifetime sifting through body parts, telling parents their children are dead, and trying to pick up the pieces that are left behind when innocent lives are shattered." He licked his fingers. "I don't have any sympathy left."

"Well, when you put it that way, guess I'm lucky to be alive and I'll just put all this pain and drama behind me."

"At least while we're working. You're welcome to start feeling sorry for yourself when you're off the clock."

"Gee, thanks."

"Anytime." He pulled himself from the desk. "Now, let's go see Suzanne Astor." His face and collar were stained with chocolate.

"You might want to freshen up before we go." I alerted him to the various specks of food that had been so ambitiously collected and proudly displayed.

"Oh," he said. "Thanks." Running the back of his sleeve across his face brusquely, he said, "Okay. I'm fresh. Let's go."

37

The Mediterranean didn't look as picturesque beneath a dark and stormy sky. The trees that lined the private road blew violently in the wind, tossing gold and brown leaves onto the windshield and rattling the foundation of Bennett's archaic automobile. Gray clouds rolled overhead. The house sat on the hill like a monster, monolithic, powerful.

Suzanne was standing in the doorway, a white silk robe hanging from her svelte and tan shoulders, her hair in rollers, diamonds in place. It wasn't even noon and the woman was wearing more yellow canary than the entire Harry Winston store. I was jealous and a little in awe. She closed the door behind us, and said, "What an awful day. Weather Channel says it's going to be like this into the night, with the possibility of golf-ball-size hail."

"It's pretty bad," Bennett admitted. "Wind about destroyed my hood, and you're not going to have any leaves left on those trees out there."

"My yard boy will have his work cut out for him." She walked into the living room and offered us a seat on the plush sofa, smiling at Bennett as he wiped the rainwater from his forehead. "I've got a fresh pot of Columbian on the stove and blueberry scones from Fred Segal, if anyone is hungry."

Bennett's thick head swung in her direction. His face was flushed with joy. The thought of food did for him what romance did for others. "I'll take a cup of coffee and a few of those . . . whatever."

"Scones," she said formally, as if teaching him a culinary lesson.

"Yeah. Them."

She nodded politely and then looked at me.

"Coffee would be lovely," I said, crossing my legs.

When she left the room Bennett leaned over and said, "She's one of the few broads I seen that looks good in the morning."

"She's *not* a broad," I said defensively. "And when you are a guest in one's mansion, and the host offers you a light snack, you should politely accept one instead of requesting every last morsel in the house."

"Thank you, Emily Post." His lip curled, sneering at me.

Suzanne returned with Bennett's order and set the silver tray on the coffee table in front of us. He started in on one of the scones and I sipped at my coffee. She excused herself to get dressed and take the rollers out of her hair. Fifteen minutes later she returned to the living room wearing a black Michael Kors sweater and pink Escada pants that were small enough to fit a supermodel. More jealousy flooded my veins, especially when I noticed the white-diamond necklace that must have been purchased from a private jeweler, because I had never seen it on the market and it looked to be a one of a kind.

She sat down on the sofa across from us and I caught a slight whiff of Chanel No. 19, which was a nice contrast to Bennett's personal scent. He was finishing off the fifth scone when she said, "I'm assuming Mark was not cooperative yesterday, since you're back today."

"Not true," Bennett said with a full mouth. "He was fine. It's just that we'd like to take a look around his room. See if there's anything of interest. Do you mind?"

She was quiet for a long time, got up, walked over to the bar, thumbed the Stoli, and then sat back down.

"Guess it's too early for a drink."

"Not in my book," I said. "Somewhere in the world it's happy hour."

She smiled as though it hurt her face. Looking at Bennett with eyes that reminded me of shined emeralds, she asked, "Mark's a suspect, isn't he?"

There was thunder in the distance, rattling the endless liquor bottles and providing a certain background music from Mother Nature. "Not a suspect, per se." Bennett washed down the remainder of the scone with cold coffee, the china cup disappearing behind his enormous hand. "Your son was quite close to the victim. And although he seems to be a volatile fella, I'm not here to wrap his belongings in plastic and ship them off to the penitentiary." Bennett kind of laughed, more of a snort, and Suzanne Astor remained stone-faced, wringing her hands and looking over at the bar.

She pulled herself up from the sofa, and I assumed she was getting ready to make herself a drink. Her diamonds sparkled in the gray air when she waved a hand at us. "C'mon," she said. "I'll give you two a tour of my home, and you can see Mark's room."

We climbed the stairs behind her and I could tell Detective Bennett was impressed with himself, manipulating the rich, skirting around search warrants and cranky judges and defense lawyers. Suzanne Astor seemed grateful for the company.

The second floor was lined with gray and white marble. A Tiffany chandelier hung above the top of the stairs, adorned with enough bulbs and wattage to light a small country. The artwork on the walls was French Renaissance and reminded me of the stuff I had seen at the Louvre, gold-framed and expensive even by European standards. The furniture was thick and sturdy and antique, depressing and heavy, too masculine for a woman's house. We walked down the corridor, and Bennett made some phony comment about how nice everything smelled and looked.

Suzanne stopped at a door and reached for the gold knob, twisted it slowly, and then pushed open the heavy oak. She stepped inside the room and crinkled her nose at the musty odor. Flipping the light switch, she said, "This is Mark's room."

Bennett stepped inside. I followed.

It took everything not to burst into laughter.

The place was every fourteen-year-old's fantasy: A full-size bed with a light blue comforter covered in race cars. Nascar wallpaper and a closet full of muscle magazines and comic books. His desk was made of wood, nothing fancy, and painted the color of caramel and covered with miniature plastic wrestlers that came equipped with interchangeable body parts and WWF clothing. The lampshade next to his bed had Superman on it, and the ceiling had been victim to glow-in-the-dark stickers. Suzanne Astor's face was red as a sunburn when she said, "Mark never really outgrew his boyish phase. Mentally, I still see him as a kid, a teenager. He chose to keep his room like this, after all these years."

"Is he mentally ill?" I said.

"You met him," she responded defensively. "What do you think?"

"I think he's different. And I think the steroids have really affected his mind and body, and there's no going back. He has a lot of anger and a lot of that comes from being messed up chemically, the hormones out of whack."

"He's out of wha—" She cut her sentence short and stepped into the doorway, arms crossed in front of her chest, still on the defensive. "You can look around if you'd like. I'm going to make myself a drink." She looked at me, feigning a smile. "Because it's happy hour somewhere in the world." Her footsteps faded on the polished marble.

"Look at this place," I whispered. "No normal person would be caught dead or alive in this room. Friggin' race-car comforter and Superman lampshade and glow-in-the-dark stickers on the ceiling."

Bennett paced the room, opened desk drawers, thumbed the sweat pants hanging in the closet. When Suzanne returned, she had a martini glass in her right hand and a sudden flush to her face, the booze settling in her veins, taking off the edge. "Well," she asked, "anything else you need in here?"

"No." Bennett shoved his hands into his pockets.

"What exactly are you looking for?"

"Something that might tell me more about your son's relationship with the vic."

"Evidence?"

"You could call it that."

"Did you think Mark would have a room full of knives and guns and body parts?"

"Based on my meeting with him yesterday, I wasn't sure what would be in his room. He's hard to read. I just wanted to get a feel for how he lived when he wasn't at Babylon with the rich kids or at the gym with the musclemen."

Her eyes circled the room. "Well, this is it. Not much to see, really."

"Thanks for letting me have a look around."

"Sure."

Thunder blasted in the distance and rattled the Tiffany chandelier. She politely walked us to the door, shook Bennett's hand, and didn't seem to want to let go. "I hope you find what you're looking for, Detective."

"Me, too."

"Come by anytime."

I felt like a third wheel, inappropriately perched between the two of them, while she worked him over with those eyes.

38

The sky was granite-gray and looked hard and violent as we headed toward the car.

I envisioned the rest of Suzanne Astor's day being spent tossing back eighty-proof martinis, reading *Vogue*, filing her nails. My old life.

The new life: Bennett farted the moment he slid across the leather seat. "Those scones gave me gas or something," he said.

I rolled down the window. "That's so lovely."

He edged the Buick through the gates and we were on our way toward Sunset. The storm was still full of life, and blue lightning streaked across the gray sky. "What are we gonna do for lunch?" he asked.

"It's only eleven in the morning. And you just had five scones."

"I'm just thinking ahead, planning. I'm dreaming about a sloppy joe, somewhere like Pete's Deli or Dupars."

Sunset was bumper to bumper. It took us an hour to get to Pete's Deli, so technically, it was lunchtime. Bennett was staring hungrily at the menu when I said, "I think Suzanne Astor has a little crush on you."

His cheeks flushed as if he had suddenly caught a fever. "Oh, stop." He waved dismissively.

"I'm serious. The woman didn't want to let go when the two of you shook hands. Didn't you notice?"

"No. You're being ridiculous." His eyes drifted back down to the menu and I could tell by the silence he didn't want to discuss it.

"She probably thinks you're this rough and tough Dirty Harry type. That's appealing to a woman like her—sheltered, bored, lonely. You must seem kind of exotic and heroic to her."

His cheeks flushed again. Eyes frozen on the menu, he chose to ignore me.

Referring to Bennett as exotic and heroic was almost amusing, but it didn't sit well in the back of my throat.

Finally he tossed the menu onto the table. "She's a nice lady," he said. "And that's all I'll say. There's nothing further to discuss, and I didn't notice anything flirtatious about her behavior in the least."

I decided to leave it at that and tried to order a Waldorf salad, at which point I was met with boisterous laughter from both Bennett and the waitress. My culinary desires were constantly being mocked, while Bennett enjoyed a daily feast of cholesterol and lard.

39

After lunch we drove out to Pasadena to pay Mark Astor another visit. Trinity Rehabilitation Center looked even more bleak and dreary beneath the storm-laden sky, and Mark was less than enthused to see us. "Back so soon?" he groaned. "You guys must be hard up for a suspect." He pulled himself up from his twin mattress and flexed his right arm, then slipped his tan feet into Reebok tennis shoes.

"We saw your room," Bennett said ominously.

"So? You gonna arrest me for having bad taste?"

"You never outgrew dolls and race-car sheets."

"Fuck you." His eyes turned to stone. "I'm not a killer, man. Big deal if I'm into muscle mags and glow-in-the-dark shit. I didn't have much of a childhood. It was comforting to surround myself with youthful things."

"Including fifteen-year-old girls?"

"That was a long time ago," he said bitterly. "And she looked eighteen. And, supposedly, I have the brain and emotional capacity of an eleven-year-old. So it all evened out. Of course, my mother never let me live it down 'cause it cost her, like, thirty grand. She could've bought a really nice purse with that kind of cash."

Mark was standing close to me now, towering, breathing deep and fast like he was about to explode. His breath smelled metallic, and when I handed him an Altoid he threw it across the room as if it were a football. "Take your fancy mints somewhere else, lady."

"I'm just trying to help."

"Yeah, right. As long as you're riding shotgun with the police, you ain't trying to help me. So take your Beverly Hills beaver and hit the road." That was meant for Bennett, too, and I took a step closer to the door.

Bennett got into his face. "Listen up, kid. I could pull you from this joint and stick you in a five-by-eight cell just for fun. With guys that would eat you for breakfast. And your mother wouldn't be able to buy your way outta this one. I'd make it impossible. She might have lawyers in her pocket, but I got federal judges and lieutenants in mine. And we're tight that way. Blood brothers."

"You don't have a single piece of evidence on me, man."

"Your volatile personality is enough," he said. "You got a history of rage and you got one arrest for statutory rape. And you're a chronic drug-user. And, frankly, I just don't like you."

"Don't like you either, pal."

I stepped between the two of them, braving Mark's breath and possibly risking injury. "Guys," I said in a teacher's voice. "Let's solve this argument peacefully, without violence. My outfit is brand new and I'd hate to have it stained with blood."

Mark's beady eyes fell upon me. "You sound just like my mother," he said. "Bet the two of you get along quite nicely."

"We do, in fact."

"Figures."

Mark stormed out of the room. Bennett and I followed him as he sulked his way down the corridor and into the communal game room. There was a TV blaring, and Trinity patients engaged in card games and Ping-Pong and feckless chatter. The furniture seemed to be made of foam, and the carpet was muted gray. The windows were thick and covered with bars. Mark slumped dejectedly on the couch, crossing his arms in a huff. Bennett pulled up a chair and sat in front of him, facing him straight on. I took a seat next to him and wondered how anyone could concentrate in a room full of white noise. The volume on the television was obviously adjusted for the deaf and the Ping-Pong game was loud and monotonous, the plastic ball reverberating off the table in a constant, repetitive fashion.

"This is where we come to have fun," Mark said angrily. "Look at this place. Fucking asylum. Bars on the windows, freaks playing board games. I hate when it rains. I'm stuck inside with these morons watching Bob Barker interview retarded people. The noise. It makes me crazy. And I can't lift inside. The weights are forbidden. And I can't work on my tan. I love the sun."

"That's pretty obvious," I said. "You have a few moles on your neck that should be checked—"

"Shut up," he interrupted. "Told you to take your Beverly Hills beaver back to the Westside."

Bennett cracked his knuckles. The patients wearing hospital gowns stared our way, intrigued, fascinated. The Ping-Pong game finally came to an end and I could almost hear myself think. And then someone on Methadone walked over and raised the volume on the television. Mark kicked his foot out and rolled his eyes.

Bennett wanted a piece of him. "You hate women, don't you?" he whispered.

"I hate people."

"But mostly . . . women?"

"Not true," he said. "You're trying to make me out to be a monster."

"Well . . ." Bennett shrugged. "Aren't you?"

Mark's eyes glared at him and I felt as though I could see the man's soul, empty and tortured. "You really like pushing people's buttons, don't you?"

"Just want some answers."

"I don't have any."

"I think you do."

Mark twisted and arched his torso, slowly, as if a snake was slithering inside him, unraveling. "I didn't kill the girl," he said. "And I don't hate women. I hate life, man. And I hate nosy cops sneaking around Trinity, trying to get answers that I just don't have. I don't know why Valentine was killed, or who did the honors. She shanked a lot of guys, you know. But not me. I haven't had an erection in five years. But that's another story entirely. She crossed some bad dude. But I ain't got a clue as to who. Take your pick. It's L.A, man. Fuckin' sin city."

Flushed with anger, Mark got up, walked over to the television, ripped off the volume knob, then pushed the entire thing off of the metal stand. The patients scattered, card games stopped, and a nurse came in carrying a hypodermic needle, followed by two male orderlies. They wrestled Mark to the ground, secured his arms, and injected him. Within thirty seconds he had stopped fighting and a calm gaze washed over his face. He had succumbed to the power of narcotics, and no amount of testosterone and rage could wake him. The patients resumed their activities, moving around clumsily, and the orderlies began picking up pieces of the television.

The nurse stalked over to us, a grim authoritative look on her face. "Visiting hours are over," she said.

40

I awoke at dawn, my bedroom bathed in purple light. A hint of thunder rattled the Monet. Wind whispered outside my window like a lost soul searching for a place to rest. A dreamlike morning unfolded before me. I made coffee, showered, dressed in imported silk. Then I sat down on the sofa and surfed through all the static and infomercials that clouded the television networks this early in the morning. It was a flashback to my old life. Tranquillity. Freedom. Luxury. More Tranquillity. Endless freedom. Excessive luxury. Boredom. Lots of it. Aimless days and lonely nights. Monotony. More boredom . . .

I thought about Mark Astor and how it might advance the investigation if I could get him alone. Bring him a gift, something he'd cherish. If I weren't standing in Bennett's shadow, maybe he would see me differently.

It was half past six when I got in the car, headed to Pasadena, and found myself sitting in the parking lot of Trinity. It was an intimidating presence even in the peace of morning light. The guard on duty was sleepy-eyed and barely audible behind the glass.

"I'm here to see Mark Astor," I said. "My name is Claire Fontaine."

"It's a little early for visitors."

"I should be on the list."

His eyes lowered to the clipboard. "No one is on the list. And visiting hours don't start until ten. Come back in a couple of hours."

"It's urgent, sir."

"Are you of any relation to the patient?"

"No, but—"

"Then come back later, when you're actually on the list. We're exhausted around here. Last night was a bad one. Without a TV, we had a virtual riot. Complete lockdown."

"Yes, well, I can help you with that."

"How so?"

"I'm making a donation to Trinity. It's a tax write-off, of course. I'll have a sixty-three-inch plasma here by noon. Largest screen available. Integrated set. Surround sound."

"No, shit?"

"Yes shit."

"What was your name again?" He picked up a pen.

"Claire Fontaine."

"Seems that you're *on* the list."

He buzzed me in with a generous smile and whispered, "Mark's not a morning person."

The halls were quiet, and the lights were dimmed to a hazy yellow. Bleach tickled my nose.

I knocked on the door gently, then pushed it open a few inches and stared into the darkness. Bob the Prophet wasn't in his bed, and I figured he'd been sent down to the psych ward for a little one-on-one with the Holy Spirit. The white sheet that draped

Mark Astor's body rose and fell with each breath. He snored like an animal in the wilderness. I looked at my watch and realized I didn't have a lot of time to procrastinate. Bennett would want me at the office by nine.

I flipped on the light switch. As I entered the room, the nerves in my neck came to life. This sleeping monster was about to be roused awake.

Astor hadn't budged. I reached down and tapped his hand, then thumped his arm.

He let out a manly groan, opened his eyes, and then pulled himself into a sitting position.

"What the fuck!" He moved dizzily.

"Listen, Mark, it's okay. I just wanted to talk to you without Detective Bennett."

"Are you nuts, lady?" He dropped back onto the bed. "It's the crack of dawn."

"Actually, it's well past dawn."

"Scared the livin' shit outta me." He reached for a barbell. "Get the hell out."

"You don't have to pull that tough-guy routine with me. I'm not an asshole like my partner. I just thought, maybe, we could talk. Like normal people. I'm not asking to be your friend or anything, and when this is all over, I'm sure you'll never see me again."

He placed the weight on the floor. "Why're you here?"

I reached into my satchel and unloaded the arsenal of products. "I just think you're not trying hard enough to remember your friendship with Beth Valentine. You've pushed it all to the back of your mind and washed your hands of it."

He eyed the Lancôme bottle in my hand. "You bring me a gift?"

"It's nothing much." I handed it to him. "Self-tanning lotion. Streakless. Long-lasting results. Leaves skin feeling soft and moisturized."

"No sticky after-feel?"

"Nope."

He pretended not to be amused, shrugging. "Huh. That's good stuff. I've been using the Fake Bake crap for years. It's cheap and I don't gotta step into a mall to buy it. But sometimes it makes me look orange and I feel like a gigantic pumpkin walking around the yard."

We shared a tense laugh.

"I have more." Now for the big guns. "Clarins."

"Damn." He snatched the bottle like a kid on Christmas.

"Personally, it's my favorite. Very lightweight. I like the Tinted Self-Tanning Face Cream."

I tossed the last bottle over to him. "Dior Bronze. Has the potential to turn very dark. And it doesn't dry out your skin."

"This is, like, awesome." He raised his head proudly. "No more carrot spots on the ankles and elbows."

I sat down across from him and could tell he was dying to lather it on, wait an hour, and then admire himself in the closest mirror. But that would have to wait.

"I want you to think real hard," I said. "But don't hurt yourself."

"Think about what?"

"Her." My eyes met his. "Conversations. Names. Places. Faces. We've been through Babylon, followed up on leads that led us nowhere. Even though you broke a nice TV yesterday and have, at times, been unbearably rude, I still have faith in you."

"You do?" A little shock was evident in his voice.

"Yes."

He placed himself firmly at the end of the bed, feet evenly apart on the floor, head bowed. "I'm thinking," he whispered.

It sounded like a warning.

Ten minutes passed. Then twenty. Then thirty. I feared he had fallen asleep, and just when I was about to speak, his eyes rose to mine. "I thought of something."

"So quickly?" A little cynicism was unavoidable.

"Yes."

"Go on."

"Wait." He raised a finger and closed his eyes. "I just forgot what I was going to say."

"Try to get it back, that one thought."

His head dropped into his hands and he squeezed his temples hard. "Got it," he said.

A gasp of relief. "Tell me quickly."

"Beth liked to slum 'cause it wasn't in her nature to act like a rich kid. I mean we'd hang at the club plenty, but that shit got boring. I just remembered this dive called Absinthe. She was into it. Real dirty joint down on Vine. Cheap booze, lots of guys on the lam. The girl was into danger that way. Taking risks. Guess she got off on it. I'm not sure if you've already been there. Maybe somebody else told you about it."

"Never heard of it."

"Cool. Then maybe it's, like, somethin' new. A lead. Or whatever you call it."

"She go there with anyone else? Hook up?"

"Probably. But she didn't tell me about it. The place is for bottom-feeders. Too many ex-cons. Not my scene."

"You said it was on Vine?"

"Yeah. Couple blocks south of Hollywood."

"I'll check it out."

"That's all I can think of for now." After taking off his shirt, he reached for the Dior bottle, popped the top, and poured half the contents into his palm. "Can't wait to see how this shit turns out."

So consumed by the tanning process, covering every nook and cranny, he didn't even notice when I left the room.

I called Bennett's cell phone from the car, a little nervous about his response, even though I had managed to get a tidbit of information out of the giant.

"Bennett," I said. There was so much background noise I was sure he wouldn't be able to hear me. "It's Claire," I shouted. "What's going on?"

"I can't talk right now."

"Sounds like hysteria." I could hear. Hurried and sporadic voices and sirens.

"There's been . . ."

"What?"

"I'll call you back later," he said firmly. "Now's not the time." A burst of static. "There's a fresh one."

I had seen enough episodes of *C.S.I.* to know what a "fresh one" was, and I was hardly going to spend the day at the mall, being ignored, while Bennett got to be a part of the action.

"Wait . . ." I was begging.

"Gotta go, kid. I'll call you in an hour or so." That was forever.

Just before he hung up, I overheard bits and pieces of the hurried chatter in the background and was able to comprehend the words "Ivy Hill Road."

I sped toward the Westside and made it to Venice in just under fifty minutes. Crime-scene tape and police cars were being used to block off the entire block. The warehouse, all too familiar and ominous, was host to a variety of investigative activity. The medical examiner's van was ditched at the curb, and forensic experts were walking in and out with containers and plastic bags. Henry Bennett was standing next to an ambulance, and I thought it optimistic to think paramedics would be needed at this juncture. A fresh one.

I got as close as I could on foot, joining the rest of the lookie-loos and all their video equipment. Tourists were taking photographs, a Kodak moment to show the kids back home. A fresh one.

Agitated and crammed between two obese townies, I phoned Bennett again.

"Yeah," he groaned.

"It's me."

"I *said* I'd call you *later*."

"I'm *standing* across the street, between Dumb and Dumber. I'd like *some* respect, please. Give me a break. Let me over this yellow tape."

"You pick up the location on the news?"

"No—overheard the info while talking to you."

"Impressive."

41

A land developer named Lance Morton found the body.

Bennett said he was covered in his own vomit and crying like a baby in the back of the squad car. His company had planned to bulldoze the warehouse in less than a week and he was doing a walk-through. Wearing a three-thousand-dollar pinstriped Armani suit, he stumbled across the remains, fell to his knees, tossed his breakfast on the concrete, and turned into a weeping boy. Finding a dead body can do that to a man. I could see only the back of his head, as I was still being forced to wait on the sidelines. Lance Morton looked like he was having a seizure, his head swinging side to side, then back and forth, as he sobbed. I could only imagine the incoherent babble spewing from his mouth.

Bennett was talking to a couple of badly dressed detectives as the body was rolled out of the warehouse. The crowd finally came to a hush, transfixed by the corpse on the gurney. I knew then I could never have the stomach for straight police work, but I'd never tell Bennett that. I had to wait another twenty minutes for him to come and acknowledge that he actually *knew* me.

Pulling me aside, he said, "You can't be here."

"What?"

"This is LAPD territory. It's a fresh crime scene and there's a lot of business going on inside the warehouse." It sounded subversive.

"LAPD territory? What does that mean? We found this place first."

"No, we didn't. They were first on the beat when Beth's body was found."

"Didn't do much good."

"Hey, don't knock 'em—they did the best they could given the resources."

"Can't you tell me anything about the victim?"

"Not now. Go back to the office and wait for me." He practically shoved me toward the car.

His eyes had a darkness to them that I had not yet seen, an uneasy gleam that caused my stomach to stir. It wasn't that he looked frightened, the man certainly didn't scare, but his features seemed a bit sunken.

The office was cold, and I noticed my hands were shaking as I made coffee. It wasn't quite the chill in the air that had caused the trembling, I knew. As I sat at my desk, still wearing my jacket, I listened to the distant sounds of the old building shifting from age. Halls that creaked on their own, vents that foamed with mold and lint, elevators that screamed from floor to floor. It was a nice break from the silence, but I had to admit it was a little creepy for a girl on her own. Especially since I'd been treated to the recent vision of a new body being rolled out of that warehouse and the look of black dread on Bennett's face.

I sat there for five hours. Literally five hours. Waiting. Wondering. Hoping he'd call. Anything. Bastard never rang, and he certainly didn't show up. I figured he was so immersed in the new case he'd forgotten about the old one. I wanted to be angry, my pride a little hurt from the rejection, being sent away. But I knew his instincts had taken him to a far-off place, somewhere civilians didn't go.

I drove home in a daze, my eyelids heavy. I thought about drinking vodka, heavily, maybe straight from the bottle. That might take the edge off, enable sleep to come easy. But, unfortunately, when I stepped from the car, I saw the thick silhouette and slow swagger of Rosa in the kitchen. I knew drinking myself into a coma wasn't going to happen.

"Why're you still here?" I said, tossing my purse onto the counter.

"Nice to see you, too."

"Didn't mean it like that."

"Sure you did." She diced tomatoes like a madwoman. "I see on the news, dead body in Venice. Reminded me of your new job. Thought maybe you'd want company, dinner."

"That's nice." I couldn't eat to save my life. "I was there today, you know. At the crime scene. That building has claimed two lives in as many months. It's a good place for a body dump. Dark. Abandoned. Gives the guy plenty of room, and time to run. Always takes a couple of days to find the body."

"You think they tear the joint down?"

"They were just about to. Land developer found the vic this afternoon. It was supposed to come down next week, but now I don't know. Maybe they'll need it for evidentiary purposes."

"I made broiled whitefish," she said. "The omega oil will be good for you."

"Whatever." I reached for the Stoli.

"You better watch yourself with that stuff, Claire. It's poison and it makes you fat."

"You think I'm fat?"

"No." Pause. "But, at *your* age, you have to be careful. If not, you end up looking like me. I've got an ass like a Buick and I'm too old to fix it. That drink is poison, clouds the senses, turns to sugar in the gut."

"What do you mean, at my age?"

"You're no spring chicken no more. Twenties are gone, thirties will fly by, you'll see. When you hit forty, you have no metabolism at all. Everything starts to spread out, no muscle tone left, you see."

"Thank you, Rosa, for this uplifting conversation. I'm going to bed now. Without supper. Or the drink."

I climbed the stairs, listening to the tomatoes being dissected. Her voice trailed after me like a gnat in my ear. "No barbiturates either! They make you depressed."

"*You* make me depressed."

"I just try to help. Offer guidance. Do my best to keep your mood stabilized. It's all about balance."

"Yeah. You're a real Sigmund Fraud."

I couldn't sleep without the meds or the drink.

Rosa ran the blender, then the dishwasher, then vacuumed, making as much racket as humanly possible. I tossed and turned for an hour, and just when I was going to watch the Home Shopping Channel, Bennett rang my cell.

"Sorry it took me so long."

"That's okay. I'm just glad you finally called. Thought maybe you'd found another partner."

"Hardly."

"Where are you?"

"At the Los Angeles County Morgue. Come on down."

"Come on down, *where?*"

"To the morgue. I know it's late, but the fanfare has died for now and it'll start up again in the morning. There's something I'd like to show you."

"Okay." I was terribly hesitant. "Did they do the autopsy?"

"Yes."

A sigh of relief. Bennett almost laughed. "Don't worry, I wasn't going to make you watch the postmortem butchery. But there is *something* you'll find of interest, and I think you're adult enough. Besides, you've proven yourself to be an important part of the Valentine case."

"You're going to show me the victim, aren't you?"

"Yes."

"And I'm supposed to absorb her, right?"

"Yes. Have a good look. You'll never forget your first dead body. And, well, there's something else. Just come down. Be here at midnight. Manning is on duty and I'll be in the lobby waiting for you."

"Midnight?" I sat up. "At the morgue."

"That's right. Whaaaat? You're not scared are you?"

"Me? No way. Never. I'm there, buddy."

Before he hung up, he said, "Oh, one more thing: Do not dress up for this one! Wear something you can throw away later. The stink will get in your clothes and you'll never be able to get it out. Don't waltz in here wearing some Gucci ball gown with rhinestones and shit."

His words made me indignant. "I have never, and I mean *never*, worn rhinestones."

42

It was exactly midnight when I turned onto Mission Road.

Before I knew it, I was standing in the light that was spilling from an open bay. A morgue attendant was on duty, as there would be ominous deliveries throughout the night: black body bags, victims of everything from murder to methamphetamine.

Bennett met me in the lobby and we pushed through the door and headed toward the autopsy suite. He looked as though he had aged ten years since this morning. The fluorescent light was cruel to him—his haggard skin was as gray as a ghost. I'm sure I faired no better when we walked into the coldest room on earth and saw the girl on the table. . . .

Her skin had once been white, but now it was marbled by death and decomp. She was naked, arms to her side, scrubbed clean of blood, stitched back together like a doll. It was my first dead body and I knew I would never forget it, no matter what I stumbled across in the years to come. Her nails were clipped, hair washed and pulled back from her face. She was young, flesh still supple, with the kind of bone structure that seemed carved from stone, arched brows, square jaw. There was a quiet peace about her, something unsettling yet tranquil. All the violence had been washed away.

Bennett didn't say much as we stood over the body. I'm sure he was hoping I was "absorbing" every last detail, from the toe tag to the throat. My eyes watered, my lips curled, my tongue retreated to the farthest corner of my mouth. And the cold—it had settled into my bone marrow. Bennett looked over at me, as solid and unemotional as a statue. I turned away, not wanting him to see the moisture forming beneath my lids.

Ralph Manning was standing over the sink, scrubbing his hands. He took a long time, his back to us, not saying a word. I tried to speak, but nothing came out. All I could focus on was the girl.

"Bastard slashed her neck so deeply, the . . ." Bennett lowered his head.

"The what?" I prompted.

"The tracheal cartilage was laid open."

I swallowed hard and thought I tasted blood.

"Who was she?"

"Name is Olivia Berkshire. Twenty-two. Dropped out of junior college last year, and took up waitressing. Both parents died in a car accident ten years ago. No priors. Lived paycheck to paycheck."

"You don't know a whole lot, then?"

He moved around the table. "I do know this." His hand disappeared into the girl's hair. "She's missing a few strands."

I had hoped her body turning up in the warehouse was just a coincidence, but the M.O. was frighteningly similar. "He took her hair, just like the other one," I said.

"That's right."

"We're dealing with a serial?"

"Looks that way. The blade used on her has the same edge."

"Could it be a copycat?"

"Hardly. The first one didn't get enough press coverage for anyone to care. The guy would have to know about the hair. That information was never released to the public. So far, my instincts are telling me this is our doer."

"Aren't your instincts always right?"

He was too exhausted to give me the Sherlock Holmes routine.

"This guy won't quit."

"Not until he's dead, or caught. Either way, he's out there and he's hunting. Took him two months to do another girl. I'd say he knows this one, too. If you think about it, there are certain similarities between this vic and Beth Valentine. Both are blondes from lower to middle-class families. They traded on their looks, never went to college, party girls for life. Willing to bet"—his eyes drifted down to Berkshire—"this one was quite a flirt, too. Never met a stranger. She was a real looker."

Manning turned from the sink, his face beaming from the shadows. "She was also a real drinker."

Bennett looked confused. "What?"

Manning stood over the body, drying his hands. "She had a liver like pâté. And she was only twenty-two. Had to be putting away some serious alcohol over the years to do that kind of damage. I've seen fifty-year-olds with better looking organs."

Bennett rubbed his face.

Manning tossed the towel into a biohazard container. "She also has some scars on the fallopian tubes. I'd say from repeated bouts of gonorrhea. She was no virgin, that's for sure."

"Seems our perp likes his girls on the wild side. Probably likes them pumped full of the chemicals, too."

"Well, whatever the case, this girl lived fast and died young. You know the story: serious boozer, the hard stuff. We're not talking Merlot and Michelob."

"Ninety proof."

"Straight outta the bottle."

With all this talk about liquor, I was starting to want a drink.

But more important, I wanted to corner Bennett and tell him about my little talk with Mark Astor and how self-tanner bought me some information.

Manning covered the body with a sheet. "We'll have to wait for toxicology, hair and fiber, and all the other reports to come back from the crime lab. But for now"—his eyes drifted down to the corpse—"we'll just let Olivia Berkshire rest."

We left Ralph Manning to his necromancing ways and walked out to the parking lot. I embraced the fresh air, and a light rain tickled my nose.

"How're you doing?" Bennett asked softly.

"Fine."

"Holding up okay?"

"Of course." It was a lie. "This morning when I called you, there was something I wanted to tell you."

"Yeah, well, sorry I hung up on you."

"I met with Mark Astor, on my own, at Trinity Hospital."

"What?" He turned to me abruptly, eyes narrowing. "Why?"

"I thought if I could get him alone, maybe he'd open up. I brought him a wide variety of self-tanning products. That pretty much did the trick. We bonded. He has respect for me."

Bennett was swollen with anger. "He doesn't have respect for anybody!"

"Would you calm down. There's a dead body lying in the building behind us. Let's put things into perspective."

He waved at me dismissively. "There's gonna be another dead body lying in the building behind us if you don't wise up and stop going on these excursions alone. He could've gone into a rage, really hurt you."

"Puh-lease. Once he saw the Clarins bronzer, he was putty in my hands."

Bennett let his shoulders drop; the exhaustion from the day had finally worn him down. "And what fascinating information did you get out of this character?"

"He said Beth liked to slum at this place called Absinthe. Thinks she went alone. Liked the rough ones."

"Never heard of the place."

"So you might've just learned something new?"

"You got me. I'm too tired to deal with the bullshit, Claire, so just give it to me straight. Where is this joint?"

"Hollywood."

"We'll check it out tomorrow. It could be an interesting direction. But for now, I'm exhausted. Haven't felt this tired since I was working nights on the force."

"I'm sorry I gave you flack. The timing was completely inappropriate."

He gave me a weak smile and started walking to his car. Looking over his shoulder, he said, "Thanks for coming out here in the middle of the night. For being a part of . . . the life."

The man disappeared before I could even respond.

His taillights faded into the night.

The parking lot felt exceptionally empty and cold. I suddenly had a strange and uncomfortable feeling come over me, like I was being watched. A woman knows these things. I moved quickly to my car, slid across the front seat, and locked the door. The windows had fogged over, but I started the engine, hit the gas, and sped onto the highway.

I had only put a mile between the morgue and myself when something terrible happened. My car rattled and clanked and I could hardly control the steering wheel. At first I thought the engine was burning, and then I realized it was rubber. Stinking like hot tar on pavement. I pulled the Benz to the side of the freeway and switched on my hazards. Then I called Bennett, trying not to panic. "Help! Ohmigawd! Something is wrong with my car."

"Where are you?"

"Just got onto the highway, pulled over to the side. I think I might have a flat. I smell burning rubber."

"Stay right where you are," he said. "I've got to turn around. It'll probably take me about five minutes."

I got out and was walking to the back of the car when someone's headlights nearly blinded me. I knew it wasn't Bennett because we had just hung up. Someone had pulled off the highway and was edging his car about fifty feet behind mine.

A man got out and just stood there, still as a stone statue.

He kept his brights on and didn't say a word.

I couldn't make out any specifics other than the silhouette of his physique. But I sensed he felt comfortable knowing his face was hidden behind the glare.

This was not a Good Samaritan and I wondered if there was truth to the feeling of being watched. I stepped back, almost tripping on the strands of rubber. "I don't need any help, sir!"

He didn't say a word, but inched a few steps closer.

"I've already called nine-one-one!" Trying to play it cool, I added, "And I'm a cop, anyway! Thank God for the Second Amendment. Anyway, my partner is on his way. Name is Henry, quite a big fella . . ."

The stranger, still very cool and subtle, made his way back to his car, got in it, hit reverse, and sped backward, kicking up dust and gravel. I watched in silence as he pulled onto the highway and raced past me. He was going so fast I couldn't get a make on the car. It was a four-door sedan, dark in color. That's all I knew.

Bennett arrived two minutes later. I was a little shaken by the experience, and he tried to calm me. "It's *only* a flat tire, honey. Don't cry over it."

"No, that's not it. There was someone here. . . ."

He looked over my shoulder. "What? Where?"

"He's gone now. Kept his brights on." I looked back at where he was parked. "Got out of the car, just stood there. It was the weirdest feeling. He wasn't normal."

"Most people cruising the highways at this hour . . . aren't."

"He just watched me. Like he was giving me some kind of warning."

"Did you get a description of the vehicle?"

"No, it was too dark and he went by too fast."

Bennett tried to keep the drama to a minimum. "Sounds like a pervert to me. Gets his rocks off by blinding women on the side of the road."

We called AAA and waited for the car to be towed.

Bennett drove me home. "I shouldn't have left you alone. I'm so tired I can't even think straight, you know."

"It's not your fault."

"Feel a little guilty. If I had followed you onto the freeway, none of this would've happened."

"I'm fine." My house looked so dark. "Thanks for coming to my rescue."

"I was a little late."

"I think you were right on time." I reached for the door handle. "What's the schedule?"

"We'll check out this Absinthe place in the morning. Then I might meet with some techs working the Berkshire case."

A fresh one.

He waited for me to enter the house, giving me plenty of time to turn on all the lights and set the alarm. I heard the motor of his car fading in the distance. I felt very alone, still thinking about that hazy silhouette on the side of the road, taunting me with nothing more than silence and shadows.

I was too antsy to sit in the bathtub, didn't care about exfoliating, and took the shortest shower in Claire Fontaine history. Not sure I even used soap. It was close to three o'clock when I fell asleep.

I dreamed about Nelson Rockefeller, Givenchy suits, Steinway pianos, and Italian marble. Some things never change.

43

Absinthe was the kind of place your mother warned you about: a dark bar with red leather chairs and rotten mahogany that had long ago lost its luster. Concrete floor, black as day-old blood, littered with cigarette butts and beer bottles. The walls seemed to move as Bennett and I let a cold draft in behind us. But when I got a closer look I realized they were draped in rust-colored velvet. The bar was lined with bottles of unusual spirits, things only someone from Transylvania could pronounce. Putrid smells and gothic ambience. I hated it immediately.

It was too quiet, not a soul in sight.

It felt like a coffin.

Bennett eyed the knife carvings on the bar, caught a gloomy reflection of himself in the mirror, and then shouted, "Anybody here? Hello?"

His voice interrupted the strange silence and I felt a chill run down my spine.

"Hello?" he called out again.

This time something moved.

The velvet behind us parted. We came face to face with more grime, this time in the human form. He was wearing the worst outfit I had seen in days. Oil-stained blue jeans tucked into green cowboy boots. A black leather vest that barely buttoned over his hairy chest. Heavily tattooed arms, wrists and fingers glistening with gold nuggets. A silver bicycle chain looped around his left leg.

"We're closed," he grunted. "Don't open until nine o'clock."

"We're not here for the party," Bennett said. "You own this place?"

"Why? You wanna buy it?"

"Only if I can collect the insurance money after it burns down."

"Do I look like the kinda guy that has insurance?"

"Nope," Bennett said. "You do look like the kinda guy that's done time. Hard time."

The man's lip curled. "Knew you was a cop." He pushed past us and found his way behind the bar. "Could smell it on you ten feet away."

Bennett shot back, "You got a meth lab in the basement?"

"You got a warrant?"

Things had not gotten off to a good start. And the urine-soaked wood paneling was starting to give me a headache. I nudged Bennett. "Let's get this over with. I feel an outbreak of lice coming on."

"Calm down," he whispered. "I'm just warming the guy up."

"You're insulting him. He's already on the defensive."

"Give me time."

A roach the size of my thumb crawled across the floor. I started to feel dizzy.

Bennett sat on a stool and dropped his elbows to the counter. "Is it too early to have a drink?"

"Like I said, man, we're closed."

"Just give me a little shot of whiskey."

"What's this about? You with DEA or ATF or Vice?"

"None of the above." Bennett slid a twenty-dollar bill in the man's direction, pointed to the rotgut. "Just give me a shot and we'll get down to business."

The man pocketed the cash, snatched a bottle from the bar, and poured Bennett a stiff one. "Here." He set the glass in front of him.

I took a seat next to the detective and tried, in vain, to order an Evian.

Bennett tossed back the shot and then said, "Now let's get down to business. What's your name?"

"Everybody just calls me Wyatt." He folded his meaty arms, exposing the blue and black ink that had been garishly etched into them: a naked woman on a Harley, mysterious daggers, skull and bones. I thought of Pecker Talbott and his Cobain artwork and how, by comparison, he seemed so young and innocent.

"Do you know Morris Weaver?" I asked cheerfully. "He has a parlor in West Hollywood."

"No, why?"

"He does some good work," I said.

"How would *you* know?" He eyed my David Yurman bracelet.

"Because I've seen it firsthand. Does a lot of the musicians. Very big in the rock-and-roll scene. Nice guy, too. Very organized. Keeps a good filing system—"

Bennett kicked my foot. Wyatt just stood there in a daze.

"What?" I shrugged. "I know a good tattoo when I see one."

The lights grew dim as the generator started to hum, and I could hear water dripping behind the velvet. Our possible witness had not succumbed to my charm, as so many others had. The air still felt congested with smoke and last night's sins. Wyatt twisted the gold nugget around his pinky. "You two just get off the freak boat?" He smiled and I caught a glimpse of tobacco-stained teeth. Leaning into Bennett, he asked, "What's *your* name? And what's this *bidness* you got with me?"

"Henry Bennett," he replied, sliding a fresh-faced photo of Beth toward him. "And *this* is my business."

He caught a glance. "Oh, yeah. She used to come in here all the time. Haven't seen her for months."

"She's dead."

"Guess that's why." He picked up the photo and squinted his brow. "How?"

"Murdered," Bennett said.

"Wow." He seemed lost in the photo. "You catch the creep?"

"Do you think I'd be standing here, talking to you, if I had?"

"Right." He poured Bennett another shot of rotgut. "Here, this one's on the house."

They were bonding over dead bodies and cheap booze.

"Got a solid lead on this place yesterday," Bennett said.

"Yeah, how so?"

"Let's just say this joint came up in a conversation."

Wyatt leaned back and took a swig from a black bottle with no label. A mysterious pulpy liquid stained his lips until he conjured up enough manners to wipe his face with the back of his arm. He belched out the words, "You think this murderous asshole is one of my customers, that what you're saying?"

"It's certainly a possibility," Bennett replied. "I'm not looking to disrupt this successful operation you've got here, but I am looking for a killer. Might just be a coincidence. But I don't have the luxury of assuming anything."

"Hey, man, you wanna come back tonight and check out the customers, that's fine with me. It's a free country. Just don't arrest anyone while the place is jumping. I'll lose half my business if these guys think I'm friendly with the law. Which, obviously, I'm not. Got these tats in prison, where I spent twelve years. Didn't learn no love on the inside." His voice thick with anger. "But I don't like the killin' of girls, either."

"Do you remember Beth being cozy with anyone in particular?"

"Hard to say. I'm not here every night. I like to consider myself half-retired. You oughta ask the bartender, Doyle. He's been here every single night for the last twenty years. But you need to get him while he's still coherent, somewhere between nine and ten.

"Thanks." Bennett reached into his wallet and pulled out a card. "If you think of anything else." He shrugged. "She was a good kid, you know. I'm doing this for her old lady. Been busted up since it happened, can't sleep, hitting the bottle, seriously despondent."

Wyatt pocketed the card. "No problem."

When we left the place I felt a sense a relief, but it didn't last long.

"We're coming back *tonight*," Bennett said. "First thing. Nine o'clock. While Doyle is still standing."

"I would imagine, at night, when there are actually customers, it's even scarier."

"You got that right. Wanna stay home?" He flashed me a smile.

"No."

He edged the car onto the boulevard. "Claire." The way my name rolled off his tongue I knew I was about to get the third degree. "You can come with me tonight on one condition."

"What?

"Don't wear that outfit. In fact, don't wear any of your *outfits*. Dress down. All the way down. Torn jeans, black T-shirt, and boots. Anything that'll help you fit in. Blend. You walk in dressed like that and we're *made*. No one will talk to us. Might as well walk in with the SWAT team and start making arrests."

"You're saying I'm an embarrassment?"

"Noooo. I'm saying your threads stand out like tits on toast. I mean, did ya get a look at that place? It's like a Hell's Angels hideout, mixed with a little bit of eighties goth. You cannot, and will not, wear pearls and diamonds and pink scarves. Or carry that ridiculous purse. Think of Absinthe as an undercover operation. You must lose your sense of self in order to fit in."

44

My car was waiting for me at Firestone. Bennett and I walked into the garage and talked to the technician who had replaced my tires. "Not sure what happened, miss. They could've been slashed."

"Slashed? Like with a knife?"

"That's how it usually happens." He rolled his eyes. "Or you coulda driven over something sharp in the road. Kind of unlikely, though. Car is in good shape, nice ride."

"Thanks."

Bennett pushed out his chest. "There was no way to tell if the tires were cut open?"

"There wudn't much left when the tow-truck brought it in last night. No way for me to give you a proper flat-tire-diagnosis. I think it's odd, I'll say that. Both back tires. Wouldn't of taken much to stick a hole in them, sharp knife is all. Everybody these days got one of those."

"How comforting," I said.

I drove home, thinking about the possibilities. Kind of assuming, whoever pulled off the highway last night to scare me, was also responsible for the slashing. It was all meant to slow me down, throw me off track. I was not alone. He was watching.

I could have obsessed all day over this man, this stranger, but I was about to go deep undercover and I had to have something to wear. Nothing in my closet seemed appropriate for this kind of gig, and I was tired of taking the hits from Bennett.

It occurred to me, as I thumbed through all the silk and satin, that John Armstrong was just the person who could help me on this one. I would have to swallow all of my pride in an effort to score the proper attire. It was an awful feeling.

He was home when I knocked.

And looked quite delicious in a blue oxford shirt and old jeans. Had a five o'clock shadow and smelled of expensive aftershave. I wanted to fall into his arms. It took a lot of nerve to stand there, with a plunging neckline and crimson lips. "I'm sorry to bother you," I said, choking on humble pie.

"You're not bothering me."

"That's good. The thing is . . . I've got a covert job tonight and I need your help."

"Covert job?"

"Undercover," I whispered. "The detective I work for wants me to blend. I think he'd like for me to look masculine, macho, lots of black. I was thinking you could put me in touch with someone . . . maybe the wardrobe department. Something like that."

I sensed melancholy between the two of us, despite the phony neighborly cheer. But then I caught a glimpse of humanity in his blue eyes, thought I saw the ocean in them. "We don't exactly have a wardrobe department," he said, slipping his feet into Cole Haans. "Do you want to take a drive with me?"

"Okay."

"The Santa Monica Airport," he said. "We might be able to hook you up with some threads there."

"Great," I said, taken back by his generosity. I didn't say anything else, afraid to open my mouth for fear of ruining this unexpected adventure.

"I've been thinking about you," he said with a trace of awkwardness.

"Really?"

"Yes." He choked on that same humble pie.

"That's nice." My insides were turning. "I've been thinking about you, as well. Funny thing, I was thinking about you before we were even formally introduced. Like before Sergeant tore up your lawn."

He didn't say anything, but his face was red as roses. Fingers tapped the steering wheel, and I glimpsed a flash of teeth behind those perfect lips. "I don't mind being of assistance, helping you out with the homicide gig." Back to business. "My door is always open for you . . . and the job. I'm a real professional, you know that. I respect law enforcement."

"I'll certainly keep that in mind with this investigation. And the next one. Need all the help I can get. Being a woman and all, I get kicked around a lot, pushed aside, really have to prove myself."

"You're a lot tougher than you think."

"Yes, it's true. I'm made of steel."

If you only knew how often I cried myself to sleep since you went away.

We parked in a private hangar. A couple of mechanics were working frantically on the engine of a corporate jet. The place smelled like fuel and plastic and cement. Armstrong didn't tell me where we were going, only that I would probably have to be "fitted" for the garments. I asked few questions and followed his lead, grateful for the time and the tailoring.

45

Instead of honking like a brutish rogue, Bennett actually got out of his car, walked to my front door, and rang the bell. Like a gentleman. I thought maybe my presence in his life was having an effect on him, possibly teaching him some manners. He stepped into my foyer, gave me a disapproving once-over, and exclaimed, "You're *not* wearing that!"

"Why?"

"It's a military flight suit. And it's ridiculous."

"You said dress down, no frills."

"I said *blend*, Claire. Not waltz in there like you're George W. Bush doing a 'Mission accomplished' speech."

I tossed the helmet into the chair and stormed to the kitchen. Pouring myself a glass of Pellegrino, I tried to shake off the anger. "You're never happy," I muttered.

"That's because I work undercover and you're always making a spectacle of yourself."

"What do you want from me?"

"Jeans and a T-shirt."

"They'd never fit you."

"No." He shook his head. "That's what I want for you. Average attire, nothing shiny or fluffy. And nothing issued by the federal government. Like a regular gal, below the radar."

"I can do that." False confidence.

"You've got five minutes to change out of that *Top Gun* uniform and into something realistic. I've got work to do. You're either along for the ride, or you're at home doing . . . whatever it is you do."

"Fine."

Twenty minutes later Bennett sped from the curb, jerking me back into the seat, and leaving skid marks on a perfectly good Brentwood street. It was just past nine when he pulled into the parking lot and found a space behind the bar. There were four or five Harleys parked at odd angles and two Dodge trucks that hadn't passed inspection in ten years. As we headed toward the entrance I glanced down at my Earl Jeans, black T-shirt, and old sneakers. I felt stark naked without jewelry or makeup. I was carrying cash in my back pocket, since Bennett would not allow me to carry a purse. This undercover business was a lot tougher than I imagined.

Absinthe was barely noticeable at night, tucked between topless bars with blinking lights and grandiose nightclubs that offer VIP seating to celebrities while the bourgeoisie stand in lines wrapped around the block. Bennett was in front of me, wearing a wrinkled gray shirt and dirty Levi's, looking over his shoulder suspiciously.

We stopped abruptly in front of the entrance and I almost tripped over Nick Nolte.

The old lantern that hung above the door cast a pale yellow light onto the sidewalk, revealing all the lost souls floating around me, dank buildings rife with booze and ex-convicts and velvet drapes that came to life after midnight.

Bennett looked down at me. "Just follow my lead."

"I always do."

He snarled and pulled open the door.

We stepped into the shadowy world of night crawlers and took two seats at the bar. The place wasn't jumping yet—too early for the vampires and subversives, and too late for people on parole. There were two others sitting at the bar, hardcore drunks, slumped over, slurping bourbon through toothless gums. They didn't even notice me when I sat down a few feet away. I leaned over to Bennett. "I'm *blending*," I said proudly.

"What?"

"You wanted me to blend. I'm doing just that. Take a look around. No one has even noticed me."

He rolled his eyes. "There are only two customers, Claire. And from the looks of it, they've been comatose for quite some time."

Bennett signaled the bartender. He was pushing seventy, with a shriveled face and a sunken, somewhat crippled body. Gray eyes seemed to be floating in bile. He was too scrawny to be a real threat and too old to run fast. He smelled like an alcoholic, his breath acidic, invading my space like black mold.

I figured his name was Doyle. "You two wanna try the house drink?" he asked.

"What is it?" Bennett replied.

"It's called a green demon."

"What's in it?"

"It's a secret," he whispered, "but it'll knock yur socks off. You'll forget your worries." He reached for the pear-shaped bottle of emerald liquid—no label, no ingredients. "We get it from Amsterdam, where the good shit is still available on the black market."

"You trying to tell me that that's really absinthe?"

He didn't answer and put the bottle back. "Look, pal, I'm offerin' the house drink. That's my job."

"Just give me a whiskey," Bennett said.

Doyle looked at me. "And for the lady?"

"Do you have a menu?"

"Do I *look* like I have a menu?"

"Sorry I asked." I sank down on the stool. "I'll take a glass of Napa red, preferably 'eighty-five."

"We ain't got no Napa and we don't serve nuthin' by the year."

Bennett leaned over, put his mouth to my ear. "You're *not* blending."

Doyle's eyes were on me, cloudy with suspicion.

I snapped into undercover mode. "Give me your hardest stuff, man. I mean, like, you know, Everclear and shit. Yeah, that house drink, the green demon, I'll take that. And where the hell can I get a decent tattoo around here?"

Bennett shut his eyes, holding his anger inside. Doyle just stared at me in silence, then poured my partner a whiskey and passed me the emerald liquor with a sinister smile. "You'll like it. Everyone does. We're the only 'stablishment in town that got it."

"Thank you. I'll remember this place for private parties."

"Now, about that tattoo—"

The door swung open and in walked the kind of crowd that would set off alarm bells at the police department. I imagined every single one of them had once been in a lineup, been touched for something illegal, had had broken bones. Biker-types, wearing an assortment of chaps and leather. Weathered and scarred faces. Scraggly beards. Stinking of cigarettes and body odor. Unapproachable and unruly, they sat at a table in the corner and didn't seem to want to be bothered.

Bennett slid a twenty-dollar bill across the bar. Doyle lifted it and gave me a smile. "You ain't from around here, huh?"

"Why do you ask?"

"You got that look, like you ain't never seen a riding crew, them guys that just walked in. Probably scared the crap right out of your—"

"I'm fine," I said defensively. "And I'll have you know, I've been to the edge, man. I've seen the dark side—so don't even mess with my bad self. Busta move on you so fast, old man, you wouldn't even know what hit you."

Bennett had turned away. I didn't know whether he was laughing or crying, but Doyle was certainly amused. "You're a doll," he groaned. "Not like the rest of this bunch."

He walked over to the biker clan and started taking drink orders. Bennett's face looked ancient beneath the dull light. "You're really setting us back," he said. "I've got to get to the girl. That's why we're here."

"I'm just bonding with the ol' chap. Building some trust."

"There's not a single person within a city block that would 'trust' a girl like you."

"You know . . ." I thought about downing the green demon. "I just can't please you. I ditched the fighter pilot threads, changed into this depressing outfit, left all my makeup on the dresser. I'm sitting here, exposed, feeling embarrassed about who I really am. Ashamed for having good taste and great skin. For being classy and cultured. I'm just as interested in finding the killer, Detective, regardless of my ridiculous antics and fluffy clothes." I wanted to leave, storm out of there, but my integrity would not allow it. "If you think back, real hard, you'll remember that my charm has opened a few doors, actually jumpstarted this investigation."

He was tired of hearing it, but he nodded his head. "You're right.

Calm down. I didn't mean to insult your character or your clothes. Time is of the essence and never on our side."

Doyle came back and chided me for not having made much progress on the house drink. I wondered if it was tainted with GHB or morphine.

Bennett slid another twenty across the bar. "What's your name?"

"Doyle," he said.

"Well, Doyle, I'm looking for a girl."

"Aren't we all?"

Bennett didn't laugh. "It's really quite serious. My niece has been missing for about two months. I hear she used to frequent this place, maybe hang with some of the clientele."

"What's her name? I'll ask around."

"Beth Valentine. About five-six, one hundred and twenty pounds. Real pretty." He nonchalantly removed a photo. "Here's a picture of her."

"Yeah. Yeah. She been around. I 'member those eyes, pretty like an actress."

"I was hoping maybe you'd be able to tell me if she was close to anyone. Any regulars? Any boyfriends? Stuff like that. It's been a year since I've seen her. And I wasn't really privy to her social life. You know how girls are, keeping secrets from parental figures."

"Especially the sluts," he replied.

He didn't say anything more, and the bar seemed to get quiet. There was something uncomfortable about the silence, and then the door swung open and a flurry of night crawlers spilled into the place. Absinthe was starting to show its teeth, coming alive as the night wore on. Music thumped behind the velvet drapes, glasses clattered, voices overlapped and crawled into my ears like hungry bees. I still hadn't touched the green demon and that, alone, probably blew my cover.

Bennett didn't give up on Doyle. "So, you callin' my niece a slut? Or you just making a general reference?"

He waved a scaly hand in the air. "Oh, heavens no. Just making conversation. You know how it is with women. . . ."

"No," Bennett said. "How is *it*?" He finished off the whiskey. "Been a long time since I been with one. They're mysterious creatures."

Doyle let out a sigh of relief. "Yeah, man. That's fer dang sure. I had me a wife once, back in 1970, kind of a hippie-type. Don't even know what happened to her, we drifted apart." He shrugged.

"My niece is a very private person." Bennett's voice had grown somber. "Beth kept things to herself. Scares me to death when I think of where she might be, what someone might have done to—"

"Don't know nothing," Doyle interrupted. "I'm just a bartender with a habit and she was just another fancy face in the crowd. You're wasting your time, mister. I ain't a Rolodex and people come and go in this city. It's a revolving door, and sometimes it just swallows you."

The edge was back in his voice. Flinty eyes. Furtive glances across the room. He didn't like being watched. Bennett and I had been sitting there too long, asking questions, drinking at a beginner's pace.

Doyle leaned into me, forcing a humorless smile. "Why don't you two go have a seat in the back? I got work to do and some of the regulars like to sit at the bar."

"That's a polite way of asking us to leave," I said.

"I try."

Bennett dropped another twenty on the bar and we took our glasses to a corner booth. Doyle nodded and forced another smile. By midnight, the place was wall to wall with bikers and hitchhikers. We tried to work the room, cozying up to regulars who might've have known our victim. Several recognized her photo but had nothing conclusive to offer. The rest just avoided us.

"We're not getting anywhere," Bennett muttered.

"*You're* not getting anywhere."

"What does that mean?"

"If I were working this place alone, I bet I could get some answers. Some of these guys would loosen up."

"Before or *after* they kill you?"

"Har, har."

He was sliding out of the booth when I said, "I've got to go to the restroom."

"Fine. Then we're outta here."

All the velvet curtains made for a confusing trip, but I finally located a door with the word RESTROOM spray-painted across the front. A sense of danger came to me when I opened it and found a steep flight of stairs looming below me. Staircase to hell, unfolding into a labyrinth of darkness. The solitary lightbulb above me flickered like a candle in the wind. When I reached the bottom I caught a whiff of fetid urine.

The bathroom door slid open with a shriek and I found a rusted light switch by the sink. It was quite obvious every single health code was in violation. The urinal was full of cigarette butts and beer bottles, the toilet bowl was cracked and stained, soggy newspapers were tossed into the corner. I backed out of the room, holding my breath, panicked by the brief encounter with human filth. But just before I could dread the onslaught of hepatitis or tuberculosis, I realized the stairwell had succumbed to complete darkness.

The puny light from the bathroom barely cast a shadow into the corridor and I had to fumble my way up the stairs, feeling the wall for guidance.

I think I was on the fourth step when I realized I wasn't alone.

My bladder almost gave out. I stopped for a moment, listened.

He was close.

I was afraid to take another step. And when I did, that's when I felt the hand.

Cold and clammy. He gripped my wrist so hard I thought it would break. "Please don't," I begged. "I'll give you money. I've got a nice car, too. Some stocks and bonds."

"Shut up," said the voice.

His breath danced through my hair.

"What do you want?" I took another step. His grip tightened and he pulled me back.

The voice again, hair-raising. "Stop this. You hear me. Stop."

"Stop what?"

"You know *what*."

I couldn't even scream, but I let out a whimper.

"Shut up and listen close. Next time you step foot on my turf, it's over. You got lucky t'night 'cause all them people are upstairs and that fat man is waiting for you. I say go out that door and don't look back."

He released his hand from my wrist, leaving my fingers numb. It was so dark I didn't know up from down and found myself crawling toward the slash of light beneath the door upstairs. Gasping for air, I pushed open the door and light spilled onto the stairs.

But when I looked back he was gone.

My head was spinning, my heart racing. I shoved my way out of the place and found Bennett standing next to the curb, looking at his watch. "Took you long enough."

"He's here—" I fell into him.

"What?"

"The basement," I said, still gasping. "Grabbed me on the stairs, Bennett. My Gawd, he's in there. Somewhere."

A surly group filed out just as Bennett was helping me steady myself on both feet. My eyes glanced over at the crew, with their dark clothes and dirty hands. Could've been any of them. Or not. They were on their bikes and gone in a flash.

Bennett put me in the car, gave me a pocketknife, and then said, "I'm just going to give the basement a walk-through. I'll be back in less than two minutes. *Do not get out of the car.* For any reason."

"You're giving me a *pocket*knife to protect myself?"

"You'll be fine out here, Claire, sitting in a public parking lot. My guess is he's already split."

I held the measly little blade in the air. "I have tampons that are sharper than this."

His face flushed with embarrassment. "Don't start." He slammed the door.

Drunken voices drifted from the boulevard, and the parking lot was teeming with undesirables. I looked in the backseat. Too many horror movies had clouded my sense of reality and I had terrible thoughts of this creature seeping into the car, taking my life, playing with my blood.

Bennett was back so soon I wondered if he chickened out and didn't take the stairs all the way down to the basement.

"There was no one," he said. "Did you get a look at this guy at all? Any sense of his size, his features?"

"It was pitch black. He had a voice like razors. And he was strong. That's all I know."

He started the engine. "Could he have been drunk?"

"No way. He was as sober as I am right now. You think I'm overreacting, don't you?"

"No, I didn't say that. We were in a bar, it's a valid question. I saw a lot of heavy drinkers in that place."

I handed him the pocketknife. "Thanks for the blade," I said archly. "Really made me feel safe. Take me home, please."

"Don't get all huffy."

We pulled onto Vine. "Do you not find it odd . . . ?"

"What?"

"Last night, someone slashes my tires in the parking lot of the medical examiner's office. Then I'm blinded by some stranger who pulls off the highway to taunt me. And now this. I'm cornered in a dark stairwell, physically assaulted, and told to stop what I'm doing, which, I figure, he's talking about my investigative talents."

"You were physically assaulted?"

"Yes. My wrist. I told you, he grabbed me so hard I thought the bone would break. I know there's going to be a bruise and I'm going to have to wear long sleeves until it subsides."

He drove recklessly toward the west, probably dreaming about Mel's Diner and fried chicken. "To answer your question," he finally said, "yes, I find it a little odd. The incident last night. And now this. I have to use logic and not get all emotional and paranoid. That's your job. If you feel like you're getting too close to the fire, you can take a break."

"Not an option, Detective. I've worked too hard, put too many woman-hours into this. I think, in an effort to ease all my fears and feel secure, I need a gun. Can you arrange this? There's like a five-day waiting period, right? Maybe with all your connections they could waive that rule for me."

"No way." He pressed down on the gas. "You will never have a gun. Ever. I'm not in the business of supplying firearms to girls."

"What about a really small one? Something that would fit in my makeup bag. Maybe it doesn't even kill people, it just really injures them. Can you score me something like that?"

"The only thing I'm going to *score* you is an appointment with a psychiatrist."

My house looked bright and warm. Lights were burning on the inside. I was actually happy that Rosa was around. Bennett reached over and grabbed me as I was climbing out the door.

"I'll check out Absinthe again tomorrow. I'm not just brushing you off, Claire. I believe you when you say you sensed danger, that this man is not just a coincidence."

"Thanks."

I walked into the house and found Rosa sitting on the sofa reading the Spanish version of the paper, her feet propped up on the coffee table, sloppy clothes draping her like a tent. "Can't believe you're here this late," I said.

She had to do a double take, making sure it was me dressed in such mediocre attire, no makeup, not even lip balm. "What's going on with you? Never seen Miss Claire look so . . . normal."

"I'm working undercover, Rosa."

"Under whose covers?"

"That's real cute," I said. "You won't believe who actually spoke to me today."

"Mr. Goodbar next door?"

"That's correct." I sat down next to her. "I needed wardrobe help. Swallowed my pride long enough to stand on his front porch. Thing is, well, he was so darn polite I wanted to kill him. Drove me to the Santa Monica airport, hooked me up with some clothes. It was real nice, Rosa. The way he talked to me in the car."

"You give it time. He'll come around."

"I've had a tough couple of nights. Don't really want to go into it, but it's getting a little scary out there."

"The Boogeyman," she whispered, half mocking me. "He come for you?"

"I think maybe he has."

"Then I go clean David E. Kelley's house down the street."

"You do that," I retorted defensively. "It's five times as big, and I'm pretty sure he won't let you put your feet on the coffee table."

46

The next morning Bennett was nowhere to be found. He didn't show his face at the office, and I got no response at his home or on his cell. I figured Krispy Kreme was having a sale. By noon, I was bored and antsy and *almost* concerned. I called his mobile forty or fifty times, and then finally gave up. I started thinking about painting his office again to piss him off. Just as I was calling Home Depot to get some paint swatches delivered, he rang the office.

"It's about time," I said angrily.

"Didn't know you were keeping tabs."

"It's noon. I've been sitting here twiddling my thumbs for, like, two hours."

"Least you could do is . . . file."

"I've alphabetized the flavored coffees. There is nothing left to file."

I heard voices in the background. "I'm down at the crime lab. They got some reports on the Berkshire girl."

"Like toxicology reports?"

"Not yet," he replied. "But some preliminary results from Hair & Fiber."

"What does that mean?"

"They found a few strange hairs at the crime scene."

"What kind of hair?"

"Animal."

"What kind of animal?"

"That's the problem," he said. "It something rare, too exotic for an immediate ID."

"How long will it take to get a positive?"

"Could take a day, a week, a month. I don't know. We're not talking your average household pet here. It's not a Labrador retriever, if you get my drift."

"Aren't you people supposed to be wired with all the technical advancements?"

"The lab can only do so much. They can't work miracles. It might take time to break down proteins, do some comparisons. We're dealing with an *exotic* here. Could be a South American jungle rat for all I know."

"Eeewww."

"The relevance here is also where the hairs were located. Not on the victim, not even near the victim. They were on the edge of a bloody footprint close to the warehouse door."

With a thrill in my voice I asked, "You guys got a footprint?"

"Hardly. Sorry to get your hopes up." He sighed. "It was the partial of a heel. Forensics thinks the guy was wearing some kind of boot, but didn't get enough of a print to make identification. Could be any type of boot from anywhere in the world. They think the hair sample might be a better lead. They also think since the hair was along the perp's footprint, that he tracked the hair in. Possibly it was already on the bottom of his shoe, maybe in his car, his house, whatever."

"Guy left a partial bloody print. . . . He must be getting sloppy."

"Or he was in a hurry, or just having fun. Or he's fucking with us."

"Makes me sick, knowing he's out there."

Bennett belched. "Want to grab a bite to eat?"

"How can you think about food right now?"

"Easy," he snorted. "Let's meet at the Potato Factory, mid-Wilshire area."

"Can't wait."

Bennett was first in line at the all-you-can-eat buffet.

I waited politely in a stained booth, drinking my own filtered water, watching obese people fight over the last of the macaroni and cheese. This place, no doubt, was one of Bennett's favorites. He set his plate on the table, gave me a smile, and then shoveled saturated fat down his throat. With a mouthful of french fries, he said, "The human hairs found at the scene all belonged to Berkshire." He swallowed and then took another repulsive bite. "But the four separate strands are quite puzzling. It takes a real *atypical* hair sample to throw off the crime lab. They know their shit, their equipment is tops." He moved on to the chicken-fried steak.

"You don't really think it's a South American jungle rat?"

"No, that was a joke."

I know I looked stupid when I asked, "Eventually they'll be able to pinpoint the origin, right?"

He shrugged. "I certainly hope so. There are no absolutes in this business, though."

"These animal hairs," I said. "They could be the key to catching this guy."

"That's why it's so important to track their origin."

"But we might have to wait days? A week? At worst case a month?"

"Possibly." He was on to the baked beans. "I know it's frustrating, but trust me. Los Angeles County has an excellent crime lab, great technicians. But they've also got four measly strands of hair from some unidentified animal. We're not the Pentagon, can't just snap our fingers and expect an answer."

That got me thinking. "I might be able to help," I said.

"With what?"

"Speeding up the identification process. I know a guy."

"Uh-oh." He dropped his fork.

"John Armstrong. This guy has access to incredible technology. He's on the *inside*, you know." I had lowered my voice to a whisper and felt foolish. "We're talking covert operations, the federal government, unlimited connections."

"What, exactly, are you thinking?"

"Let me talk to him, see if he has any advice. Maybe, just maybe, he offers to help me because he likes me. And he's into catching bad guys, just like you."

Bennett furrowed his brow. "Didn't he dump you?"

"Thanks for bringing that up. We're on speaking terms. He's the one that got me the flight suit. But never mind about that."

"Okay, so you talk to the guy, he's got some fancy comrade that knows animal hair like the back of his hand. Then what?"

"You let me borrow a strand of the hair sample and I get it to the right people."

He burst into laughter. "You can't just *borrow* evidence. There are strict rules and regulations with regard to hair and fiber and trace."

"Since when have you ever followed rules and regulations?"

He looked away, grabbed his fork, and disappeared behind a brownie the size of my hand.

I left him sitting there, in his own pile of lard, and drove back to Brentwood. Standing on Armstrong's front porch, I felt a little nervous about facing him again so soon. And I wasn't exactly having a good hair day.

He was dressed casually, a smirk on his face. "Hi," he said coolly. "Is this a social call?"

"No, it's not," I said, getting right down to business. "I hate to ask for you another favor. You were so kind already, helping me out with that wardrobe issue."

"No problem." He stepped onto the porch.

I didn't want to get too comfortable. "Here's the thing," I said. "We've got an obscure hair sample. It was lifted from a partial shoe print at a crime scene. It came from some kind of animal. They call it 'exotic' and the lab hasn't been able to trace its origin. Time is key here. This guy we're dealing with is a monster, and he'll kill again."

"You want to know if I can help you out with the sample?"

"Yes, that's right. I don't want to wear out my welcome, John. It's just that lives are at stake here. Girls are dying. And I need to find this animal, whatever the hell it is."

He crossed his arms. "There's a crazy scientist that used to work for the agency. Dr. Eugene Speck. He's a friend. I can call him."

"You have a friend?"

"Shocking, isn't it?"

"Yes." Back to business. "So . . . you think he could help me out?"

"Absolutely. The guy is brilliant, has his own lab in the back of his house. But he would need the sample, a piece of the hair, to run the tests."

"I'll see what I can do. Bennett is very weird about me borrowing evidence."

"Do you want me to call him?"

I didn't know what to say. He was being so generous, forthcoming. It was so out of character. *He must really miss me,* I thought.

"Yes, that would be great," I replied. "Since you have government clearance and all. He'd probably take you seriously."

I gave him Bennett's cell phone number and he walked into another room, kept his voice to a whisper. The conversation didn't last long, five minutes or so. Armstrong came back to me and said, "Okay. You'll have a single piece of hair by late this afternoon. I'll call Dr. Speck and see what I can arrange."

"Thank you. You have no idea how much this means to me."

I let myself out slowly, hoping he'd come calling after me, ask me to dinner, anything. That didn't happen, of course, and later in the day when I met up with Bennett, he seemed more enamored with Armstrong than I was.

"Quite a fella," he said, biting into a king-size Butterfinger. "Did you know he was a strategic analyst during the first Gulf War?"

"Thought he was a field man."

"Guess he does both. Real nice of him to put us in touch with Speck. I read about him a few years ago in *Time* magazine."

"And to think you mocked me earlier—less than four hours ago, to be exact."

That night Armstrong called to confirm a meeting the next morning with the crazy scientist. There was nothing flirtatious about the call. It was business pure and simple. I fell asleep alone, as usual, thinking about our whirlwind of a romance and how it had all come tumbling down around me.

47

Armstrong and I left Brentwood just after dawn. The city was still quiet, with little traffic. We took Highway One all the way to Topanga. The sea to my left sparkled like floating diamonds beneath a purple sky that could've been copied from a painting. It was a beautiful morning and I was happy to be riding shotgun with the most handsome man I'd ever met, not to mention the most elusive. We climbed high into the Santa Monica Mountains, edging around sharp corners, and winding our way into the fog. The altitude changed, the sky and sea no longer visible, and I felt my ears go numb. Suddenly we had entered a different world, somewhat secret, closer to the heavens and far from earth. We passed through wrought-iron gates and drove another mile, a bumpy ride, as the pavement gave way to dirt and gravel.

Dr. Eugene Speck owned three acres of countryside, rustic wilderness really, offering complete seclusion. I imagined City Hall didn't even have this address on file, not even the Pentagon. As I stepped from the vehicle, I heard eucalyptus leaves rustling and noticed a bamboo garden and a citrus orchard. "Nice place," I said. "Two thousand feet from civilization." I couldn't tell the clouds from the fog.

There was something disquieting about being in the middle of nowhere. But when Dr. Speck came out to greet us, most of my fears subsided. He was a small man, no taller than five-six, with thick glasses perched on a beak nose and gray hair that hadn't been combed in days. He smelled like formalin and printer's ink and looked exactly like the "mad scientist" you imagined working in the basement of a federal building.

Armstrong towered above him like a statue. "This is my friend, Claire Fontaine."

"Aaah, yes." Speck nodded. "You're in the business of death."

"Seems that way."

"Both of you come inside. Let's have a look at the sample."

The front of the house seemed artificial, as if no one really lived there. An air of mildew clung to the stone walls. There was a gigantic fireplace that seemed to have never been used. Too many books to count. Dust on the remote control. The man probably never turned on the television, and I would bet that pop culture repulsed him. The scientist, the loner. He brought us into the kitchen and I noticed a pot of vegetable stew on the stove, Fiji water on top of the fridge, plenty of Irish oatmeal, and fresh fruit in a ceramic bowl.

"Coffee?" he offered pleasantly.

"Please."

Armstrong nodded.

Eugene Speck made a fresh pot of European blend, rich and toxic, the last legal addictive stimulant available. He noticed my girlish figure, blushed a little, and eyed Armstrong. He was titillated by me, I guessed, and by Armstrong, as well. "So," he said, eyes floating up to the big man. "I forgot. How did you say the two of you met?"

"I didn't." A smirk.

"Can't slip one past you, ol' buddy."

"We're neighbors," he admitted, letting out an embarrassed laugh.

"That's convenient."

Nothing else was said about our residential or romantic status. Speck led us down a long hallway that seemed endless and when we could go no farther, metal doors opened upon our arrival, and we stepped inside a high-tech laboratory. There was an assortment of steely computers, their screens buzzing with confidential information. Onyx tables were lined with medical equipment and liquid-filled jars. A bizarre labyrinth of animals filled aluminum cages, everything from angora rabbits and Indonesian rodents to a couple of miniature monkeys and a few exotics I couldn't even identify.

"This is where I work," he said. "I consider myself a student of biology with an interest in cold fusion. Not to mention, an expert in trace evidence and a professor of computer science."

"Do you still work for the, you know . . . the Company?"

"CIA?" He smiled. "I'm retired, but on occasion I'll do some consulting. I'm out of the game these days. Like to be with my equipment, not big on bureaucracy. Don't like people all that much, either. Humanity is at its worst."

"Thank you for doing this." I reached into my purse, handed him the evidence envelope. "They removed four pieces of hair from a shoe print. Said it was animal hair, something very rare. I was hoping with your expertise, we could cut the identification time in half."

He took the envelope from me. "Let's see what we can do."

Armstrong hung back, arms crossed, mouth shut. He seemed to be a little fascinated and amused to watch me work.

Speck washed his hands, slid them into gloves, and removed the paper from the envelope, sliding the hair onto a petri dish. Then he looked at it under a microscope, mumbling to himself. "Definitely nonhuman, based on the complex structural pattern of the medulla. Unidentified origin. Very interesting. Haven't seen anything like this in a while. I have a feeling it's . . . dog hair."

"You're kidding?" I walked to the microscope. "The lab said it was exotic, too rare to identify without further research."

"I'm not talking about an ordinary dog, like a pomeranian or a poodle."

"Then what?"

"I'm not sure yet." He removed the sample and walked over to another strange piece of equipment, gray in color, octagonal in shape. "This is called a Quantum 500XRQ. Only federal agencies have them. Fastest identification system in the world, has millions of hair and fiber samples preprogrammed into memory, from carpet to cotton to cats. Too expensive for state organizations. The only reason I have one is because I helped design the thing."

He put the slide into a mechanized holder, entered a few numbers, and held his breath. We stood there like gamblers waiting for a triple seven on the slot machines. The Quantum 500 was a magnificent testament to technology and the new age of detection. It only took thirty seconds to get a positive result.

Speck hit a few more buttons. "We got a definite match."

"What is it?" My heart was aflutter.

"The hair belongs to a timko."

"A what-co?"

"A timko." He was proud to be a nerd. "It's a canine, a very rare breed. And very expensive. I've never seen one in person, and few people actually own them. Have to go through specialized breeders to get one. They're very very inbred, more so than golden retrievers or dalmatians."

"Why would someone want one, go through the effort and cost of breeding?"

"The fur," he said. "It's not coarse or dense. It's incredibly soft, like mink or chinchilla. They're small dogs, generally. High-maintenance. Neurotic. But enthusiasts love their velvety coat. They'll pay up to twenty grand for one."

"Twenty thousand for a dog?"

"Yep."

"That's totally ridiculous. You could buy a decent bracelet for that kind of money. What a waste."

"Not to timko lovers."

Armstrong was still quiet, just observing.

Speck moved across the room to another computer and hit the keys like a madman. "I'm now going to find the closest breeder to see if we can narrow down the possibilities. I don't think there will be many. It's such a rare animal."

My coffee had gotten cold, and when I set it down on the counter, a marsupial took a swipe at me through the bars of his cage.

"Here we go." Speck had pulled up the information. "Got one licensed breeder in the California area. Name is Roger McCormick." He leaned his head back like the screen hurt his eyes. "Ooohhh . . . no."

"What?"

"He's deceased."

"That's not good."

"Looks like he died of cardiac arrest last year, no foul play. He was eighty-five. Let me see if I can pull up his client list. Find the current owners."

We waited in silence again. The computer beeped. Speck nodded. "Two clients. One in Nevada and one in the Southern California region."

"Let's zero in on the SoCal customer."

Speck scrolled down the page. "Name is Ellen Shaw. Forty-eight years old. Lives in the Pacific Palisades. Doesn't list any personal information. She bought a timko from McCormick about three years ago. Do you want her address?"

Feeling defeated, I gave a listless shrug. "Okay."

"Sorry," he said. "I know you were hoping for Ed Gein or Jeffrey Dahmer."

"No, no, this is great. I'll check it out. I can't thank you enough for your help. My partner is going to be so impressed."

Speck wrapped up the sample and handed it back to me. "This was, um, well, fun for me. Don't get out that much, certainly don't have many visitors. Come back any time you need a fast ID on hair, fiber, dirt, metal. Whatever."

"You can count on it."

I had a new friend with a Quantum 500.

He walked us to the car and shook Armstrong's hand. I gave him a quick kiss on the cheek and he blushed like a schoolboy.

"Thanks again," I said. "You're a real genius."

"If you ever want to ditch James Bond for a geek, you just let me know."

"I'll do that."

Once in the car, Armstrong and I edged our way back down to a normal altitude; the sky and sea were visible once again. I touched his hand lightly. "You have amazing friends," I said. "I'd like to meet more of them, you know, someday."

"We'll see."

"I mean I'm not pressuring you or anything, just a suggestion. It would be a way to get to know you better, since talking isn't one of your strong suits."

"Don't push it."

"I won't. I promise. When the time comes, maybe we could throw a party, invite *everyone* we know. I have a great caterer who does excellent Chilean sea bass and—"

"You're pushing it."

It was quiet for the rest of the drive.

He pulled up to my house, and as I was getting out of the car, he said in a serious tone, "Claire, maybe we could have dinner sometime soon?"

"Tonight?" So much for playing hard to get.

He looked at his watch. "Late dinner maybe. Nine o'clock?"

"Works for me."

"See you then."

I was hoping for a new beginning. A real relationship with a real man, heartfelt, ripe, full of truth and passion and trust. I knew the only way to secure such a fantasy was to be anyone *but* myself.

48

I couldn't reach Bennett.

I tried the office, his cell. I figured I had lost him to the Berkshire girl, and all that went with her. He was getting to be one of the boys again, working with the department, probably hoping to find new clues that would solve an old case. I was patient enough to wait five minutes for him to return my call, but he didn't. . . .

So I went alone.

The Shaw house was small for Palisades standards, set back off the road, tucked behind old trees that swayed rhythmically in the breeze. Even though it wasn't fancy or ostentatious, it didn't look like the kind of residence that wanted strangers standing on the doorstep. I parked along the road, got out, and walked up the narrow gravel trail. The house was white, ranch-style in architecture, old-fashioned. I listened to the trees in the wind, took pleasure in the fact that I could barely hear the traffic on Sunset Boulevard. The place was isolated, a little rustic for my taste, but there was an air of old money that kept it from being mediocre.

I knocked on the door. A woman in her late forties appeared, broad-shouldered, no makeup, wearing a pink bathrobe. Her dark hair was pulled back into a bun, and her pale skin didn't seem to have seen the sun in forty years. Her voice was thick with inconvenience when she said, "Whatever you're selling, lady, I don't want it. Especially if it's Avon."

I tried not to wince at being called an Avon Lady and thrust myself into undercover mode, even though I was certain there was nothing to be *uncovered.* "Ms. Shaw?" I asked politely. "I'm sorry to barge in on you like this. Got your name from a local breeder. I'm doing an article on timkos, and, well, you're the only person in Southern California that owns one. I know I should've called first. . . ."

"Come in," she said, the edge gone from her voice. "Yes, yes. I have a Timko. The love of my life. I'm sorry I'm still in my robe. Goodness, if I had known the press was coming . . ."

"I'm not the press, ma'am. Just your basic dog lover who happens to be a journalist."

"Is this article for the *Los Angeles Times*?"

"No, it's for a magazine called, er, *Diva Dogs.* We have a few thousand readers. It's a small publication, but the subscriptions are growing."

"Diva Dogs." She smiled. "That's just dandy. Can I offer you anything? Water? Tea?"

"No, thank you. I don't want to take too much of your time."

She told me to have a seat in the living room and she would go and get her prized timko. I sat there on the sofa, surrounded by chintz and flowered wallpaper and grandfather clocks. Looking around the place, I found nothing out of the ordinary, except too much paisley on the chair in front of me. I knew I was wasting my time, and the clock on the wall clamored loudly with each passing second, reminding me about the dead bodies that were piling up, the killer on the loose.

Ellen Shaw returned, still in her bathrobe, holding a small gray dog under her right arm. She set it on the floor in front of me. "Her name is Tessa. She's a real joy."

The *thing* chased its own tail for the next five minutes.

I pretended to be amused and fascinated, while the clock on the wall grew even louder. Dead bodies piling up. Beth Valentine. Olivia Berkshire.

I finally reached down to stop the dog from getting dizzy, and it bit my left finger. Ellen was mortified, grabbed the thing, and lifted it into her arms. She leaned into me, face red, voice full of shame. "Oh, dear. Are you okay? I'm so sorry. They're very territorial, don't like strangers. Sometimes they react, but they're still good pets. I hope this won't reflect poorly upon the timko in the *article*."

I had forgotten, with all the spinning and now the blood. "Oh, the article. No, don't worry about it. These highly inbred dogs are moody. I know that. She's a beauty, though. Could I get a Band-Aid?"

"I'm so terribly embarrassed." She set Tessa on the chair. "Let's go to the kitchen, run some water over your finger."

Standing over the faucet, I played the good journalist. "What made you want a timko?"

"My grandmother had one. I remember being a kid and hoping someday I'd have one. Of course, it died right after Nana did." Long sigh. "And then, when my father died and I inherited this place along with some insurance money, I decided to get one. Cost me a pretty penny, but I'm sure you know that."

"About twenty grand."

"That's right."

"You could buy a used Volvo for twenty grand."

"Oooh." She waved a hand. "But a timko will bring you sooo much joy."

I looked at my bleeding finger and tried not to laugh. "Yes, I can see that. I understand they have the softest fur."

"That's true. Feels like a chinchilla coat. Tessa really is a good dog. I'm sorry she bit you. I hope you'll write good things in the article. I'd like for people to know about these little dogs and how special they are."

"Of course. That's why I'm here. The article will be in a positive light. Can I send you a copy?"

"Oh, most definitely." She reached in a drawer and handed me a Band-Aid. "Let's go back into the living room. Maybe Tessa is ready to play now."

We were crossing through the dining room when I caught a glimpse of a photograph.

It was hanging on the west wall, a little lopsided, black and white. I stopped in my tracks. The face staring back at me belonged to a man. I got a strange feeling in my stomach—maybe it was instinct, but it could've been nausea. Ellen Shaw was already in the living room and I could hear her talking to the timko. My eyes were firmly glued to the photograph, this man, this darkness. He had a small mouth, a sharp slender nose, and an unusually long face that was as pale as the moon. His dark hair was cropped close to the scalp. And he had the most violent eyes.

Ellen was standing in the doorway now, head tilted. "Tessa is ready to play."

"Who is this?" I tried to sound steady.

"That's my son."

I was certain my upper lip had accumulated a bit of moisture. "It's a . . . nice . . . picture."

"Taken last year."

If I told her he was handsome she would know I was lying and was probably in her house under false pretenses.

I don't even remember walking back to the living room, but I found myself sitting on the sofa feeling a bit dizzy. The timko was chasing its tail again, and I had a phony smile frozen across my face. Ellen was laughing and taking pictures of the thing. "I'd love to have Tessa's photo in the magazine. Do you think that's possible?"

Robotic answer. "Of course." I reached down and touched the fur. "Do you have any more children?"

"No. Cooper is my only one."

"Does he live here?"

"Out back." She jerked a thumb toward the window. "In the

guesthouse. But, funny thing, I haven't seen him for a couple of days."

I pretended to enjoy my playtime with the dog, all the while wondering where Cooper Shaw was lurking.

"Are you worried?" I said

"About what?"

"Not seeing him around for a couple of days."

She shrugged. "No. He's had some girl problems."

I'll say.

Tessa jumped into Ellen Shaw's lap. "Cooper is an odd kid, can't hold down a steady job, but he's smart as a whip. Always been real shy, especially around the ladies. But he's starting to come around. He's getting stronger, more confident. We've never been that close. He's too aloof and I'm too controlling. He lives in the guesthouse for financial reasons; it's a free place to stay until he can get a salaried job."

"Where's he working now?"

"Last I heard, he was fixing cars at Ray's Auto Repair, down on Pico Boulevard. He likes to work with his hands, physical that way. Been good with tools and mechanics since he was a kid. Never into sports or anything like that. The girl problems have really taken a toll on him. I think he gets a little too possessive and scares them away."

I couldn't wait to get out of there.

The dog was chasing its own tail again, frantic, psychotic. A waste of twenty grand.

"When will the article run?" Ellen asked.

"In about a month." I was gathering myself. "Can't thank you enough for allowing me in your home. It's been a real pleasure getting a firsthand look at this marvelous creature. The timko. I've been fascinated with them forever."

"Me, too." She stood up and walked me to the door. "So you'll send me a copy?"

"Absolutely."

"Hope you enjoyed meeting Tessa."

"I'll remember it, *always*."

And with that, I was heading back down the trail, wanting to sprint to my car. The distance between me and the road seemed endless, a football field of separation.

49

The next thing I knew I was sitting in front of Ray's Auto Repair watching two guys change a tire and frantically trying to reach Bennett, who was still out of pocket. I pulled the car closer to the shop, slid down in the seat, and attempted to separate all the grease from the grungy faces.

I sat there for ten minutes debating what to do next, on my own, and tried to shake the feeling of abandonment, solitude. I got out of the car and walked into the garage. A man in a gray jumper came over, wiping his face with a red bandanna. "What can I do ya for?"

"I'd like an oil change, please."

His eyes floated over my shoulder, staring longingly at my red automobile. "Nice Benz," he grunted. "That's a classic, ain't it?"

"I think so."

"How many miles ya got on it?"

"Close to seventy thousand, but she still runs like a gem."

"We'll get her fixed up." He took the keys from my hand and walked past me, inundating my olfactories with motor oil. "It'll take about thirty minutes. You can watch if you like." He made it sound sexual.

My eyes scanned the place, frantic, obsessive. "Listen," I said to the man, "is Cooper Shaw around?"

He seemed shocked by the question. "What's a girl like *you* want with Coop?"

"Nothing really," I said, waving a hand in the air. "I'm just . . ."

"Just what?" He had gotten suspicious, wasn't so interested in my car anymore.

"I'm a friend of Ellen Shaw, his mother."

"Oooh, I see." All the doubt faded. "So, you don't really know Coop?"

"No."

"That makes more sense."

"How so?"

"Well, let's just say, Coop ain't your kind of fella."

"Where is he?"

"Fuck if I know. He went on a rampage a couple days ago, and the boss told him never to come back. Ain't seen him since."

"Define rampage."

"He and I had a disagreement over a 'ninety-eight Plymoth that some guy brought in. It was stalling on him, and I told Coop it needed a new transmission. I been in this business long enough to know my shit. He didn't like my assessment, said the engine needed a new fibulator and not a transmission. We went back and forth for fifteen minutes, arguing over it. Call it 'mechanic competition,' and it can get in the way of fixing a car in a timely manner. So, anyways, he just finally blows a gasket, starts throwing pliers and kicking tires. He looked nuts. Came at me with a crowbar, but then bossman walked in and tackled him. I thought he was gonna kill me, his eyes were all crazy and shit."

"That sounds awful."

"It was, and of course I was right. Plymouth needed a new transmission, that's all. Hope you don't go tell his mama what a bad boy he is."

My cell rang and I knew it was Bennett. I quickly excused myself and went around to the side of the building. "Where've you been?" I snapped.

"Working."

"You just won't believe what I've done."

"Try me."

"We traced the origin of that sample hair to a timko."

"A what-co?"

"That's exactly what I said." I could feel my spine tingling. "It's a rare breed of dog. Found this woman in the Palisades that owns one.

Went to her house, posing as a journalist. Just wanted to snoop around, see if there was anything out of the ordinary. Everything seemed kosher until I saw this photo on the wall. Turns out she's got a son named Cooper Shaw. It's our guy. I just know it."

"Where are you now?"

"Getting my oil changed."

He let out a sigh. "Of course."

"No, no. Shaw worked here as a mechanic. Ray's Auto Repair on Pico. He hasn't been around, got fired for trying to kill a guy with a crowbar. Without a doubt, Bennett, it's him. I knew it the first time I saw his picture hanging there in the dinning room, those eyes staring back at me."

"I'll be there in twenty," he said. "Don't go anywhere."

I clicked off the phone and walked around to the front of the building, then stepped into the garage. The mechanic was standing behind the hood of my car. He poked his head out and said, "I think I just saw him. Can you believe that?"

"Who?"

"Coop."

My cell came tumbling out of my hand and I quickly grabbed it, desperate for composure. "Where?"

"Across the street." He pointed. "Hard to tell. But I could have sworn he was standing by that pay phone, looking this way. I lost sight of him when the traffic picked up. A couple of trucks went by, and when I looked again he was gone. He's probably pissed about being fired from this place, planning to burn the garage down. Control freak." He opened a can of Penzoil.

I held up a hand. "Wait!"

"What?"

"On second thought," I said frantically, "I don't want my oil changed."

"Christ, lady, I just did all the paperwork. We're talkin' about thirty minutes here. Gotta keep this baby juiced."

"No, I just remembered, I've got an appointment. Please. I'll pay you for your time. Just give me my keys and let me get out of here."

He slammed down the hood. "Man, you're a piece of work."

I threw a fifty-dollar bill at him, grabbed my keys, slid into the front seat, and pealed of there. As I cruised Pico Boulevard for the next five minutes, my eyes scanned every parking lot, pay phone, nook and cranny. Finally I called Bennett and told him about the possible sighting and we met at a Jack in the Box. I was certain he wanted to go through the drive-thru, but time would not allow.

I slid across the front seat. "He's out there. Watching. Waiting."

"Calm down."

"I am calm."

"I have to say," he said, "I'm really impressed about the thing-co."

"Timko."

"Whatever. That John Armstrong, he's the real deal."

"Speak for yourself."

"I am." He pulled out of the parking lot and we cruised by Ray's Auto Repair, and then checked out the phone booth across the street.

"Mechanic thought he was standing right there." I pointed. "Then he was gone."

"You said he was living with his old lady?"

"Guesthouse, out back. I think we should stake the place out tonight."

"He won't be coming home anytime soon. He's into the cat-and-mouse game now, seems to really be enjoying it. You might think you're chasing him, Claire, but he's chasing you. And I would imagine he feels pretty powerful having the upper hand."

"But eventually he'll need more."

"That's right." He looked at me levelly. "And I'd hate to see you end up like . . ."

"Don't say it." I held up my hand to his face.

"Better watch yourself, then. Don't be going on these little treasure hunts by yourself. He'll overpower you. He'll have a jagged edge. Your moxie won't be able to save you."

"Hence the reason I asked you to get me a gun."

"No guns. Ever. Never. Don't start with this shit again."

"Then don't lecture me about safety."

"All I'm saying is, don't get yourself isolated. Don't go looking for trouble."

We were forced to wait it out, not knowing where he'd gone, but certain he'd never be home. I figured he had become too preoccupied with me to be stalking someone else. I had become the chosen one, the flavor of the week. That was good in that I was pretty sure he wouldn't be cutting some party girl's throat. On the other hand, he'd be dreaming about mine.

Bennett alerted the LAPD about the new suspect in the Berkshire case. We learned that Cooper Shaw had no priors, no warrants. We got the sample hair back to the lab, and I imagined, by sundown, Ellen Shaw's house would become a virtual police haven. The place would be crawling with cops and criminalistics, tearing apart the house and the guesthouse, overturning mattresses and collecting fiber. Tessa the timko would be chasing her tail for the next several hours, spinning like a Tasmanian Devil until all the uniformed strangers filed out of her house. I would not be able to face Ellen Shaw. She would have to assume that I, the *Diva Dog* journalist, had something to do with the sudden onslaught of sirens, the search warrant that was handed to her on the front porch, the endless parade of questions about her son, who, for now, was missing.

I had trespassed onto her property, earned her trust, manipulated her into telling me personal things, and completely *lied* to her when I told her I liked her dog.

The only humane thing I could do was stay away.

I sat in the car, at the edge of the road, while Bennett joined the team of investigators. It grew dark quickly, always does on the West Coast. There was a full moon and I thought I saw a face in it. Hovering directly above the Shaw estate, it was like God's spotlight. It was cold when I finally got out of the car. There was a bite in the air that reminded me of winter. I stood among the trees and watched the house from afar. Every single light was on, and five or six police cars were ditched along the trail, as was an unidentified van with government plates.

It must have been over an hour when I finally couldn't take the chill anymore and got back in the car. My face felt frozen, and the vapor of my breath lingered in the air like cigarette smoke. I noticed Bennett walking toward the car, hands in his pockets. It was too dark and he was too far away to make out any of his features, but I'd know that fat silhouette from ten miles away.

He slid into the car and looked over at me. "You doing okay?"

"Feel a little guilty about Ellen Shaw."

"She'll be fine, kid. Trust me. Cares more about that crazy fucking dog than her own son. You should've seen this thing chasing its tail. Twenty-fucking-grand for a pile of fur. You know what I'd do with twenty grand?"

"Can't wait."

"I'd buy every single George Foreman Grill on the market. The portable outdoor grill, over a hundred and sixty square inches of grilling surface. Then there's the the indoor grill. Double-coated non-stick surface. Oh, and let's not forget the stainless-steel propane grill."

"You've got to be kidding me. . . ."

He snapped his fingers. "And, of course, the mother of them all—the jumbo grill. We're talking two hundred inches of surface. You can grill up to twelve burgers at a time."

I was nauseated. "Take me home."

He started the engine. "Forensics found hair in the guesthouse, plenty of it, too. Human, most likely two X chromosomes. Berkshire and Valentine, I'm willing to bet."

"Where'd they find it?"

"Under his pillow."

"He'd been sleeping with it?"

Bennett thought about the question for a long time. "I would imagine, at night, he would probably lie in bed, holding the hair, touching it, smelling it, remembering every single thing about the girls. Killing them. Taking control. The blood. The look on their faces. It was just enough to keep him going, keep the dream alive. Relive the fantasy."

"But he's still out there," I said. "Dreaming, fantasizing."

"You want me to spend the night?"

"Gawd, *no.*" I looked at my watch. "I almost forgot. I've got a date at nine o'clock. Do you think I should cancel?"

"Why?"

"Well, with all this going down, I guess I'd feel guilty."

"You've got to live your life, remember? Can't lose yourself in the horror of this job. And you need to try to work things out with this Armstrong character."

"Why so interested in my love life?"

"I'm not," he grunted. "But it would be nice if we had access to some of his, shall we say, advanced technology."

"Yes, that would be quite an asset."

"And the way I figure, you'd be in a better mood if you was, you know, bein' romanced. I know how life is when things are dull and flaccid. It's boring as hell."

"Don't be gross."

His head swung in my direction. "I'm not being gross."

"Promise me that you'll never use the word *flaccid* in my presence again."

"Such a wimp."

"I'm a lady."

"If you say so."

50

It had been the longest day of my life. And it wasn't even over. In some ways, it was just beginning.

Armstrong showed up at nine o'clock, dressed in a suit and tie, looking unforgivably handsome. I was wearing a black Caroline Herrera dress and burgundy Manolo Blahniks. Despite a desperate attempt to appear drop-dead gorgeous, I was afraid all my effort had been wasted and I just looked *dead*.

Thankfully my date didn't feel the same.

"You look lovely," he said as we walked toward the car.

"Thanks, so do you. It's been a long day. Believe it or not, Ellen Shaw, the owner of the timko, was a valid lead. Been trying to chase down her son all day."

"No kidding?"

"Thanks for putting me in touch with Eugene Speck."

"Anytime."

We drove toward the sea and then headed north. I rolled down the window and felt the autumn chill.

"There's a nice little place up here," he said. "Thought we could eat and then walk."

"Walk where?"

"On the beach." He was trying to be romantic. It was awkward pure and simple.

I looked down at my Blahniks, which weren't quite appropriate for salt and sand, and with a happy shrug I said, "Sounds great."

We had dinner at a chummy place called Le Ducememe. It was quiet and out of the way, not yet pretentious enough to be annoying. Armstrong ordered a bottle of wine, and I felt like it was our first date. The butterflies were back and, boy, were they dancing. I could hardly eat. Before the liquor could make me loopy, I switched to water. It felt weird being sober at this hour.

I tried to be elegant and mysterious when I said, "So, are we getting back *together*?"

He looked at me for a long time, eyes level with mine, no expression on his face. "I just thought it would be nice to have an evening."

"Have an evening?" I repeated, haughty. "What does that mean?"

"Dinner. Conversation. Candlelight. What do you want from me, Claire? A written contract? A marriage proposal? A six-karat Harry Winston on your finger?"

"That last one would certainly be okay."

He finished off his wine. "I'm not good at this, you know that."

I suddenly felt guilty. "You're doing just fine. I'm a lot to handle. There's a lifetime of neuroses that you're up against. I can't tell you how grateful I am to be sitting here, with you, talking like normal people. I never thought . . ."

"I'd ever actually speak to you again?"

"Correct."

He could barely look at me. "Just let it happen."

"I promise I'll try. From here on out, it's a brand-new Claire."

After dinner we walked down to the beach and I took off my shoes, let my feet sink into sand that felt like shards of ice. It was almost too cold to be enjoyable, the wind whipping off the water. He put his coat around my shoulders and we walked for a while, still a strange distance between us. We were so far north I could hardly see a trace of the city, just an endless stretch of the shoreline, a moonless sky, and a black ocean.

Armstrong was walking beside me, but I could hardly feel his presence, like a ghost that was out for his nightly walk.

There was no escaping the grim, the unanswered, the faceless people that now flooded my thoughts and showed up in my dreams. Nightmares. Ghost stories. Strangers. I reached into my purse and removed my cell phone. Turning to him and feeling terribly unromantic, I said, "Mind if I make a call?"

"No problem." He let me walk ahead of him, giving me some privacy.

I already felt miles from him. The fog was rolling in, and white-capped waves rose and fell with the rhythmic purity of nature's finest achievement.

"Bennett," I said, when the detective answered.

"Yeah?" he grunted into my ear.

"I'm just checking in."

"Aren't you on a date?"

"Yes."

"Then what're you doing calling me? Is that the ocean I hear?"

"Look, I just wanted to know if I've missed anything. We haven't been in contact for a few hours."

"Hey, I offered to spend the night," he snorted.

"Ewwww. Stop."

"Enjoy yourself, kid. If anything goes down, I'll call you. How 'bout that?"

"Fine."

Armstrong and I headed back to the car, made our way through the fog, and soon found ourselves sitting idly on our street. This is when dating your neighbor gets really awkward.

He had not made any physical advances toward me, and I felt it was best to leave on a proud foot. "I had a lovely time," I said, reaching for the door handle.

"Wait . . ."

"What?"

"Since it was so important for you to see my house, I thought maybe it would be appropriate to give you a proper tour."

The butterflies about sank me. "Are you asking me in for a nightcap?"

"Yes. I am."

I was quiet for a nanosecond. "Gladly, I accept."

We stepped from the car and his hand brushed mine.

I glanced up at him, playing cool. "I'm going to run home real quick to freshen up. Can I bring you anything?"

"Just yourself."

51

In a real dark night of the soul it is always three o'clock in the morning.

—F. Scott Fitzgerald

He had given me a proper tour, kissed me the way I always wanted to be kissed, and when the night was finally slipping away, I picked myself up from the fantasy and went home alone. I felt whimsical, still sober and still dressed, my house had the kind of warmth I had always wanted. Or maybe it just seemed that way because I was so heated from his touch. Either way, I didn't care.

It wasn't until I walked into my bedroom that I sensed something was wrong.

Standing there, holding my purse, stiff from the endless day, I thought about the whirlwind of an evening that had come and gone, and how, in such a flurry of passion, I hadn't set the alarm on the house. My mind wasn't as focused on the case, the killer, the shadowy man on the highway and in the stairwell. The only man on my mind was John Armstrong. Unfortunately, my new profession didn't allow for such frivolous escapes. One mistake, one second of thoughtlessness, one alarm gone unset, and the next thing you know you're looking down your own hallway as if it's the barrel of a shotgun.

Suddenly the lights went off. Clocks stopped. Silent all around. My house had died, succumbed to a man who was good with his hands . . . knives.

He was near.

His presence was dreadful and dark, rife with violence and rage. As I started moving down the corridor, I caught a whiff of unfamiliar air. The stairs felt endless and steep, and I sensed Cooper Shaw was waiting for me in some unforeseen corner. He would need to possess me, own part of my soul, and take something tangible with him on his way out. He had come for me the way the devil does, in the middle of the night, impervious, without shame.

I was standing in my living room now, soaking up the blackness, listening to him breathe. I recognized his odor from that night in the stairwell at Absinthe. Something sulfurous about it. He was all around me, moving, confusing me. I didn't know up from down, left from right. And I was dizzy with fear, spinning until I heard the sound of my own voice. "I know who you are," I said. "And I know what you did last summer."

"Stop talking." That voice had been conjured from the basement of hell. "Or I'll cut you. . . ."

"I've seen your work."

"It's beautiful, isn't it?" His breath was on my neck.

"If you're into that sort of thing."

"I am," he whispered. "Now be a good girl, and do what I say, darling."

"Can we turn on the lights?"

"Why?"

"Because I'm dizzy. And don't you want to see me, Cooper?"

He clicked on the flashlight and blinded me with the beam. "I *seeeeee* you."

When the light fell away, I caught a glimpse of the knife's jagged edge. I put my arm up to shield my face. "If you want my hair, I'll give it to you. Don't need to kill me for it. Take all you want, but don't give me a buzz cut. I'll look too masculine."

"Shut up." The blade touched my chin. "I'll take what I want because *I'm* in control. The only thing you know right now is that I am God, the most powerful person in your life. Think about that. *I decide!* I decide whether you live or die, whether you suffer, whether you bleed out, or get your head smashed in. Do you understand?"

"Yes. Yes, I do."

"Then don't get smart with me. All your fancy footwork, trying to get me cornered like some kind of animal. I watched you, waited. Should've killed you that night on the stairs. I warned you. And you didn't listen, kept on sticking your nose into my business. And that fucking dog hair. No way I'm doing twenty-five to life 'cause of some shit like that. Nobody beats Cooper Shaw, hear me?"

"The timko is what got you—"

"No! Nothing got me, goddammit. That's why I'm standing in your living room with a knife to your face. You don't know what power is, real power. Taking lives. That's power. Showing those girls they can't just walk all over me. Lie to me. Leave me. Cheat on me. There are consequences when you fuck with Cooper Shaw."

"Could you please stop talking about yourself in the third person—"

His hand went firmly around my neck while he hit the light switch. And then I came face to face with the man that had plagued my dreams. He was uglier in person, with eyes dark as marbles, face too long for his neck, uneven yellow teeth. I could see why women lied to him, cheated on him, and left him. He had figured out a way to compensate for his insecurities, to finally obtain control over the situation. Shaw's thirst for blood, for absolute power, had cost Beth Valentine and Olivia Berkshire their lives.

His body tensed.

He was readying himself to make the cut, to feel my blood, to rip into my scalp for a souvenir. I slowly brought my right heel from the floor, and with all the strength I had left in me, slammed that razor-sharp Blahnik heel into the top of his foot. I knew I broke the skin because he yelped like a child and knelt to the wound. Blood was seeping from his shoe and onto the carpet. His metallic eyes looked up at me, shocked by the sight of his own fluids.

He rose from the floor, unsteady, a little broken by the woman standing in front of him.

He could not regain control and lost his balance completely this time, tumbling backward at full speed and crashing into my coffee table. The glass splintered into a thousand pieces. His head was stuck somewhere between the sharp edge and the ground, his face awash in blood. He convulsed for ten seconds, twitching as if electric currents were running through his veins.

Then he went still.

I waited. And waited.

He never came back to life, the way they do in the movies.

I sat there for a moment, trying to make sense of it all. His eyes had lost their violent glare. His fingers had curled upon themselves. I called Bennett first, and then 911. There was so much blood, a crimson river still flowing onto the carpet. The demon had come for me in the middle of the night, but I had not fallen victim to such evil. Left with no other defense mechanisms, I had used the heel of a very expensive shoe to disable him. The feeling was euphoric. A wonderfully powerful moment in my life. A turning point. Like when you realize that getting a perm is no longer the answer; it's about texture and shine.

The paramedics arrived first, Bennett shortly thereafter.

He was leaning over Shaw's body, shaking his head. "I can't believe this son of a bitch is lying dead on your living room floor."

"Tell me about it. My decorator is going to be so pissed."

"How the hell—"

"He came at me with the knife. I just, you know, slammed my heel into his foot. He cried like a baby, fell backward, and totally ruined my coffee table."

"It cut his head wide open." He moved toward me, reaching out sympathetically. "Are you okay, Claire? You hurt anywhere?" He let out a sigh of relief. "Do you know how lucky you are?"

"Lucky?" The insult registered on my face. "This isn't about luck, mister. It's about raw talent, instinct, all that crap you've been preaching about for weeks now." Diva snap. "And it's about my ability to kill any creep that breaks into my house and destroys my limited-edition furniture."

"Claire . . ." he said in that voice. "Don't get me wrong. I'm extremely proud of you. But you didn't exactly kill him with your bare hands. The guy took a bad fall and hit his head on the table."

"Bare hands?" The audacity. "I wouldn't break a nail over this freak. And my Blahniks did the trick, really threw him off course. As much as you'd like to chalk it up to timing and the sharp edge of my coffee table, I take full credit for his death."

I was sulking on the front porch when the police arrived. I gave my statement to some uniform that looked like John Stamos, and then I watched Armstrong emerge from his house. The blue air of night circled around me, the world slowed down for just a moment, and then he was standing before me with that chiseled face. "What in the world is going on?" He pulled me close, and for a second I forgot all about Cooper Shaw.

"It's classified." I buried my face in his chest. "And it's over."

The paramedics rolled the gurney out of my house, and what lay beneath the plastic was dead. Armstrong got the picture. He knew someone, something, had died tonight in my house. And that I was still standing.

He embraced me. "I've never been prouder."

My confidence was at an all-time high. "Maybe someday I could come work with you at the CIA."

He waited too long before he said, "We'll see."

"You're turning me down?"

"I think you're doing just fine in homicide. The federal government would only hinder you. Too many rules." He was politely rejecting my offer.

"You don't think I'm good enough. . . ." I pulled back from him. "*H-e-l-l-o.* I just killed a sadistic monster with my shoe."

Bennett was standing behind me just in time to say, "No, you didn't." He nodded at Armstrong, and they shook hands like tough guys. "Cause of death is being cited as arterial damage to the brain—inflicted by a sharp object penetrating the skull. Your coffee table killed him."

"Well, in my defense, I'd like to point out that my actions forced him to fall on his head. If you'll notice the damage to his foot, caused by another 'sharp object' driven into his flesh, you'll realize that I'm the real bad ass here. If, for one second, you could give me a little credit and stop giving it to my coffee table, we'd have a much better working relationship."

Armstrong kissed the top of my forehead. "I'm going to leave this one alone and give you guys some space to figure things out. Call me if you need me. Hell, just come on over. I'll be around for a few days."

It was just Bennett and myself now, sitting on the front porch, as the dark gave way to a ghostly gray. No sirens and cop lingo. My neighborhood felt like a vacuum, all the violent air having been sucked out during the night. I felt a strange sense of peace, along with a sense of duty to the dead.

Bennett interrupted my thoughts with his rough voice. "You did good, kid. For all the lipgloss and perfume and annoying chatter, you've got real potential in this business. I know someday I'll kill myself for saying that, but not today. You've got the right instincts to survive, and judging from the amount of blood on the floor, you've also got the right footwear."

"So, what you're saying is"—hand on hip—"it's time to make me a *partner.*"

"Not quite. I'm saying you can stay on for a while, work the next case with me."

"Will I get dental? Medical?"

"No. And no," he replied. "But you'll have somewhere to go every day, you'll have purpose."

"Even better."

The best part of our job came next.

52

The Pontiac was in the driveway.

A sliver of pink came over the horizon as dawn fell upon us. Bennett turned the engine off and we watched the place. He was too quiet and I felt alone in the car. I knew he was probably thinking about the case, the victim, how it all played out. A sense of relief that it had come to an end. "What're you thinking about over there?" I asked.

"Nothing." He reached for the door handle, distant and fatigued.

"Liar."

"You're in my interpersonal space, kid. Get out. Leave me be for at least a minute. I'm usually doing this kind of thing on my own. It's an adjustment with you around."

"Didn't know I was such a burden." Total lie.

We were standing on the front porch, the chimes singing in the Pacific breeze. We could see a constant flicker of light inside, blue and gray flashes on the opposite wall, and we heard the muffled sound of the television. Bennett knocked softly, and it didn't take long to hear the patter of footsteps. Nina Valentine looked ancient when she pulled open the door, with eyes that were perpetually burdened by sleepless nights, and a face that was permanently set in a frown.

She had to catch her breath when she saw the two of us. "My God . . ." She swung the door open all the way. "Come in. What's happened? My goodness, I'm shaking terribly."

Bennett had to help her to the sofa, as her legs could not withstand the tremors.

"We have some excellent news, Nina." Bennett placed a hand on her shoulder. "The man that so viciously took your daughter from you . . ."

"He's been caught?" She swallowed.

"You could say that."

I edged Bennett out of the way. "He'll *never* take another life, Nina. Ever. That's for dang sure. The guy bled out on my—"

Bennett interrupted. "Cooper Shaw was his name."

Tears were flowing liberally down her face. "Cooper Shaw." She digested the words.

"That's right." Bennett nodded. "He had taken a second girl. Left her in the same place. We were able to track him based on hair evidence that—"

"Cooper Shaw," she repeated, like a mantra.

Then she turned to me, flushed and excited. "You said he *bled* out? Is he dead? Please tell me he's gone."

"Oooooh, he's gone. Trust me. The guy broke into my house last night because I was hot on his trail, let me tell you. I watched him die on my living room floor. All the life twitched out of him."

She held her chest tightly, wheezing. "I'm . . ." She was somewhat capsized by shock. "Free."

"Yes. Yes you are. Beth is smiling down upon you, grateful she had a mother who cared so much. So very much." I was in tears now, but Bennett kept his face of stone. It was his job to be a man of steel, to push emotions to the wayside. I, on the other hand, was a weeping willow, not yet hardened by my new profession.

"Why?" she finally asked. "Why'd he take my baby that way?"

The lump in my throat was the size of a plum. Bennett answered flatly. "Seems he liked control, and we're guessing your daughter could not be controlled. Shaw was a jealous predator, with a history of OCD, dangerously possessive. I think he was just getting started. Your daughter was probably his first. Claire and I feel she probably angered him by having other lovers. And he couldn't let her live in the same world. The only way he could feel power was to—"

"I get it." She closed her eyes. "Had a feeling it was something like that, some jealous creep."

Nina sat there for a long time, saying his name, wiping tears from her face. The memory of this moment would never fade. I would never forget the joy and relief on this woman's face. I would never forget the feeling of sitting in her living room at dawn, Bennett's hand on her shoulder. The way she said Cooper Shaw's name over and over. The sudden flush of life that washed over her. I felt Beth's memory all around us, no longer sidled by pain and dread. There was an air of freedom; she had finally been released from the purgatory of waiting for her killer to be caught.

Bennett and I stayed with Nina for a couple of hours, going through old pictures, talking about the case, letting Nina in on some of my eccentricities. She opened Beth's bedroom door and a few of the cardboard boxes, finally able to acknowledge her daughter's scent again.

When we left her house, I didn't feel as euphoric as I had hoped.

There was too much exhaustion, as well as tension that would take weeks to subside. The train graveyard faded into the distance, a constant reminder of what it was like to live in a forgotten neighborhood.

Bennett let out a big sigh. "I'm starving."

"I couldn't eat if my life depended on it."

"So you're not up for a Hungry Man special at Denny's?"

"Hardly." My stomach was still in knots. "Maybe we can have brunch in the morning. The Ivy on Robertson. I'll call and make a reservation."

"Don't bother," he grunted. "I ain't hanging out at one of those hoity-toity places."

"It would be good for you, Detective. You might learn some manners, get some culture in your life."

"All them celebrities with fake tits and teeth? Gimme a break. That ain't culture. It's pretentious bullshit and I won't have it."

"I'll go by myself, then."

"You do that."

I removed a nail file, slowly trying to put myself back together again. "I'm not dropping this issue of partnership," I said. "Not after what I've been through."

"You just keep on jabbering, Barbie. You'll be selling shoes in no time. Bet you've already got your own parking space at the mall."

"Hey, don't knock it. Works out nicely over the holidays, when there's a thousand people in the parking lot."

"Whatever."

His phone rang, and he brushed me off rudely. He mumbled incoherently for about five minutes, keeping his voice to a whisper, then he clicked off the cell and retreated to that very dark private place.

"What's up?" I said. "You're all serious and mean and unhappy again."

"Death does that to me."

"Who died?"

He looked out the window. "A girl."

"Another case come your way?"

He nodded. "Something like that."

"You gonna share the details with me?"

"If you'd shut up long enough to hear them."

I kept quiet for the duration of the drive.

We of course ended up at Denny's for lunch, where he gave me a few details about the new job he'd just been offered.

Homicide is a growth industry, and Bennett would certainly be working the beat until he died, which, based on his cholesterol level, could be quite soon. I was already thinking about funeral attire. What color I'd paint his office once I moved in, installed a treadmill, and threw out the rest of his crap.